"Coyne is an inc kable and well-realized Tapply's deftly re ckdrops are a p

Detroit News

"The plo is complicated and satisfying."

Publishers Weekly

"Tapply imbues well-worn themes and plot devices with a remarkable freshness.... Brady Coyne is a most beguiling mouthpiece for the Brahmins."

New York Daily News

"Brady Coyne, even though he is a lawyer, is an engaging sleuth, and he manages to juggle his thriving practice with his detecting sideline with admirable integrity."

The Miami Herald

THE
MARINE
CORPSE

A Brady Coyne Mystery

William G. Tapply

BALLANTINE BOOKS • NEW YORK

Library of Congress Catalog Card Number: 86-15408

ISBN 0-345-34057-4

This edition published by arrangement with Charles Scribner's Sons, a division of The Scribner Book Companies, Inc.

Manufactured in the United States of America

First Ballantine Books Edition: October 1987

For Martha

Author's Note

My thanks once again to Betsy Rapoport, my estimable editor, Rich Boyer, my good friend, and Cindy, my dear wife. Their contributions to this story—and to this writer's spirit—have been beyond measure.

PROLOGUE

Felix Guerrero hunkered down into the beige windbreaker he had stolen from the big department store and wondered why the hell he had ever let Paulo talk him into leaving Miami.

The sign outside the bank near Faneuil Hall told him it was minus four degrees centigrade outside. Dirty, hard mounds of week-old snow lay against the buildings and edged the sidewalks. Puddles of frozen slush glittered dully in the reflected yellow light from the phony gas lamps that illuminated the brick-paved plaza. Felix was wearing low-cut sneakers. For speed. Good, leather New Balance. Also stolen. His toes ached from the cold. It was *muy frio* in Boston. Very damn cold. Nothing like Miami. Nothing like Cuba.

The sign blinked, and then it told Felix the time: 6:42 PM. He had another eighteen minutes to wait before the man would arrive.

There wouldn't be much of a crowd, they had told him.

Just enough for him to lose himself, but not so many people that he wouldn't be able to run. He'd be able to get close to the man.

Felix kept his hands in the pockets of his jacket. He had to keep them warm. His right finger caressed the trigger of the little square automatic they had given him. A lady's gun, he had called it. But they told him that it was clean and it would do the trick, and he should shut up.

He kept his finger on the trigger, rubbing it lightly, lovingly, the way he would rub a woman's nipple to make it grow hard.

Get close to him, they had told him. When he gets out of the black limo, just walk up to him. Smile, as if you wanted to shake his hand. When you are standing in front of him, take out the little automatic and stick it at him and yell the words—be sure to yell the words, they told Felix, that was very important—and start pulling the trigger. Then run away. Run for the crowds of people and they won't shoot you. Go around the building and turn down the alley. Run to the end of the alley. A car will be waiting. Get into the car. You'll be in Miami the next day.

Felix had walked through it that morning. He knew where the alley was.

He hugged himself and shuffled his feet. *Maldito!* It was cold. He made fists, rubbing his fingers together inside his pockets. He couldn't do the job if his hands were numb.

But it sounded easy enough. Already it was dark outside, and the people were beginning to gather there, their breaths coming in little white puffs. They were young, most of them, jolly and fat and full from expensive meals in fancy restaurants, and now they were gathering to see the man with the pig face that Felix was going to kill. Men and women, just hanging around in their expensive, warm coats, furs and big wool topcoats and colorful ski parkas. Felix thought he should have stolen a ski parka.

He patted his shirt pocket. The thin envelope crinkled. A comforting thing, that envelope. It contained five big ones. There were five more to come after he finished the job. And then the sunshine and all the *niñas guapas*, the pretty white girls on the white beach, and a few lines in the evening for his nose and some good Jamaican weed and he wouldn't be cold anymore.

Felix would buy himself a tight little black bikini bathing suit to show the *niñas* on the beach what he had. He'd wear a big gold cross and stroll up and down the white sand, and the girls would see him and he'd look them over and pick one out.

Cousin Paulo had said there'd be work in Boston. *Chinga* cousin Paulo. Fuck him. There was nothing in Boston but snow and snotty dried-up women with zippers between their legs and big black dudes who liked to beat up little Cubans.

Now Felix had a job. It was work he knew well enough. It was work he'd done before.

Just like Americans, thought Felix, to make speeches on a day of national disgrace. Pearl Harbor Day! The day the Japs kicked the *mierda* out of the American Navy. And they celebrate it with speeches by important men like the one with the pig face.

Cuba had a day like that. The day of *Babia de Cochinos*, the Bay of Pigs. Felix wondered why the Americans didn't celebrate that one, too.

The man with the pig face, they had told Felix, was an important man, *mucho hombre*, a man of the government, and Felix would be a big hero when he killed him. They had tried to explain it to Felix, that the man was going to tell why the Americans were giving weapons to the government of Haiti to kill the guerillas. These guerillas were young men just like Felix, they had explained, so this man was an enemy of Felix and an enemy of Cuba and an enemy of the great communist revolution in Haiti.

Chinga these Haitian guerillas. *Chinga* their revolution. *Chinga* this pig-faced man who wanted to make a speech in the old square brick building in Boston. All Felix wanted to do was get away from this frozen hellhole of a city where everybody wanted to kick his ass and Cousin Paulo was in jail and therefore unable to introduce Felix to the men who would pay him to carry drugs.

He turned up the collar of his thin windbreaker and shivered. The sign told him that the temperature had dropped another degree. *Tan frio.* Too damn cold. It was 6:56. He eased himself closer to the front entrance of the building. His finger lightly stroked the trigger of the little gun in his pocket.

Two uniformed policemen stood by the steps. Warm orange light shone through the windows of the building. The policemen looked cold and bored, as if they'd rather be inside. Felix tried to look bored, too. He didn't have to try to look cold.

The two black limos pulled up, close to the steps, closer to the entrance to the building than Felix had expected. A tall man with a child perched on his shoulders stepped up beside him, and he could feel people pushing up in back of him. They had seen the limos, and they were gathering around to see the man with the pig face.

They had shown him a picture of the man. He was an old man with round pink cheeks and a flattened-out nose and white hair and tiny eyes. A pig-faced man. Felix had looked at the picture for a minute and nodded. He wouldn't forget the face. The man's name, they told him, was Thurmond Lampley. Felix had shrugged. He didn't care what the man's name was. He was the Deputy Assistant Secretary of State for Latin American Affairs, they told him. Felix rolled his eyes. He was an enemy of the brave guerillas in Haiti, they continued, an enemy of Castro, an enemy of Cuba, and Felix didn't even bother to tell them that he didn't give a shit who the man was or what he believed.

They told him it would be a good and brave thing to kill this pig-faced man. Felix remembered what he had said. "I do not hate this man," he had said. "But I am happy to kill him. *Tengo cojones.*" I have plenty of balls.

The one thousand dollars, the trip back to Miami, these

were the things that made Felix happy to kill this Thurmond Lampley with the pig face.

The first one out of the limo was a big blond man without a topcoat or a hat. He stood there for a moment, not smiling, looking all around. Felix saw him nod to the policemen and then bend back to the open door of the limo. Then the man with the pig face climbed out. The blond man stood straight and looked around some more. He stared right at Felix. It seemed that he was staring right into Felix's soul, and Felix eased himself back behind the tall man with the child on his shoulders.

When Felix looked again, the blond man was no longer staring at him. The man with the pig face was smiling at the crowd and at the same time speaking to another man who was standing beside him. *"Chinga tu madre,"* cursed Felix under his breath, trying to hate the man, because that always made it easier.

Then the pig-faced man and the two others began walking toward the building. They had only a few steps to go. If they made it into the building, Felix would have missed his chance.

"Excuse me, please," mumbled Felix to the tall man in front of him. The tall man glanced down, smiled, said something to the child on his shoulders, and moved aside. Felix stepped forward, gripping the gun in his pocket, and began to run toward the man with the pig face.

"Haiti libra!" he yelled, as they had told him to. And he yelled it again as he took out the gun and pointed it at the man. He saw the startled look on the pig face, a flash of fear that Felix liked to see. But then the blond man turned and calmly stepped in the way. Felix pointed his gun. As he yanked on the trigger, something pushed him from behind, and Felix felt his foot slip on some ice and his shots went into the air. *"Mierda!"* he muttered. He tried to stop, to regain his balance. He felt hands clutching at him, and he saw the blond man reaching inside his jacket.

Felix managed to turn and darted back into the crowd of

people, who moved quickly to step aside for him. He didn't feel cold, now. He felt warm and alive and he moved quickly. The crowds seemed to open a pathway for him, and he followed it across the brick-paved plaza, around the building, and there were no bullets coming after him.

He was running very fast, feeling strong. He came to the alley. It was dark and deserted. At the end would be the car, waiting for him. He heard shouts behind him, noise, confusion, anger in the voices. But he would make it. He was running well, the way he would run on the hard-packed sand along the water's edge on the beaches, knees high and elbows pumping, head up, breathing easy, all the muscles of his good hard body working together.

He was nearing the end of the alley where the car would be waiting for him. He looked. The car was there, and two men stood beside it. He could see the exhaust coming from the back of the car, a big gray cloud in the cold air.

He slowed to a jog. He would make it easily. When he was about twenty-five feet from the car he began to walk, a nice, slow, cocky stroll, like on the beach in Miami. The two men were grinning at him, saying something, he couldn't hear what. Felix grinned back at them. *"Haiti libra,"* he said, the password, so they'd know it was him for sure.

The two men, still smiling and speaking to him in loud voices he couldn't understand, showed him the guns they held in their hands. Big, ugly revolvers with short snouts and wide bores. Felix stopped, hesitated, started to speak. He held out his hands to the two men. One of his hands, he suddenly realized, still held the little square automatic. He opened his mouth to explain. The two men were pointing their guns at him.

"Chingado!" Felix muttered, seeing it all now. "I've been fucked!"

He whirled around and began to run back down the alley. He heard shouts behind him, more voices ahead of him. He ran harder. He heard the first shot, loud in the narrow alley, and he felt it shatter his elbow and spin his body through the air.

He didn't hear the second shot, because the bullet got there before the sound registered in his brain, and it shattered his shoulderblade and crashed through his chest and killed him before his body landed in the dirty snow.

That, as well as I can reconstruct it, is how Felix Guerrero died. The newspapers, with their usual instinct for irony, called him ''The Happy Warrior.'' Mickey Gillis, in her thrice-weekly column for the *Globe*, hinted darkly at conspiracies and cover-ups. But the government did not see fit to respond to her hints—which, in turn, gave Mickey fodder for another series of columns.

The attempted assassination of Thurmond Lampley at the annual Pearl Harbor Day Public Forum at Faneuil Hall was big news for a long time, because it finally confirmed our government's claim that Cuba was involved in the Haitian revolution. Thurmond Lampley gave his speech as scheduled. He appeared a bit shaken, according to reporters who were there. But he didn't forget to emphasize the Cuban role in Haiti.

Lampley was a big hero. So, in his way, was Felix Guerrero.

Stuart Richmond Carver died less than a month later, also in Boston. He got no headlines at all—partly because of the intercessions of his uncle, former United States Senator Benjamin Woodhouse, and partly because Stu's wasn't a very interesting death.

But Stu Carver's death was more interesting to me, because he was my friend and my client.

1

Homicide detective Al Santis hung up the phone and sighed. He jammed his forefinger into the styrofoam cup on his desk, frowned, and wiped it on the front of his shirt. "Cold," he muttered to himself. "Figures. Story of my miserable life. Cold coffee. Cold bodies. Cold trails. Cold women." He belched into his fist. " 'Scuse me," he said. "My digestion ain't so hot these days, either."

He snapped the plastic cap back onto the cup and dropped it into the wastebasket beside his desk. He ran his fingers through what was left of his hair and peered at me. "I kept you waiting. Couldn't be helped. That damn shooting at Faneuil Hall's got us all jumping, you know?"

"That was a month ago," I said.

He shrugged and nodded, as if to say that he'd prefer to get on to more important things than an attempt on the life of a Deputy Secretary of State. "Jurisdictions, see?" he said. "You got your Secret Service, you got your FBI, you got your State cops, and then you got us City cops, all tryin' to figure out which of the other guys fucked up the worst. Spend more time these days fighting among ourselves than we do trying to catch bad guys." He put both hands to his head and pressed against his temples. "Driving me nuts, I'll tell you. Anyway, where were we?"

"Stuart Carver."

"Yeah. Right. The stiff we found New Year's. What was I saying?"

"You didn't say anything, actually. I came in and introduced myself and then the phone rang and then you got up and left and fifteen minutes later you came back in with your coffee and the phone rang again and you said 'Yes, sir' into it several times. Then you put your finger into your coffee."

Santis grinned. "And it was cold already. Yeah, yeah. Right. And you're the dead guy's lawyer or something. Coyne, it was, right?"

"Brady Coyne. Yes."

"Okay. I got it right here." He rummaged through a drawer in his desk and came up with a manila folder. He opened it and glanced through the papers in it. "See, we thought it was just another wino. Naturally. I mean, there he was, laying under some newspapers in the alley, frozen stiff as a haddock, wearing this raggedy old coat, and them eyes staring up at the sky. There was no blood or bruises. He was just laying there."

"Frozen," I said. "Sure."

"Hell, the Medical Examiner came and looked at him. You know, didn't really examine him. It was colder'n a witch's tit out and only like five AM in the morning. But the ME kinda tried to move his head around, felt of his fingers a little, went through his pockets. Routine, understand? Didn't find much, naturally. You don't expect to, these bums. No engraved gold watches or billfolds with credit cards or college rings. Okay, he coulda been rolled. Even so, those boys'll kill each other for half a jug of Guinea red quicker'n they'll say please, and those shitbum teenagers do it just for fun. But, you look at this one, you figure he just lay down and froze to death. Another dead bum. With that beard and them old clothes—shit, he had newspaper in his shoes, no socks—you know? First of the year, but there'll be plenty more. Cold weather's here now, missions're filled up, they go get boozed up so they feel warm, then they pass out in the alleys. Routine, you figure.''

"You don't have to apologize," I said.

"I ain't apologizing," said Santis. "Explaining. See, every winter we get ten, maybe twelve, just like this one. Mostly old guys, though nowadays it's a little different. We get women too, now, and even young guys like this one, since they started letting them out of the nuthouses. The home guard, they call themselves. Lots of 'em born right here in Boston. 'The homeless,' as the Welfare folks call them. But that ain't necessarily right. They *are* home. This is their home, the streets and the alleys, the parking garages, the subways. We get more in the summer, the tramps and the bindle stiffs. They come in on the freights from Atlanta, Phoenix, St. Louis. They like Boston. We got lots of churches and missions and clinics and whatnot. Nice weather here in the summer. Nice benches on the Common, lotta nice people to give 'em handouts, lotta nice squished vegetables down at the marketplace. Boston's a good city if you happen to be a bum, especially in the summer. Most of 'em tend to head south in the winter. Those that stay around tend to freeze to death in the winter. Like your friend there.''

"Stuart Carver was my client."

Santis shrugged.

"Stu Carver wasn't a bum," I said.

"Well, that depends on your definition, I'd say. He damn well looked like one when we found him. Now, understand, this is technically a Medical Examiner's case. Unattended death. Usually they lay around in the morgue at City Hospital for a few days. Then Welfare buries 'em.

Oh, they'll send the guy's fingerprints to Washington. That's routine. Maybe he was somebody. Usually not. Anyhow, coupla days later it comes back. He was the Senator's nephew. That changed things a little."

"I imagine that changed things a lot," I observed.

Santis nodded. "The Senator still pulls a lot of strings in this city. But, hey, it ain't our fault his nephew went on the skids."

I took a pack of Winstons from my shirt pocket, tapped one out, hesitated, and said, "Do you mind?"

He waved his hand. "Naw. Go ahead."

I lit the cigarette. "So when you learned it was Stuart Carver . . . ?"

"When we learned it was Senator Woodhouse's nephew, somebody suggested that maybe the ME ought to do an autopsy."

"That's not done routinely?"

"Supposed to be, I guess. But they got stiffs piled up in there like cordwood, if you know what I mean, and I guess it's up to them who they want to cut open. Some wino who froze to death ain't high on their list of priorities."

"The nephew of the leading Republican in the Commonwealth ranks right up there, though."

"Sure. See, we've all got the same problem. Too many dead guys, not enough time." He scowled at me. "I mean, maybe with lawyers it's different."

"It's a little different, yes," I smiled.

"So, anyway, that's when they found the wound. When they did the autopsy."

"Tell me about that wound."

Santis shuffled the papers in the manila folder, glanced at one of them, grunted, and looked up at me. "You can read it, if you want," he said. "Amounts to this. Somebody stuck an icepick into his brain, is how he died."

"That," I said, "would do it."

"That would do it very nicely. See, the entry wound was in his left ear." He demonstrated on himself with his forefinger. "A wound like that won't bleed hardly at all, especially when it's like ten above out there. You'd never see it if you weren't looking for it. Puncture wound like that, inside of the ear. No blood, hardly."

"Sure," I said. "But now it's a homicide."

Santis's laugh startled me. "Well, now, it don't exactly look like an accident, does it? Probably not what you'd call self-inflicted, either. I mean, we don't want to go out on a limb or anything, but we're guessing it was maybe a homicide. That, I imagine, is how come you're here talking to me."

"That's part of it, yes. What can you tell me about your investigation?"

He stared at me for a moment. Then he sighed, leaned back in his chair, and tilted his head to study the ceiling. "Mr. Coyne," he said softly, "you gotta understand. First, we've got this assassination thing. This little Spic goes running up to the Deputy Secretary of State yelling 'Free Haiti,' or something, and starts shooting, which means already our security was shitty, and then the little Spic gets killed so nobody can ask him any questions. Mickey Gillis at the *Globe* won't leave it alone. Every goddam day, an editorial, seems like. And Internal Affairs is going bananas trying to pin the blame on somebody, and the Commissioner is trying to keep a lid on the whole damn thing." He shook his head.

"What are you trying to tell me?"

"Look. Whatever this Carver guy used to be, he was a bum when he died. When that icepick went into his brain, he was drunk. Not just legally drunk, understand, but absolutely shitface. So says the ME, even though I expect Senator Woodhouse didn't like to hear it. He had probably passed out. He wasn't wearing socks, Mr. Coyne. He didn't have on any underwear. He was filthy dirty. Sores all over his body. He had about two weeks' beard on his face, and there were pieces of dried-up puke caught in it. You know what I'm trying to say?"

I stubbed out my cigarette in the big glass ashtray on Santis's desk. "You're trying to say that the death of a wino isn't worth investigating."

"You tell me something," said Santis quietly.

"What?"

"Was Carver a drunk?"

I hesitated. "He *got* drunk from time to time. But he wasn't an alcoholic, if that's what you mean."

"What I mean is this," he said. "He certainly looked like a drunk to us. A bum, a derelict, is what he looked like. And he looked like a bum to everybody else, no matter whose nephew he was. You want me to investigate the murder of old Ben Woodhouse's nephew, and I'm telling you that we're trying to investigate the murder of an anonymous bum. Because that's what whoever stuck that icepick into his head thought he was."

"That's your theory."

He sighed. "Okay, then. It's a theory. You got a better one?"

"No. I don't have a theory. But I don't believe it was just a random, arbitrary killing, either." I shrugged. "I guess you know more about this sort of thing than I do. What have you found?"

He shook his head. "Found? What we'd expect to find. Which is to say, not much. Listen. It was three days before we even realized he'd been murdered, you know? Three days before we knew who he was or anything. We got no suspect, no weapon, no motive, no witness. Nothing. Just a theory. We checked the missions. Showed his photo. Couple people recognized him. Know what they called him?"

"Cutter, probably."

Santis squinted at me. "Yeah. That's it." He shrugged. "Anyhow, he started showing up in the middle of October, near as anyone could recall, though none of them like to talk to cops. Best we can tell, he had no friends to speak of. No enemies, either. Just a few folks who recognized his face is all. They'd say, 'Oh, yeah, that's Cutter,' and we'd tell 'em Cutter was dead, and they'd say, 'Yeah, that happens.' " Santis shrugged again.

"This is not very encouraging," I said.

"You got any reason to think somebody wanted Ben Woodhouse's nephew dead? You think this is political or something? If you think we're on the wrong track, let me know."

I shook my head. "I can't help you there."

"Well," he said, spreading his hands palms down on the littered top of his desk, "we haven't given up. Look. You wanna know something?"

"Tell me."

"I'll bet some day soon we find another bum with a little hole inside of his ear. And then another and another. And then we'll put some cops out there in raggedy clothes, with radios in their pockets, pretending to be passed out in the alley. And eventually we'll catch some crazy guy with an icepick, who gets a big hard-on when he pulls it out of his pocket, and who creams his jeans when he sticks it into somebody's ear." He nodded, as if he had persuaded himself. "That's my personal idea."

"That's a neat theory," I said, smiling so that Santis wouldn't think I was mocking him. "They didn't find anything in Stu's pockets, then?"

"Like clues, you mean?" Santis's grin did mock me.

"Specifically, a notebook."

"I don't remember any notebook. If there was a notebook, I guess I'd remember it. That," he said, his eyes twinkling, "would be a clue, huh? There were a few odds and ends, as I remember it. Hang on. There's a list in here somewhere." He peered into the manila folder and extracted a sheet of paper. "Okay. One matchbook. One meal chit for supper at the kitchen at St. Michael's. Two nickels and a quarter, which might or might not eliminate robbery as a motive. A pencil. Handkerchief. Probably not freshly laundered or pressed. That's it." He closed the folder and placed his hand on top of it. "No notebook. So listen, Mr. Coyne. Tell me. What the hell is this Stuart Carver, who calls himself Cutter, and who happens to be the nephew of Senator Ben Woodhouse himself, doing, passed out in an alley on New Year's Eve, anyway?"

"Research," I said. "He was working on his new novel."

2

Ben Woodhouse had introduced me to his nephew two years earlier. Ben and I were sitting on the patio outside the men's lounge at Ben's country club in Dover, sipping vodka tonics and watching the afternoon's last foursome straggle up the sloping fairway toward the eighteenth hole. Ben slouched down in his white wicker chair, his long legs propped up on the low brick wall that fronted the patio, his shoulders hunched up against his ears. Ben had served one term in the United States Senate during the Eisenhower years. Since then, he preferred to wield his considerable political clout from behind the scenes. But he was still called "The Senator"—as if he were the *only* Senator—by most people in Massachusetts.

"My sister Meriam's boy, Stu Carver," he was saying to me. "The family black sheep. I'm rather proud of him, myself, but then, I've always been a bit out of step with the rest of the clan."

Ben had ascended gracefully into his seventies, with his

unruly shock of slate-colored hair still as intact as his political influence, and his patrician nose as long as his memory and as straight as his ethics. "It wasn't bad enough, he grew a beard and marched around Washington carrying a candle during Vietnam. Hell, Chub Peabody's mother did that, too, though my brother and sisters didn't think that should absolve Stu. After all, Peabody was a Democrat, so that sort of misbehavior might be expected. But it wasn't dignified for a Woodhouse. And, of course, moving in with that Jewish girl—well, his mother admitted that it could have been worse." Ben chuckled.

"He could have married her," I said.

"Yes, I've mentioned that to you before, haven't I, Brady?" He gazed out over the rolling fairways. "Stu thinks this place here"—he waved his hand, taking in the green sweep of the golf course and the big rambling clubhouse "—is a shameful example of conspicuous consumption. Of course, he's right."

I nodded absently. The golfers had reached the green. By the way they squatted behind their putts, dangling their putters in front of their faces and squinting along some imaginary line of sight, I supposed large sums of money rested on the number of strokes it would take them to knock the balls into the holes. I was thoroughly relaxed in Ben Woodhouse's company, and not the least bit concerned about consumption, conspicuous or otherwise.

"He'll be late," said Ben. "He's always late. It's his way of protesting."

"Protesting what?" I asked.

Ben grinned. "Doesn't matter. In this case, I imagine he'll rant and rave against the tyranny of time. He likes to say that the wristwatch was the invention of a fascist mind. 'You're never free,' he says, 'when you have your arm shackled onto one of those things.' But if it isn't one thing, it's another. That's why I admire him. He holds his principles firmly, even if they're silly."

"And the closest you ever came to protesting was hiring a lawyer from Yale," I observed.

"I've got to admit, Brady, my boy, the family didn't take too kindly to it. We're all Harvard, as you know. But that wasn't it. You were the only one who wouldn't let me beat him at golf. I can't trust a man who won't try his damnedest, and accept the consequences of victory as graciously as those of defeat. It's blasphemy, I know, but I find those Harvard Law School types mealy-mouthed at best."

"Well, Ben," I murmured, "I've enjoyed our relationship."

"And well you might. Ah, here he is now."

Ben unfolded himself from his chair, and I stood up beside him, as a dark-haired man of middling height approached us. He wore baggy corduroy pants, a blue dress shirt open at the neck, and a broad smile. He was, I guessed, in his early thirties. He moved with the quick grace of a gymnast to shake Ben's hand. "Uncle Ben," he said. His ice-blue eyes narrowed impishly. "I'm surprised that you risked permanent ostracism from the Woodhouse clan to do this for me." He looked at me. "You must be Mr. Coyne."

I extended my hand. His grip was firm. "At your service."

"You know what you're getting yourself into here, Mr. Coyne?"

"Brady, please," I said. "And, no, actually, I don't. Your uncle has been very mysterious about this. But when The Senator calls, I come."

"Don't they all," smiled Stuart Carver. "You going to buy your wayward nephew a beer, Uncle?"

"A beer?"

"Well," said Carver, "a beer for starters. Just for the thirst. Then some good Cutty Sark for the serious sipping."

I detected the trace of a frown skitter across Ben's face. But he made a circular motion in the air with his forefinger and a young man in a white jacket materialized before us.

"A Beck's for Mr. Carver, Alan, and a refill for Mr. Coyne and me," Ben said.

"Very good, Senator." The waiter dipped his head and left.

Stu Carver pulled a wicker chair up beside me and Ben. We all sat down. Carver leaned forward, his knee jiggling furiously with nervous energy. "Let's get to it, Uncle."

"You have no sense of propriety, Stuart," Ben replied benignly. He sighed. "Ah, the impetuosity of youth," he said to me. "It seems that my nephew has written a book, Brady."

"Good for you," I said to Carver. "What sort of a book is it?"

"It's a novel, actually," he said. "I've been working on it, off and on, for about ten years. It's based on some field work I did in college."

"Harvard?"

He grinned. "Afraid so. Senior year, for a sociology project, I studied this religious cult. They had what they called a cell down near Central Square, and I joined them. Went through the initiation rites and so forth, and, for about two months, I lived with them. My novel is based—pretty loosely—on that experience."

I nodded uncertainly. "So where do I fit in?"

"Stu wants to publish his book," said Ben, as if that explained it.

I shrugged. "So . . . ?"

"But the family doesn't want me to," said Stu. "They think it'll besmirch the good family name. And, of course, in things that involve the good family name, the good family makes the decisions."

"Democratically," said Ben. "The family voted that Stu would not publish his novel—assuming he was able to find a publisher, which, given the, er, access the family has, he probably would."

"So this was Uncle Ben's idea," said Carver.

"What, for God's sake, was his idea?"

"It was a compromise," said Ben. "In the finest democratic tradition. Something we Massachusetts Republicans have become rather deft at accomplishing. The meat of politics, compromise. When you can win, you go for the throat. When you're going to lose, you go for the compromise. It was my idea. We let Stu publish his novel. But he must use a pseudonym. No one must know that it was a Woodhouse, by any other name, including Carver, who wrote this book. That's where you come in, Brady."

"Oh, sure," I said.

We paused while the waiter set our drinks down on the table. Stu Carver lifted his glass of beer and drained of half of it in one long draught. "See," he said, wiping his mouth with the back of his hand, "I've got to have an agent. Somebody who can keep a secret, who can handle all the business so the revered family will not need to soil its fingers." He dumped the rest of his beer down his throat. "The point is, they think it's trash."

Ben touched his nephew's knee. "It *is* trash, Stu," he said gently. He turned to me. "The other half of the story is this, Brady. We have persuaded Stu that he wouldn't want his novel published just because he wrote it, and because anything written by a Woodhouse would be instantly newsworthy. We have appealed—successfully, I believe—to Stuart's artistic integrity, and he agrees that he wants it accepted or rejected on its own terms. Through you, and pseudonymously."

"So you want me to peddle Stu's book," I mused. "I don't know much about that."

"But you do know how to be discreet, and if there should be a contract in the offing, you could certainly handle that."

"Yes, I could. And if all you want me to do is keep your name out of it and work on a contract, I don't see why I shouldn't give it a try. It goes with the territory, I'd say."

"Good, good," nodded Ben. "Then it's settled. Now. Shall we dine?"

Later that night I started reading Stu Carver's manuscript. He called it *Devil's Work*. It was a real page turner, replete with bizarre religious rites, sexually perverse ceremonies of all descriptions, torture, and death. I found scant redeeming social value in it, and it wasn't particularly well written, by my standards. Stu had decided to use the pen name "Nick Cutter," which I thought had a certain ring to it, and, all in all, I had to agree with the Woodhouse clan's verdict: Stu's book was trash.

Which was what the editor from one of Boston's biggest and most prestigious publishing houses told me two weeks after he had agreed to read Stu's manuscript. "It's garbage, Mr. Coyne," he told me on the phone, pronouncing it as if it were a French word, with the accent on the second syllable. "Drek. Crapola. Utterly, irredeemably without literary merit."

"Well, that's all right," I said. "I understand."

"No, I don't think you do," he said. "We want to publish it. We think it's going to be a big seller."

And it was. The publisher gave it a big pre-publication buildup, and when it hit the bookstores nine months later—which, I learned, is the average gestation for a book as well as a human being—it landed near the top of the local bestseller lists. I earned my hefty retainer from Ben Woodhouse just by keeping the media at bay and nurturing the mystery of Nick Cutter's identity—which did nothing to hurt the book's sales. The publisher encouraged me to accept invitations to radio talk shows to discuss *Devil's Work*, and when I told them I'd have to give my honest appraisal of it, they encouraged me to do that, too. "Call it trash," they told me. "Trash sells big."

For the first couple of months, supermarket tabloids and other gossip-brokers debated the question: "Who is Nick Cutter?" I had fun, teasing them when they asked me. Stu and Ben thought it was quite grand. Ben told me the family remained apprehensive that I'd let the pussy creep out of the sack, or that Stu would find himself unable to resist the temptations of celebrity. For my part, discretion was easy. For Stu, it was a relief that his real name hadn't been appended to the manuscript. "I guess the clan was right," he told me. "It really is trash. And anyway, it's more fun this way."

I had my own fun, negotiating the sale of rights with British and Italian publishers and movie and television option brokers. I rather enjoyed my ten percent off the top, too.

After the initial hubbub died down, several months after *Devil's Work* made its splash, Stu Carver showed up at my office. It was a golden October Friday afternoon, and I had kept my calendar clear for a golf date with my friend Charlie McDevitt, my old roommate from Yale Law days, and presently a lawyer with the Justice Department's Boston office. I told Stu I could only give him half an hour.

"Oh, that's okay," he said. "Hey, you got something to sip on?"

I produced the bottle of Cutty Sark I kept on hand for my clients who lacked sufficiently refined taste to prefer Jack Daniel's, and poured him three fingers. Stu tossed it off and helped himself to a refill.

"How 'bout you, Brady?" he said, holding up the bottle.

"I have an important engagement this afternoon," I said, thinking about how many beers Charlie would win from me if my putts wobbled. "I better keep my mind sharp."

"You got a court date?"

I thought how much easier this sort of thing must be for my attorney friends who play tennis. "A court date," I said. "Yes. Something like that. So what's up, Stu?"

"I'm gonna do another book."

I shrugged. "Nick Cutter has a big following. Good idea, if you're looking to get rich."

He grinned. "I already *am* rich, Brady. Have been all my life. That's not it. This one is going to be a *real* book."

He knocked back his second drink and splashed more Scotch into his glass. I must have frowned at him, because he tilted his head at me and said, "I drink too much, sometimes, I know. But this is by way of celebrating. Wish you'd join me."

I waved my hand at him. "Help yourself. I'll pass. What do you mean, a real book?"

"Oh, I read what everybody's saying. They're right. *Devil's Work* was pretty trashy. I didn't think so when I was writing it, and it's truer than people seem to think. I mean, all those things really did happen. It was originally going to be a kind of journalistic novel, based on sound field work. But I guess I got a little carried away with it. I decided to fictionalize it, so I could generalize. I thought I could actually tell the truth better that way, if you know what I mean. And I wanted to protect everybody's privacy. And then I found the fictionalizing more compelling than the reporting." He let some Scotch slide into his mouth, tilted his head back to swallow, and wiped his mouth with the back of his hand. "Anyway, this one's going to be different."

"This new one, you mean."

He nodded.

"Well, why don't you put down your drink and just tell me about it."

He grinned at me, to let me know he caught the disapproving tone that had crept into my voice, and I grinned back at him by way of apology. Then he drained his glass and set it down on my desk. He licked his lips and cleared his throat. "This city," he began earnestly, "is full of homeless people, Brady. Every one of them has a story. And there are people who devote their lives to helping them—priests and ministers, Welfare workers, do-gooders, and just plain nice people. I want to meet with them, live with them, talk with them, experience what they experience, feel what they feel. It'll be another field investigation. But this time I'll tell the story straight."

I nodded. "Sounds good. Another Nick Cutter tale will get people's attention. That, I guess, would be a good thing."

"I'm hoping it won't be another Nick Cutter," said Stu. "I'm hoping the family will allow this one to be a Stuart Richmond Carver book. I'd like that name to mean something. I'm a little sick of being a Woodhouse, to tell you the truth. I want this to be an important book in its own right."

"Well, good," I said. "Do it, then." I glanced at my watch—a little ostentatiously, I hoped. I didn't want to keep Charlie waiting. The sun was setting earlier every day, and I wanted to be sure we'd get in our full eighteen holes before dark.

Stu chose to ignore my hint. He poured more Cutty into his glass—just a finger, this time, which I took to be a hopeful sign—and tipped all of it into his mouth. He swallowed it with a great show of pleasure, sighed, and leaned toward me. "I will be needing your help on this one, Brady," he said.

"Your uncle hires me to help."

"I'll be in the field for several months."

"In the field."

"Yes. Living among the homeless, learning their lifestyles, their mores. I'm going to *be* homeless. No safety net. I'll be out of touch with the family. I will sever all ties. No money, no place to run to, until the project is over. I have to learn what it's like to feel hopeless, if that's the way they feel, to have nobody to bail me out or to feed me or to keep me warm. It will certainly be a new experience for a Woodhouse. I think I will bring a unique perspective to that experience, given my—privileged, I guess you'd call it—background."

"Get to it, Stu. What do you want me to do?"

"Okay. Sorry. I'll be keeping notebooks and I need a place to store them safely until I'm done."

"Here is fine with me."

"Good. That's all I wanted."

"Will you be mailing them, or dropping them off, or what?"

"I'll get them here, one way or another."

I stood up and moved around my desk, giving Stu no choice but to rise also. I shook hands with him and gentled him out of my office. He staggered only a little. Then I went off to play golf.

3

It was nearly noontime on a Monday three weeks later when Julie, my secretary, opened the door into my office and gave me that eyebrows-raised shrug of hers that said "Don't blame me."

"There's a Mr. Altoona here to see you?" she said, lifting the inflection to make a question of it.

"I don't know him. Do I?"

"No. You don't know him. He says you know what it's about."

"Well, I don't. So let's find out. Send him in."

She stood back in the doorway and murmured, "This way, please."

The man who shuffled past her wore a bulky tweed topcoat that came nearly to his ankles and heavy leather boots that looked several sizes too big for him. A rim of shaggy white hair encircled his head, leaving the top pink and bare. His eyes were pale and watery. He stood just inside the doorway, glancing uncertainly from Julie to me.

"Mr. Altoona, this is Mr. Coyne," she said, a little grin tapdancing at the corners of her mouth.

"Not Mister, my dear lady," said the man in a voice like a dull hacksaw working on a length of copper pipe. "It's just plain Altoona. Altoona is what they call me, after the singularly insignificant metropolis in Pennsylvania whence I hail."

He bowed to Julie, who winked at me as she closed the door on us. The man extended his hand to me. I took it. It felt small and bony in my grip. "A pleasure to meet you, sir," he said. Abruptly he bent over and hugged his chest with both arms. He gurgled and groaned, straining as if he had the dry heaves, and then exploded in a spasm of coughing—great, long, wracking fits punctuated by desperate wheezing intakes of breath. I put my arm across his shoulders and steered him to the sofa, where he collapsed, his head between his knees. His seizure sputtered and died like a truck running out of gas, leaving him panting and redfaced. He wiped his nose and eyes on the ragged sleeve of his topcoat and smiled apologetically at me.

"A thousand pardons, sir," he puffed. "Consumption, as they liked to call it in the literature of the nineteenth century. TB, you now. Many of us suffer from it."

"Would you like a drink?" I said, because I couldn't think of anything else to say except to ask him who "us" was.

"Ah, for medicinal purposes. Excellent, sir."

I went over to the cabinet. "What's your pleasure?"

"My pleasures, sir, are catholic. The grape and the grain, the potato and the juniper berry." He smiled. "Whiskey. Neat, if you please."

I poured a drink and carried it to him. He accepted it with both hands, sipped, and sighed. "Ah. That helps." He settled back into the sofa and regarded me expectantly.

I sat in the armchair beside him. "Are you being treated for your disease?" I asked.

He waved his hand dismissively. "After a fashion."

"I would say that you ought to be hospitalized."

"Yes. I've been told that." He sipped his drink, and I nodded. He had politely advised me not to pry.

"Well, then. How can I help you?" I said.

From the folds of his topcoat where, I assumed, it had been tucked up into his armpit, he extracted a large manila envelope. He held it out to me. "From our mutual friend, Cutter," he said.

I took it from him. Inside I found a red spiral-bound notebook. Stu Carver's notes. I flipped through it. Stu's writing was virtually indecipherable, pencil scrawls as if done hastily in the dark from an uncomfortable position. The notebook was about half full. I closed it and slid it back into the envelope and looked up at the old man. "Thank you," I said. "He said he'd be sending me some of these. And how is he?"

Altoona grinned. "Oh, he's quite well, considering. He's been studying us, you know. He has taken me into his confidence. Anthropology has always fascinated me. Cutter calls himself a sociologist, and, frankly, the distinction between the two so-called sciences has always eluded me, but if I remember my Margaret Mead, I believe the anthropologist inclines toward the study of obscure alien cultures. And that is surely what our friend Cutter is engaged in."

I had to smile at his ornate syntax. "And you . . . ?"

"I'm what Cutter calls a bum," he smiled. "Oh, yes. One of his subjects, as well as an ally of sorts. He has found me a most willing, if marginally helpful, collaborator."

"He's got you running errands for him," I said, tapping the envelope that contained the notebook.

"He indicated that you would, ah, take care of me."

"And I will. Shall we have some lunch?"

He nodded. "Most assuredly."

I put Stu's notebook into my office safe. Then Altoona followed me out of my office into the waiting room, where

Julie looked up from her typewriter. "We're going to lunch," I told her.

Altoona seized her hand and bent to it, brushing it with his lips. "It has been a pleasure to make your acquaintance, Madame," he murmured.

Julie grinned. "You are a gentleman, sir."

We walked to Marie's, my favorite little Italian restaurant, in Kenmore Square. Altoona clomped along slowly in his big boots, and I had to adjust my pace to his. Halfway there he had another coughing attack, and I held him as he leaned against a store window until it passed.

"You should wear a hat," I told him.

"You sound like my sainted mother," he wheezed. "Actually I've got a thick skull," he added, tapping his bald pate. "Plenty of insulation up there already."

Marie greeted us at the door. She hugged me and we kissed each other's cheeks in the European manner. I introduced her to Altoona, and she leaned toward him to accept his kisses, ignoring, as I knew she would, his shabby attire. Then she led us to my regular table in the corner. Altoona shrugged off his topcoat and draped it over the back of his chair. Under it he wore a faded red flannel shirt, with a blue sweatshirt underneath showing at his throat. Thick black and white striped suspenders held up his pants.

The day's specials were listed on a chalkboard. Altoona read them aloud, pronouncing the Italian words with tongue-trilling relish and translating them for me—first into French, then into English.

We each ordered a bowl of vermicelli—"little worms," Altoona told me—with a pesto sauce, a side order of deep-fried eggplant in beer batter, green salad, hot bread. Marie, as usual, provided a half carafe of red wine on the house. I poured each of us a glass, leaned back to light a cigarette, and lifted my glass to him.

"Your health," I toasted.

He nodded. "Not the best. But I thank you for the

wish.'' He touched his glass to mine. "To beautiful women."

I smiled. "My sentiments exactly."

We tipped our glasses. "An aggressive little vintage," he pronounced, after sniffing, sipping, and sloshing it around in his mouth. "Clever, but not at all deceitful."

"You must be an interesting subject for our friend," I said.

"He has made a study of me, yes. I think I have confused him. I am giving him some lessons." Altoona peered at me as if he had told a joke that I didn't get. "You are curious about me, Mr. Coyne."

I nodded. "Yes, I guess I am."

He sipped his wine. "I told you I was a bum, and that is true. It's a generic term, 'bum,' and it encompasses a multitude of sins, both of commission and omission. We so-called bums are as various as—well, as attorneys, for example. We are also called the 'homeless' by bureaucrats whose sense of propriety deters them from plain talk, but to put perhaps too fine a point on it, the term is less serviceable than 'bum.' I, for example, have a home, and even a family of sorts. I reside at the mission at St. Michael's. I sweep the floors and do a few other odd jobs—nothing terribly taxing, mind you—and dutifully go through the motions at the daily Mass. In return I am given a cot to sleep on, a clean towel and a shower each morning, a new razor every week, oatmeal and coffee for breakfast."

He paused to sip his wine again. He did it delicately, without thirst, and I felt certain that at some time in his life he had known how to enjoy fine things. But now the erupted capillaries on his nose and across his cheekbones revealed a different sort of appreciation. "Now—Cutter," he continued, running his forefinger across his lips, "Cutter is looking for something he calls typical. He's moving around, doing his research, and some nights he doesn't find a cot, and some days he gets in line too late for a chit and misses a meal. This seems to please him." He shrugged.

"He'll learn. Our culture is more complex than he knows. Wheels within wheels. Hierarchies. But he's a bright enough young man. Too eager, perhaps, to come to conclusions, too impatient with evidence. And he has yet to learn how to become invisible, to merge. As for me, what I have is as good as the hospital. Better, in many important ways. At least I'm free."

"The hospital?"

"A state mental facility, Mr. Coyne. It was my home for several years." His eyes twinkled. "Then I was deinstitutionalized. Kicked out. No longer certifiably crazy enough. Between us, it was their standards that changed, not me. So now I sweep floors for bed and board, and I get prayers instead of pills for what ails me, and the prayers seem to work about as well as the pills did."

Marie's waitress, wearing the uniform of the place—a clean white blouse and very tight blue jeans—brought our salads, and we ate them in silence. When he finished, Altoona dabbed at his mouth with the corner of his napkin and refilled our wine glasses. "I know Cutter isn't his real name," he said. "Of course, Altoona isn't mine, either. Most of us, you see, realize we aren't the men—or the women—we once were, or thought or hoped we might become. People without homes are people without the need for names. Our names are our shorthand, and a way to sever painful old ties. No one really cares about our names, anyway. The phenomenon of anomie—namelessness, rootlessness, homelessness—that so delights the sociologists."

"You are a learned man," I observed. I wanted to ask him about his time in the mental hospital, for surely this man was bursting with erudition, and if there was something wrong with his mind, it wasn't evident to me.

"Every morning, after I sweep up, I stroll over to the public library to commune with the newspapers," he went on, as if he had read my mind. "It's warm there. I feel comfortable, and nobody seems to mind. I like to know what's happening in the world, even if there isn't much any of us can do about it." He cocked his head. "So, Mr. Coyne. What do you think about this business in Haiti?"

The question startled me. I found something surreal about sitting at a table in a fine little Italian restaurant in downtown Boston discussing current affairs with an old man in a raggedy topcoat who had spent time in a mental hospital, and who cheerfully called himself a "bum."

"I suppose I hold what is generally called the conventional, knee-jerk, liberal view," I said, realizing as I began that I wanted to appear intelligent to this man, and that I feared I wouldn't. "Communism may not be the worst thing in the world for Haiti. Even the Cuban brand of communism. I know the figures. The average per capita income in Haiti is something like eighty-five dollars. Ten percent literacy. Which makes ninety percent illiteracy. Haiti is the poorest, most backward, unenlightened nation in the Western Hemisphere. And its people have been oppressed forever. Too much witchcraft. First Papa Doc, then Baby Doc, now the juntas, one after the other. All of them propped up by American—dare I say it?—by American imperialistic interests. Just like Batista's Cuba, right? Cheap labor to sew cowhides onto baseballs. This revolution is still going on. I think it's a real, legitimate people's revolution, and I really think it's time we got the hell out of it. They deserve a chance, at least, to join the twentieth century, and they won't do it as long as we continue to give support—military, economic, diplomatic, whatever—to corrupt, self-serving regimes. Listen. I hope they can finish this thing they've started. And Cuba just may be their best model. We should pull out."

My words sounded in my ears like a series of lectures I'd heard as an undergraduate years earlier from a self-avowed Marxist economist, reflecting then on recent events in Cuba. The words were fresh and exciting in 1960. Now they sounded stale.

"I don't support the administration's opposition to human rights, or the desire of American business interests to maintain the status quo there for the sake of cheap labor," I finished lamely.

Altoona cleared his throat. "I have given the matter considerable thought," he said, implying, it seemed to me—and with good cause—that I hadn't, "and I believe that this so-called revolution is not about human rights or democracy or the twentieth century at all, nor would its success mean progress for the people of Haiti. It is, quite simply, a not even thinly veiled communist takeover, orchestrated by the minions of Moscow via Havana, with the obvious aim of replacing one tyranny with another, only this new one less friendly to our own interests. All the abstractions confuse the simple issue: Which tyranny ought we to favor? It's fundamental *realpolitik*, Mr. Coyne."

"The people there seem to support the communists." I shrugged. He had me, I knew. There's so much more logic to realism than there is to idealism.

"I doubt if the people know what's going on," he answered. "The people, of course, are ignorant, superstitious, short-sighted fools. In Haiti, just as in the rest of the world. They don't know what's good for them. How could they? No, our government is right. And the liberal press once again is tragically wrong." He smiled at me. " 'Hurrah for revolution and more cannon-shot! A beggar on horseback lashes a beggar on foot.' That's Yeats, Mr. Coyne."

"Jefferson said that a revolution every twenty years fertilizes the tree of liberty," I replied, a futile try, I realized. "Something like that, anyway."

"Jefferson was wrong, as history has demonstrated, about several things." Altoona smiled. "Mao said that a revolution is not the same as inviting people to dinner, or writing an essay, or painting a picture. That man had a true sense of politics. And I have quoted him accurately."

I held up both hands, palms out. "You win. I can't beat you in a duel of quotations."

I was saved further embarrassment by the arrival of our

meals. We ate in silence. Altoona broke off chunks of bread from the crunchy loaves and then meticulously picked the crumbs off the front of his shirt and popped them into his mouth—whether from innate neatness, or an old habit born of hunger, I couldn't determine. When we finished, he proclaimed it a "splendid repast" and a "gustatory delight," and he gallantly kissed Marie's hand as we prepared to leave. She smiled, touched his cheek, and said, "You're welcome. Any time."

Outside the restaurant the November air stung my cheeks, a harbinger of winter. I huddled into my sports jacket and thought of Stu Carver spending a frigid Boston winter on the streets.

Altoona held out his hand to me. "We part company here, for now," he said. "I must get home, if you'll pardon the expression."

I hesitated, then drew my wallet from my pocket. I extracted a twenty-dollar bill and held it out to him. "For your troubles," I said.

He accepted it without surprise and tucked it into his pocket. "Cutter, I trust, will reimburse you eventually," he said.

"He most certainly will," I smiled. "How will you use it?"

His grin reminded me that I had been rude, and that his own manners were too good to mention it. "A bottle of expensive gin would be tempting, of course. But I expect I shall opt for a greater volume of cheap vodka. Such good fortune must be shared with my friends. From each according to his ability and to each according to his needs, Mr. Coyne. That is true communism."

I smiled. "Yes, I suppose it is. Give my regards to our mutual friend. I expect I'll see you again."

He nodded, lifted his hand, turned, and trudged away from me, a small shapeless figure not that much different from many of the others on the Boston sidewalks.

When I got back to my office I looked up the number

for the St. Michael's mission and dialed. The person who answered said, "Father Joe."

"My name is Coyne," I said in my most businesslike voice. "I'm an attorney."

"Yes?"

"I'm concerned about one of the men who I believe lives with you."

"Which one?"

"He calls himself Altoona."

"Sure. What about him?"

"He's very ill."

"That's right. He has tuberculosis. He probably should be hospitalized."

"Oh. You knew that already."

"Mr. Coyne, Altoona is being treated to the best of our very limited ability. Dr. Vance—he volunteers here—has him on medication. I make sure he eats regularly. He has a cot here. Beyond that, there's not much we can do. He refuses to see anyone except Adrian—Dr. Vance, that is. He will absolutely not go near a hospital. We take care of him as well as we can. That is our mission here."

"Is there anything I could do?"

I heard the voice laugh harshly. "Do? You said you were an attorney, didn't you? Mr. Coyne, there's no end to what you could do."

"I meant for Altoona."

"Of course. Make sure he dresses warmly. Be kind to him."

"I see."

"Come visit us some time. You might be interested to see what we do here."

"Maybe I will."

Altoona showed up at my office every Monday for the next several weeks after that to deliver a manila envelope containing a spiral-bound notebook, and each time I took him to lunch at Marie's and gave him a twenty when we parted. At each lunchtime he came prepared with an issue for discussion. We debated the management of the Red Sox and of the Federal Reserve, appointments to the Supreme Court and to the woodwind section of the Boston Symphony, the philosophies of Plato and Hugh Hefner, starving African children, and Cabbage Patch dolls. We argued about the assassination attempt at Faneuil Hall when it occurred. We discussed the effects of the Pope's visit to South Africa, the possibility of nepotism in the Flynn administration, and the plight of the Bruins. We wondered how many more manuscripts attributed to Ernest Hemingway would be unearthed in the coming year.

Altoona, I came to believe, was better read than I, and he had a pragmatic perspective that allowed him to see each issue separately, with a clarity that I envied. At the same time, he loved complexity, and he loved to point it out to me where I hadn't seen it. He held firm opinions which usually conflicted with my own. I found myself reading the papers more carefully, in order to prepare myself for our weekly get-togethers.

He always wore his old tweed topcoat, which was frayed at the cuffs but not dirty, and those floppy boots. He never failed to appear at my office clean-shaven. Both Julie and Marie seemed to revel in his old-fashioned chivalry. I considered taking up the practice of kissing hands and spreading my Harris Tweed across mud puddles, since both women, I imagined, had begun to look upon me as an ill-mannered dolt.

Whenever we met, I inquired perfunctorily after Stu, whom I remembered to call "Cutter." Altoona's reply was invariably, "He's learning." I glanced through the notebooks when he delivered them. Stu's handwriting remained virtually illegible to me, and since his notes hadn't been made for my eyes anyway, I didn't try to decipher them. I just built a stack of them in the back corner of my office safe.

On the Monday before Christmas I took Altoona for a steak at J. C. Hilary's. We started of with martinis—two each—and finished with big wedges of hot apple pie for dessert. When the waitress brought our coffee I took a gift-wrapped package from my briefcase and handed it to him.

"Merry Christmas, my friend," I said.

He cocked his head at me, and for once he had nothing to say. He carefully undid the Santa Claus paper and removed from the box a maroon knit wool cap and matching scarf. He pulled the cap over his ears and wrapped the scarf around his neck. "Brady Coyne, you are a kind man and I thank you," he said.

He reached into the pocket of his topcoat, which hung over the back of his chair, and took out a small package wrapped in brown paper. He held it across the table to me. "Nothing of much utility," he said. "But felicitations of the season to you."

I unfolded the paper. Inside was a wood carving of a human hand, the size of a child's, cupped as if to receive a handful of jelly beans. It had been rubbed to a satiny gloss. It was the color of bourbon, and its close grain and density suggested that it had been crafted from oak.

"It's beautiful," I said, genuinely touched. "A real work of art."

He smiled shyly. "You, sir, have extended me a helping hand during these past few weeks. Now, this is a useless thing, but I did want to find a way to give you a hand for a change. So here's a hand. Perhaps you can use it for a paperweight, or an ashtray."

"You made it, didn't you?"

"Yes. A skill I practiced at the hospital, once they felt they could trust me with a little blade. Under the most watchful supervision, of course."

I rubbed the smooth curves of the little hand with my thumb. It was exquisitely proportioned, and so lifelike I felt it might twitch and grasp my finger. "It must have taken you forever."

"I have forever," he said.

When we parted outside, I gave him a fifty and told him

to extend my Christmas greetings to his friends. He shuffled away, his new maroon cap bobbing among the crowds.

I saw him one more time, on the Monday before New Year's Day. Julie ushered him into my office, as usual, and I poured him a drink, as had become our custom. We settled into our regular seats, he on the sofa and I in the armchair. He handed me Stu's weekly journal.

I stood up and took it to my wall safe.

"Look at it," said Altoona.

"I'm not really interested," I said. "I'm just keeping them."

"Take a look at this one."

I opened it to the first page. It was blank. I riffled through the rest of the notebook. It was all blank. I frowned at Altoona.

"I know what you're thinking," he said quickly. "You think he had nothing to write this week, but he wanted to make sure I got my Monday lunch and twenty-dollar bill."

I grinned. "I guess it crossed my mind."

"He has been writing this week. I've seen him."

I held up the notebook. "Then . . . ?"

Altoona shrugged. "Not in there, obviously."

"Something he doesn't trust me with."

"Or me," said the old man. "Not either of us."

"How does he seem?"

"Different, lately. Secretive. He avoids me, now. He used to seek me out. At first, I figured he was just getting acclimated, didn't need ol' Altoona anymore. But I don't think that's it. It's more as if he were protecting me than avoiding me."

"Can you be specific?"

He coughed, cleared his throat, and sipped his drink. Then he peered up at me with watery eyes. "Specific, no. But I can tell you this. I know fear when I see it. Our friend Cutter's in some kind of trouble."

* * *

Altoona didn't appear in my office the following Monday. But I didn't expect him to. Because by then Ben Woodhouse had already called me to say that they had found Stu Carver's body frozen in an alley.

4

On the Sunday after I talked with Detective Al Santis, I drove out to the Senator's country estate in Wayland. The foot of snow that had fallen the previous night had been plowed off the half-mile drive through the meadow and up the pine-wooded slope to the low hill where Ben's Federal period colonial stood, hidden from view from the main road. Ben owned a hundred or so acres of fields and woodlands, the far side of which descended to a marshy wildlife sanctuary bordering the Sudbury River.

The house itself was much like the Senator himself—square, weathered, old, well-preserved, immaculately tended, and solid. It contained sixteen large rooms, eight on each floor, four full baths, plus a big ell that had been added onto the back for a kitchen and glassed-in dining area overlooking the pasture and river vista below it. There was a garage large enough for four cars, and above it living quarters for Ben's gardener and stableman. Out back was a barn and a stable. Old stone walls paralleled the winding driveway and demarcated the meadows, pastures, and woodlots on the property. The estate had been in Ben's family since the early nineteenth century. As keeper of Ben's estate, I knew that its market value was close to three million and appreciating at a solid fifteen percent a year.

If there had been neighbors, they would have seen automobile headlights cutting through the woods up to Ben's house at odd evening hours from time to time, as the movers and shakers of what was left of the Commonwealth's Republican Party came to pay court, and to scheme and connive with the Senator. Ben's Wayland house was the geographical locus of Republican power in Massachusetts.

I expected the parking area beside the circular drive in front of Ben's house to be jammed with Cadillacs, Mercedes, and Lincolns. As the death of a Prime Minister or President or monarch demands tribute from all the world's governments, so, I thought, would the death of a Woodhouse require a visit from representatives of Ben's former, present, and future political allies and enemies. Especially the enemies.

But there were only a dozen or so cars there, which, I realized, was more in keeping with Ben's style. It would be family and close friends only. Ben kept his tragedies in the same Yankee perspective as he did his triumphs.

I wedged my BMW in between a new Porsche and an old Dodge and started for the house. A couple was coming toward me, holding hands and skidding across the ice on the long curving pathway.

"Hey! It's Brady!" said the better-looking of the two. It was Mary Adams, and the hand she held belonged to her husband, Doc, one of my favorite fishing companions, and the best of an otherwise unpleasant lot of oral surgeons who have hurt me. Doc Adams had constructed a regular suspension bridge inside my mouth a few years earlier, and later, on my recommendation, he completed some renovations on Ben Woodhouse's bite. That sort of intimacy seems naturally to lead to friendship, at least with Doc, so I wasn't surprised to see him and Mary there.

Mary threw both arms around my neck and kissed me hard on the mouth. Doc grinned and pumped my hand.

"Can't be all that bad in there," I observed.

Mary turned down the corners of her mouth in that peculiarly Calabrian grimace of hers. "Oh, it's veddy veddy civilized," she said.

"The booze was okay," added Doc. "How're the choppers behaving?"

"Perfect," I said hastily. "Absolutely terrific. No problems at all."

"Special on root canals this week. Two for the price of one."

"Jeez, I'm gonna have to pass it up," I said.

"Too bad," he said. "Day'll come, you'll wish you had more foresight."

"Seriously," I said. "How are Ben and Meriam taking it?"

"Seriously," said Doc, "you'd think this was another one of their campaign parties, rather than a memorial get-together for a murdered nephew. We WASPs are hard to figure."

"You sure as hell are," said Mary.

We agreed to get together soon for dinner at their house in Concord—something Italian, veal, probably, that Doc would pound out and cook himself—and I headed for the house while they continued sliding and hollering their way to their car.

I followed the path to the front porch, went up the steps, and rang the bell, stamping the snow off my shoes. I don't normally enjoy the festivities associated with offering condolences to bereaved families, but Ben had put me at ease when he called the previous night. "We're having a little get-together," he said. "A few drinks, some hors d'oeuvres from the caterer. Just to make Meriam feel better. Morbid conversation strictly forbidden. There'll be no funeral, none of that ghastly viewing of the body, no moaning or wailing or gnashing of teeth, no speculating on the destiny of Stu's immortal soul, no contemplating on the wonders of God's ways. We'll have the football game on the tube and some Mozart on the stereo. The young folks will want to play that silly trivia game. If you're not too busy, I'd love to have you here."

And that, I knew, constituted a command performance for me.

Ben himself answered the door. He wore a dark blue cardigan sweater over a pastel yellow button-down shirt, open at the collar. He took my topcoat, grinned at me, and said, "For Christ's sake, Brady, take off that necktie. This isn't a funeral, you know."

He led me into the living room, where three matching sofas were arranged in a U in front of the blazing fireplace. Half a dozen people were seated there, all leaning toward each other and talking at the same time. I recognized Meriam, Ben's sister and Stu Carver's mother, an angular woman in her early sixties, and, seated opposite her, Howie Carver, her former husband and Stu's father. When Meriam saw me enter the room, she said quite loudly, "Shut up for a minute, will you Howard? Here's Brady."

She stood up and I went to her, took her hand, and said, "I was sorry to hear about Stu. Damn shame."

"Yes, it was," she said. She had the icy Woodhouse eyes and ski-slope nose. Her mouth was too big for her narrow face, so that when she smiled she looked as if she were planning to blow down some houses so that she could make a meal of little pigs. "But that is water over the dam, Benjamin," she said, impaling her brother with her quick glance, "get this poor man a glass of bourbon."

Ben smiled, mocked her with a bow, and went to a table in the far corner of the room.

Meriam seized my hand and pulled me to the sofa. I sat beside her. I reached over to Howie with my hand extended. "Hi, Howie," I said. "My sympathies."

"You're kind," he said mournfully. "I just can't believe it. One day he's—"

"Dammit, Howard, enough, already," interrupted Meriam.

"Yes, you're right," he said. Howie Carver looked at me and smiled grimly. "Did you learn anything more about Stu's death? Ben said you were talking with the police."

"Only that he was murdered. They assume it was a random sort of thing. Robbery, maybe. More likely a crazy person." I chose to keep my own opinions to myself for the time being.

"Anybody who'd murder somebody is crazy," said Howie.

"Psychologically, but not legally, a quite defensible position," said Ben, who handed me a glass nearly full of bourbon. He sat beside Howie. "No leads, huh?"

"I guess not. I wouldn't expect this to be solved, if I were you. The detective I talked with wasn't very encouraging."

"Doesn't matter," said Meriam. "Wouldn't make Stu any less dead if they caught his killer."

"But Mim, don't you want to see the bastard burned?" Howie's voice quavered with emotion, and I was again reminded of how weak men rarely survive as husbands of strong women.

"What good would that do?" she answered.

"In any case," said Ben, "murder is a crime against the state, not against the victim's survivors, so we shall let the state do what it can." He eyed me meaningfully. "And we shall stick to our own affairs."

Ben's tone defined that as the end of that particular topic of conversation. He turned to the four people seated on the other sofa. "Brady, you know Frank Higglesworth, Cal McDowell, and Harry and June Parker?" I nodded to each of them. "Harry, here, has been lecturing at the Fletcher School this semester," Ben continued. "His star has risen since that business in Haiti. The State Department is looking for good men to invent apologies for their Caribbean policies. It looks like Harry is their man."

"I'm not an apologist," said Parker, in what I gathered was his Fletcher School lecturer's tone. "I have simply pointed out that arguments on the ethics of intervention miss the point. It's not a question of some abstract concept of justice, after all. As Thucydides said, 'Right, as the world goes, is only in question between equals in power, while the strong do what they can and the weak suffer what they must.' It's that simple. If the administration's policy is wrong, it's wrong because it violates our vital national interests. I don't happen to think it does. Hence, it's right."

Meriam clapped her hands. "Oh, that is wonderful, Harry. I absolutely adore sophistry. Do some more of it for us."

"You really are such a bitch, Mim, darling," said Harry's wife sweetly.

"*Noblesse oblige*, June, dear," answered Meriam with a lupine smile.

"I should think," persisted Parker, "that after what Castro did to the Woodhouse holdings in Cuba you'd have a more sympathetic attitude to our government's firmness in Haiti, even disregarding the issue of party loyalty."

Meriam shrugged. "So he nationalized our banana plantations. I'd have done the same thing if I'd been Castro."

"In retrospect," said Ben, "I wish we'd taken a firmer stand earlier in Cuba. I don't miss the bananas particularly. But the tobacco situation is another story. A good cigar, after all, *is* a smoke." Ben made a show of checking his watch, and then put his hand on my arm. "You're welcome to stay here, Brady, and toast yourself in the warmth of the fireplace and the heat of the discourse. As for me, I've got to make a couple of phone calls."

"I think I'll freshen my drink," I said, grateful for the chance to move.

"Help yourself," said Ben, waving to the table in the corner.

I stood up. "Do come back and tell us what you think about Haiti," said Meriam to me.

"I don't have any interesting views," I said, thinking that Altoona would easily hold his own with all of them. "I go along with Harry, here. Vital national interests. Bananas and cigars. That sort of thing."

Meriam winked at me, and I went over to slosh some more Old Grand-Dad into my glass. I wandered into the kitchen, where gleaming chrome and glass contrasted with the otherwise comfortable colonial decor of Ben's home. "Neo Paul Revere," Ben called his eclectic collection of braided rugs, overstuffed chairs, oil paintings, and antiques, but that was Ben's point of view. By his standards, the rented junk in my apartment qualified as Early Conan the Barbarian.

I nodded at the group that was playing wordgames at the big trestle table and shook hands with the two Woodhouse nephews I recognized. Then I moved over so I could gaze out of the floor-to-ceiling windows. The pink late afternoon sky was studded with black submarine-shaped clouds, and the snow-covered landscape that rolled down toward the frozen river seemed to glow colorlessly as it gathered what was left of the daylight. The stark lines of a rail fence carved the pasture into neat geometrical shapes.

It was a cold, dead world outside, a more appropriate setting, somehow, for a gathering to mourn the dead than the cheery interior of the Woodhouse mansion.

I sipped my drink, grateful that nobody seemed to feel obligated to include me in the activities. I practiced no religion, but still I felt that I had been more moved, more motivated to speculate on big questions, than these members of Stu's family, who seemed content to accept his death with a Calvinist fatalism that struck me as ironic. Calvinism with no God to impose order, however arbitrary, was randomness without redemption—the bleakest of all theologies, a black existential pit.

I went to look for the football game. I had wagered a

dollar on Miami with Charlie McDevitt. I suspected I would accept that loss, should it happen, with considerably less equanimity than Meriam and Ben accepted Stu's death.

I found a big color television in Ben's study, a cozy bookshelf-lined room in the far corner of the house. There were two easy chairs pulled up in front of the tube. I took one of them. A young woman in her mid-twenties, I judged, sat in the other. She wore her black hair short. It looked like it had been chopped of hastily by a man wielding hedge trimmers. I supposed she had spent a lot of money to acquire this look.

She glanced at me, smiled perfunctorily, and then returned her gaze to the television. In the instant of that smile I saw enormous eyes, almost black, the color of strong coffee, where the smile seemed to linger after the mouth stopped. When she turned, her nose dominated her profile—not the sharp, aristocratic Woodhouse beak, but a lumpy, meandering muzzle that seemed to begin at her forehead, wander down her face, and stop indecisively only because there had to be a place left for her mouth.

"Any score?" I said to her.

"Miami by ten and marching," she said without turning.

"Best news I've heard today," I said. "I'm Brady Coyne, by the way."

She held her hand out to me without taking her eyes off the television. "Heather Kriegel," she said. "The Jewish girlfriend. The only one around here who seems interested in mourning."

"It is a rather gay celebration, under the circumstances," I agreed.

She turned and looked sharply at me. Then she smiled, as if I had said something funny, or she had noticed that my fly was open. It was a remarkable smile. I read intelligence, warmth, cynicism, and self-mockery in it. It transformed her.

Then, abruptly, she frowned. "What'd you say your name was?"

"Coyne."

She arched her eyebrows. "Aha. Now I remember. Stu mentioned you several times. You were his agent. He liked you."

"I liked him, too."

She touched my hand. "You are the first person I've met today who has said even that much about Stu. I don't understand these people. It's as if he never existed. They're all so damn dignified. These WASPs keep their upper lips stiffer than their penises."

Her eyes welled up with tears at the same time as she smiled. "I'm sorry," she said. She snuffled. "That wasn't very elegant of me. It's just—he was a nice man, Stu, and I miss him, and nobody around here seems to give a shit. Especially his Mummy."

"She probably does, in her way," I said.

Heather Kriegel tossed her head. "If she only knew," she muttered. "Anyway, it was nice they invited me. After this, I guess the Woodhouses will have fulfilled their social obligations to me."

"Aw, they're not such bad people," I said.

"Like hell they're not," she said.

She stood up and walked over to the window. She wore a black wool dress that revealed a sturdy body, constructed more of angles than curves, which, coupled with her short, carelessly cut hair, struck me as almost sexually neutral. Except that as she stood looking out the window, the slimness of her waist and the vulnerability of the back of her neck were decidedly feminine.

I turned my attention to the football game, and in a minute Heather came back and folded herself into the other chair. "You're an attorney, right?"

"Afraid so."

"Well, for Heaven's sake, you don't need to apologize."

"I didn't mean to."

She stared at me solemnly and nodded. "I could use an attorney right now. Are you by chance available?"

I smiled. My legal specialty was rich old folks. Most of them turned out to be Yankees with roots deep in the rocky New England soil. They rarely called upon me to perform difficult juridical maneuvers. I didn't consider this peculiar emphasis in my practice to be a matter of prejudice, or snobbery. It just happened to be the way things had evolved, and it had become comfortable.

"I'm not taking any new clients just now," I said. "I can recommend one, if you want."

She shrugged. "That might be good. So. Who do you like?"

"What, the game? I like Miami. I like them a dollar's worth."

"Really go out on a limb, don't you? I've got the Jets and four. Not enough. Ever since they made a rule against Gastineau making a jerk of himself whenever he sacked the quarterback, the Jets have had trouble covering the spread."

"Well, what with my big investment and all," I said, "my heart has been in my mouth all afternoon."

She grinned. "How was Stu's book coming along?"

"You knew about the book?"

"Sure. He told me what he was going to do. The last time I saw him or heard from him was in October, when he left. Did he get any of it done?"

"He sent me notebooks every week. I haven't read them."

"We talked about collaborating, you know."

"No, I didn't. In what way?"

"I'm a photographer. He had in mind a kind of documentary. His text, my black-and-white photos. He was going to do his research, make his connections, and then take me into the city with my camera. I guess that's out the window now."

"I don't see why it should be," I mused. "I do have the notebooks. Maybe there's still a project there."

"I'd really like to see them."

"Why not? They're not going to do poor Stu any good. Perhaps I could send them to you."

"Yes. I'd like that. I'm sick of taking graduation pictures and kiddie shots in K-Mart on Saturday mornings."

"My wife was a photographer," I said.

"Was?"

"My ex-wife, I should say."

"You're divorced."

"Yes."

"Good."

I looked quickly at her, but she was smiling at the television. I pushed myself up out of the chair. "Well, Ms. Kriegel . . ."

She glanced up at me. "Heather, please. Funny name, huh? You know how some parents want a boy, so they name their daughters things like Bobby and Sam and Joey? My parents wanted a WASP. They hoped I'd be tall and blonde and become a cheerleader and play the harp and go to Vassar. So they named me Heather. When they saw what I was going to look like they gave it all up. Are you a WASP, Mr. Coyne?"

"I'm a mutt," I said. "A little of this, a little of that. The surname's Irish. All sorts of other things in the genes. And call me Brady, for God's sake."

"Sturdy American stock," she said. "Stu, of course, was a WASP. His parents didn't exactly approve of our liaison. I assume there's a connection there somewhere."

I nodded.

"You sure you don't want to be my lawyer?" That mocking, wry grin was back.

I shrugged. "Sorry."

She nodded "Okay. You said you could recommend somebody."

"I can."

"Well, who?"

I took one of my business cards from my wallet and wrote a name and phone number on the back of it. I handed it to Heather Kriegel. "This is the name of an excellent young attorney. He's better than me."

She cocked her head and nodded solemnly as she took the card from me. She squinted at what I had written. "What is this guy, a Greek?"

"Why—does it matter?"

"Not at all. I'm just interested in things like that."

"As a matter of fact, he's black."

"Oh. Well, good."

I was still standing, and Heather was still curled in the chair in front of the television. I held my hand to her. "I have to leave. Nice to have met you."

She took my hand and held it. Her grip was firm. "Those notebooks. I am serious about that, you know."

"My number's on that card. Call and remind me."

She nodded. "You can count on it."

5

Ben Woodhouse called me two days later. "Couple of odds and ends," he said.

"Such as what?"

"Stu's condo, for one. The Jewish girl is reluctant to move out."

"What the hell are you talking about?"

"Stu's girlfriend. Maybe you met her. She was at the house Sunday."

"Sure I met her. What about her?"

I heard Ben sigh. "They lived together in a condominium in Sudbury. Now that Stu is gone, naturally the place ought to revert to his family. But the girl indicates she's not moving. She evidently is prepared to fight this in court."

I decided not to tell Ben right then that I had recommended a damn good lawyer to her. But it did occur to me that I was Ben's lawyer, and he was now asking me to demonstrate that I was worth that hefty retainer he paid me. "If the place is in Stu's name," I said carefully, "I don't see what the problem is."

"That is the problem. Stu put it in her name."

"Off the top of my head, then, I'd say it's legally hers."

"I don't think this is a matter that will lend itself to top-of-the-head opinions, Brady." He hesitated. "Actually, between the two of us, that's perfectly all right with me. It's Meriam. She wants it back."

"Why?"

"Oh, Christ, I don't know. She never liked Stu's arrangement. She's found some way to blame the girl for what happened to Stu. She says he bought the place with Woodhouse money, the place should belong to the Woodhouses. You know Meriam."

"Yes," I said. "I do know Meriam. Okay, Ben. I'll look into it. But unless there's something there that doesn't meet the eye, my advice is to forget it."

"Meriam is very definite about this."

"I don't doubt it. What are we talking about here, a hundred and fifty thousand dollars?"

"One-sixty-five."

"Really, Ben . . ."

"Dammit, Brady. This was a family decision."

"Sure. Democratic vote."

"Yes."

"Well, listen to your attorney for a minute, then, will you? If this place is in her name, and unless there's something funny about the documentation, then it belongs to her, and no lawyer is going to convince a judge otherwise. Even if you got that particular judge appointed, Ben."

"That's not how I play the game, and you know it."

"Yes, I do. I'm sorry. That was uncalled for. I should tell you something. I spoke with Ms. Kriegel at your little get-together. I recommended a lawyer to her. A friend of mine. A very competent attorney. He will not blow this case."

"Meriam is certain that Stu put the condo in the girl's name for tax reasons."

"Doesn't matter," I said. "You better just forget the whole thing."

"I'll have to talk to Meriam."

"Something to think about here, Ben. Are you prepared to face a palimony suit?"

"You wouldn't allow that."

"I wouldn't like it. If this gets to court, I might not be able to prevent it."

Ben chuckled. "It might be worth it, just to watch Meriam squirm. In any case, you're our lawyer, and I expect you to give us your best advice on this."

I told him I thought I already had, and he said to think about it some more, and I told him he better come up with something for me, and he said he'd talk to Meriam about it, and we hung up.

Later that morning Julie buzzed me. "Who is it, dear?" I said into the intercom.

"Don't call me 'dear.' It sounds patronizing." Her voice hissed.

"Well, bless me, I'm sorry, my good woman."

"That's not much better."

"Julie?"

"Yes?"

"Who's on the phone, huh?"

"It's Zerk."

"Well, good. Put him on."

"Certainly, sir." Julie was touchy about some things that generally seemed to elude me.

I hesitated for a moment before I jabbed the button that would connect me with the man on the other end of the line. "Zerk" was Xerxes Garrett, a young attorney with an office on Mass Ave in North Cambridge. During the year that Julie took her maternity leave to have her daughter, Zerk clerked for me and I tutored him for his law boards. When Julie came back to work, I tried to persuade

Zerk to stay on as my partner, but he made it clear that he didn't want to specialize in protecting the legal interests of my wealthy clientele.

"Don't get me wrong," he had said, his handsome black face solemn, as if he were afraid he'd hurt my feelings, "but helping rich white dudes get richer just ain't my idea of a career."

So he set about to establish the kind of practice he could live with—bringing suit against absentee landlords when the heat went of in Mattapan apartment buildings in January, watchdogging personnel moves in the Boston schools and Cambridge Fire Department, facilitating welfare and food stamp distribution, and testifying before the state legislature on bills that might affect the status of minorities in the Commonwealth.

He helped to coordinate the Jesse Jackson campaign in Massachusetts. He coached a team in the Boston summer basketball league. He negotiated a contract with the Patriots for a big offensive tackle out of Grambling. His career was shaping up.

Now and then I referred a client to him. "Don't try to work out your honkie guilt on me," he'd say. "White man's burden, all that shit. I'm scrapin' by."

"I'm just looking for a good attorney," I'd tell him. And I meant it. He was tough and smart, he knew the law, and he had a sharply honed sense of justice.

I spoke into the telephone. "Hey, Zerk. How you doing?"

Zerk's laugh was a loud, high-pitched cackle. In bars and restaurants, Zerk's laugh created instant, awed silence. Rock-and-roll bands stopped playing in mid-bar if Zerk laughed in the building where they were performing. This time he gifted me with an especially hearty one.

"What's so funny?" I said.

"My guy's suing your guy, and my guy's gonna win. Hoo hee haw!"

"You've talked to Heather, huh?"

"Sure have, old bossman. And I got the facts." Zerk liked to annoy me by mimicking what he thought I would recognize as black dialect. He pronounced the word "facts" as if it were "facks."

"But you're calling me to see if maybe we can't negotiate a settlement out of court."

"Only interested in saving you-all some aggravation, tha's all, massa. Nothing to negotiate."

"The Woodhouses do not intend to cave in on this, Zerk."

"Well, goodie! I get to drag them into court. Get to square off against my old mentor. Gonna beat the shit out of you, my man. Ms. Kriegel's got all the right papers. Plus lots of interesting things to say, if necessary."

"Like what?"

"Tut-tut. You wanna negotiate, give me something, maybe I'll give you something. But I got a secret word for the day. Wanna hear it?"

"Sure, Zerk. Whisper it into my ear."

His whisper nearly ruptured my eardrum. "Palimony!" was the word he screamed into it.

"I already thought of that," I said primly.

"You thought of it, maybe. What you gonna do about it?"

"I think you and I ought to meet for lunch," I said.

"I was waiting for that. Locke Ober's."

"Jake Wirth's," I countered.

"Parker House."

"Durgin Park."

"Uh-uh. Parker House is as far as I'm going. You want me to whisper that word again?"

"Okay. The Parker House it is. You got it."

"Just so there's no misunderstanding, Counselor, it's on you."

"It's on me," I said. "Friday okay?"

"I'll clear off my very busy calendar. One o'clock."

"See you there," I said, looking forward to it already.

Heather Kriegel's condominium was snugged back into the woods off a side road just beyond the Common in Sudbury. It was one of a series of townhouses set close together but angled strategically to provide maximum privacy. Four condos made up one building, so that each occupied a corner. Curving walkways connected them all. Scattered here and there were the gaunt winter skeletons of apple trees.

Heather's was the one with the pine cone wreath on the door and the brown Volkswagen Rabbit tucked under the carport. I parked my BMW behind the Rabbit, took the bulky package containing Stu's notebooks from the seat beside me, and went up to ring her bell. Earlier in the day I had been willingly seduced by the false promise that comes with a touch of January thaw, but now that the sun was sinking in the pale cloudless sky, the air carried a new bite, and I shivered in my fleece-lined parka. I waited several moments, then rang the bell again. I could hear music coming from inside.

The door opened abruptly and Heather Kriegel stood there on the other side of the storm door grinning at me. She had a towel draped around her neck. She wore a pink leotard and black tights with gray and blue striped legwarmers bunched down around her ankles. Her forehead was damp, and wisps of her shaggy black hair stuck to it.

She pushed open the door. "Oh, God, come on in. It's bitchily cold out there. I'm sorry. I had the music on loud—I always put on the music when I'm exercising, because it helps me forget the pain—and I guess I didn't hear the bell. Have you been standing there long?"

I smiled at her as I entered into the little flagstone foyer. "Just got here." I handed the package to her. "These are Stu's notebooks."

She took them from me. "It was really nice of you to bring them out here," she said. "You sure you didn't make a special trip?"

"It was no problem," I said evasively.

"Well for heaven's sake, come on in. Give me your coat."

I shrugged off my coat and followed her into what corresponded more or less to a big living room. The furniture had been arranged to section it off into several different parts: a sofa and soft chairs around a circular coffee table in front of the fireplace, a dining table centered on an oval braided rug, a desk in a corner by floor-to-ceiling bookcases, and, for lack of a more precise term, a gymnasium, with a rowing machine, a stationary bicycle, and a weight machine. The whole room was filled with the extravagant orchestral strains of Wagner.

"That's *Die Walküre*, isn't it?" I asked loudly.

She nodded. "Kinda loud, huh?" She went over to the stereo in the corner near the fireplace and turned down the volume a couple of notches. It was still loud. "Don't you like Wagner?"

"Sometimes, yes. Sometimes I prefer a little Bach counterpoint on a harpsichord, though. Usually, actually."

"Wagner is more inspiring, exercise-wise. You know about the Valkyries, don't you?"

"Not really."

"The handmaidens of the Norse god Odin. They hovered over the battlefield, picking out which of the young warriors would be killed. Then they conducted their souls to Valhalla. Real ballbusters, the Valkyries, flying around up there deciding the fate of the young men. Don't you love that image? The ancients knew all about how women could get pissed off at men. Great women's liberation themes in classical mythology, you know. Scylla and Charybdis, the harpies, the sirens. All of them real nut-knockers."

I smiled. "Nut-knockers."

"God," she said. "This place is a mess." She moved around the room, making little piles of the books, magazines, and newspapers that lay scattered around, and punching up the pillows. I stood there watching her uncertainly.

When she was finished, she picked up the towel and

rubbed her hair and face briskly as she came toward me. She seemed completely unaware that, aside from the skin-tight outfit she wore, she was quite naked. I was not unaware of it.

"Stu and I used to work out together," she said. "He used to kid me about being chubby."

"You don't look chubby to me."

She flexed her arm. "Feel that," she said. I did. "Hard as a rock, huh? Tell me the truth. Do you think I'm too chubby?"

"You are definitely not chubby."

She cocked her head at me and nodded solemnly. "Do I embarrass you?"

"Yes," I said.

She struck a body-builder's pose for me. "My body is a temple," she said.

I tapped a Winston ostentatiously from my pack and lit it. "*My* body," I said, "is a hazardous waste dump."

"I *do* embarrass you." She grinned. "Listen. I need a drink. And you undoubtedly would like something toxic."

"Something that will erode my stomach, yes."

"Bourbon? Scotch? Let me guess." She squinted at me. "You're a Scotch man," she said. "All Republicans drink Scotch."

"Wrong on both counts. I'm a Jeffersonian Democrat, and I drink bourbon. Plenty of ice. No water."

"A Democrat?"

"Well, I hardly ever vote for Democrats in Massachusetts, but that's an altogether different story. Bourbon I drink everywhere."

"I hear you," she grinned.

She disappeared around the corner toward what I assumed was the kitchen. I went to the stereo and studied it for a while before I identified the knob that controlled the volume. I turned it down some more. Then I went back and sat on the sofa by the fire.

She returned in a minute. She had pulled on a big baggy

gray sweatshirt with a maroon seal on it that said "Veritas." Truth. Harvard, naturally. I assumed the sweatshirt had belonged to Stu. She handed me a square glass half-filled with bourbon. She had a glass of pale amber liquid, which she placed on the coffee table.

"Apple juice," she said. "Gotta wait at least thirty minutes after my workout before I get my beer."

She retrieved the big shopping bag I had brought that contained Stu's notebooks, flopped down on the sofa beside me, took a long swig of apple juice, and pulled a notebook from the bag. "I can't wait to read these," she said. "I'm really excited about this project."

"I assume you're aware that there might be a problem if you choose to publish something with Stu's name on it."

She arched her eyebrows at me. "Oh, yes. I mustn't forget. You are the family attorney as well as Stu's agent."

"Up until now that has not presented me with any conflicts."

"Well, I have a lawyer now, so I imagine we won't do anything improper. Will we? Won't you and Mr. Garrett talk about it, work it out? Isn't that how it's done?"

I smiled. "That pretty well describes it."

She touched my arm. "Tell me, seriously. Is there a problem here?"

I shrugged. "I don't know what you have in mind. I don't even know if there's anything useful in these notes. I can't decipher them. I had them photocopied, by the way."

"Why?"

"Habit, I suppose. I have everything photocopied."

Heather drummed her fingernails on her glass. I noticed that she cut them short and square and did not paint them. "If I really wanted to, I think I could persuade dear Meriam to let me do exactly what I wanted with Stu's notes. It is Meriam that I have to contend with, isn't it?"

"You know better than to ask me a question like that, Heather. I brought you the notebooks as Stu's agent. But there are some things you and I can't discuss. Do you understand?''

"The condo, right?"

I nodded.

"You won't get it from me, you know."

I shrugged.

She touched my leg and put her face close to mine. "I have a secret," she whispered, grinning.

I felt my body involuntarily stiffen against her invasion of my personal space, and as I did she squeezed the top of my thigh. "You have lovely quadriceps," she said, her black eyes crinkling mischievously. "You don't run, do you?"

I inched away from her, and she let her hand fall away from my leg. "I don't run, I don't lift, I don't do aerobics or isometrics or macrobiotics or anything else that might prove to be painful or unpleasant or wholesome. If I have attractive quadriceps, it's probably from the stress of hitching myself up to the dinner table. What do you mean, you've got a secret?"

She hugged herself into her big sweatshirt and looked sideways at me. "You're the enemy, remember? Mr. Garrett and I shall keep it to ourselves until we need it. Isn't that the best thing to do?"

"Oh," I said. "That kind of secret." I cleared my throat. "Of course you should keep it to yourself. Consult your attorney. That's always the best thing."

"Aw, I've hurt your feelings."

"That's silly," I said.

"Poor man. Here you are, fixing me up with a lawyer, driving all the way out here with these notebooks, and being so nice, and I'm teasing you." She jumped up and stood in front of me. She reached down with both hands. "Come on. Let's go take a walk in the snow."

"In the snow? Are you kidding? It's cold out there."

She grinned. "Come on. Don't be a baby." She tugged at me. I allowed her to help me to my feet. "Let me just run upstairs and throw on some clothes. Think about chestnuts and open fires. Jack Frost nipping at your private parts. It's nice out there in the snow. It'll help me cool down from my workout. What do you say?"

"Sure. Fine," I grumbled.

"Great. I like a man who's enthusiastic. Go get your coat on. I'll be right there."

She was back in a minute wearing jeans and a heavy cableknit sweater. She went to the closet by the front door and took out a ski parka and fur-lined boots, which she pulled on quickly.

"Let's go."

I followed her outside. It was dark, except for the pools of light cast by the lamps on poles, that lit the walkways. Powdery snow sifted through the orange funnels of light.

Heather hugged my arm as we walked. "There's something you really should know, if you don't already," she said after we had walked for perhaps five minutes.

I stopped and looked down at her. "What is it?"

She frowned. "It's awkward to tell you. You might think I shouldn't, since it sort of bears on the condominium."

I shook my head. "Please don't say anything about that."

She squinted her eyes against the soft snow that fell against her face when she tilted her head to peer up at me. "I'm going to tell you this thing, and then I think you'll understand why you should know it."

I shrugged. "I hope you know what you're doing."

"Mr. Garrett said he thought it would be all right."

"You should have said that first," I said. "What is it?"

She took my arm and we resumed walking. "Stu was gay," she said.

I stopped. "What did you say?"

"I said that Stu was gay."

"Are you sure?"

She laughed. "I lived with him for nearly six years. I guess I ought to know."

"And that's your secret."

"That's it. His family didn't know, of course. That's what makes it so delicious when Meriam wants to be a bitch and take my condo away from me—hey, don't worry. You don't have to say anything." She squeezed my arm to reassure me. "Mr. Garrett would tell you this anyway, wouldn't he?"

"Probably," I said stiffly.

"See, I was Stu's cover, you might say. His camouflage. His guarantee against a scandal that would devastate his family. Actually, I think he was overreacting. I mean, nowadays who cares if somebody's gay."

"The Woodhouses would," I said.

"Well, right. So Stu thought, anyway. Tricky, though, huh? I mean, the scandal of his living with this Jewish woman was a neat diversion, don't you think? Can't you just hear Meriam? 'Poor Stuart. Hormones running amok. Under the evil spell of the Jewish witch, with her Semitic sexual wiles and unspeakable tricks. Obviously looking to grab a piece of the Woodhouse fortune. Well, thank goodness Stuart has the good sense not to marry the tramp.'"

I had to laugh. Heather had the querulous nasality of Meriam's voice down pat.

She smiled. I read a touch of sadness in it. "The condo was the deal. Stu bought it for me. The condition was that I'd live with him, in apparent sin."

"I'll be damned," I muttered.

"And I'd just as soon not have to make this public," she said.

"Um," I said.

"The thing was, of course, that Stu didn't have to buy me anything. He was a wonderful guy. I liked living with him. But he had plenty of money, and I didn't have much, so . . ."

"You and he weren't lovers, then," I observed.

"God, you lawyers are sharp!"

"What I meant was . . ." I frowned in confusion.

She patted my arm. "It's okay. Never mind. Look. Stu wasn't what you'd call a closet homosexual. I don't want you to get the wrong idea. It wasn't particularly a hangup with him or anything."

"He certainly knew how to keep a secret."

"Well, like I said, that was just for the benefit of the family. At least, that's how Stu felt about it. It was his courtesy to them. Especially the Senator, his Uncle Ben. Stu just felt that there would be a scandal if the word should get out."

"Hell, this is the twentieth century," I said.

"The Woodhouses aren't exactly the Kennedys, if you know what I mean. Stu always said that. 'We're not the Kennedys. We are the Woodhouses. We are staid, we are conservative, we are predictable, we are conventional. We are old Yankees. We behave as we are expected to behave.' That was Stu's little speech."

I thought about the fact that Stu had ended up getting murdered. While that, of itself, wasn't scandalous, neither was it the "predictable, conventional" sort of thing expected of a Woodhouse—especially given the circumstances of Stu's death. "Something occurs to me," I said.

Heather glanced up at me and frowned.

"I mean that by keeping his—preferences—such a deep, dark secret, Stu was leaving himself wide open for problems. Someone with an axe to grind could make some mileage out of it, since he wanted it to be kept secret."

Heather sniffed. "Well, he was very discreet, believe me."

"You weren't the only one who knew about it."

"Of course not."

"He had lovers."

"By definition, more or less, wouldn't you say?"

"I guess so," I said.

"He wasn't promiscuous."

"That's not what I was getting at."

"Well . . . ?"

"Look," I said. "It's really pretty obvious. Scandalous secrets—especially about public figures like the Woodhouses—are awfully hard to keep. Even you couldn't keep it."

Heather abruptly stopped walking, turned, and hit me hard on the chest with the heel of her fist. "That," she said angrily, "was not fair."

"You're right. I'm sorry. But do you see my point?"

"I'm not sure."

"Stu was murdered."

"Oh, shit . . ."

"Don't you see?"

"You mean blackmail or something?"

I shrugged. "Do you know if he spent large sums of money for mysterious things? Did he ever borrow money? Any strange visitors or phone calls?"

"I knew nothing of his finances. We kept that separate. As for the rest of it, no, I can't remember anything."

"Well, there's probably nothing to it anyway," I said. "The police are probably right. He wasn't murdered because he was Stuart Carver or because he was gay. I imagine he was murdered because someone thought he was what he was pretending to be. A homeless bum, drunk and out on the streets at night."

Heather sighed deeply. "This is very depressing."

"I'm sorry," I said. "I shouldn't have brought it up."

"Would you do me a favor?" she asked hesitantly.

"Sure."

"Hug me?"

"No problem," I said. I folded her into my arms. She pressed herself against me hard. Her arms snaked around my chest and squeezed strongly. After a moment she tilted her face to look up at me. Little droplets of melted snow glittered on her cheeks. Or maybe they were tears. I kissed them away softly. She smiled up at me and then ducked down to rub her face against the front of my coat. After a moment we headed back to her condo, I with one arm across her shoulders, she with an arm around my waist.

At her door she patted her pockets, and then she said, "Oh, shit. I did it again."

"Forget your key?"

"I always forget my key. That's why I've got one hidden out here."

She stepped to the left of the door. "Six up, six over," she mumbled. She pried up a shingle and a key fell out. She bent and picked it up. "Stu was the kind of guy who'd never forget a key," she said as she unlocked the door and jammed the key back up under the shingle. "I really did love him. Well, come on in."

We went back inside and shucked our boots off in the foyer. I put a couple of logs on the red embers of what was left of the fire while Heather went to the kitchen to get drinks for us. When she came back she put my glass and her beer bottle on the coffee table. Then she plopped down beside me, so close that our thighs touched. We both put our stockinged feet up on the coffee table. I cradled my drink on my stomach and stared into the flames of the fire as it sparked to life. I heard Heather sigh. "We were like brother and sister," she said softly. "We fought, sometimes, the way siblings will. We argued over household chores. We competed. We couldn't jog together. We had to race. But we cooperated, too, and we depended on each other. We hugged each other a lot, and we went out on dates. Movies, dinner, dancing, just like an ordinary couple. It was very nice. Really. I miss him a lot. I think I always will. When I think of him getting murdered . . ."

I felt her shudder. I put my arm around her shoulders, and she snuggled against me. "It was a senseless thing," I said.

She turned her face to look up at me. "Will they catch whoever did it?"

"The odds are bad," I said, "and getting worse every day. The police have absolutely nothing to go on."

"It's wrong, I know, to want revenge," she said, still staring at me with her huge dark eyes. "Isn't it?"

"It's uncivilized," I said. "But very human. And I'll bet you've got some imaginative techniques for revenge."

"You bet your ass I do," she said.

I grinned at her, and then I leaned down and kissed her forehead. When I pulled back I saw that she was crying. "That's just the way Stu used to kiss me goodnight," she said. "On the forehead. And just then, only at those times, I always wished he—he would come to bed with me." She snuffled and wiped her nose on the back of her hand. "I never told him that. It would have hurt him."

Suddenly she threw both arms around my neck and kissed me hard on the mouth. Her lips moved on mine, and a little humming sound came from the back of her throat. She pressed herself against me. I could feel her breasts, soft and full under the baggy sweater she wore.

Then abruptly she pulled away from me and stood up. "Sorry about that, Counselor." Her voice was shaky. "That wasn't fair. I was pretending you were Stu, I think."

I nodded. "It's all right."

She began to move around the room, touching things, avoiding my eyes, talking, as if to herself. "There was such guilt, see. He kept asking me why I didn't have dates, lovers, why there were no men in my life. He had his—his lover. He worried about me. I couldn't tell him. It was him I wanted. But he was my brother. That's how I thought of him. That's what he was to me. A brother. It was so confusing, so complicated. I wanted to make love to my brother." She turned to frown at me. "What does that make me?"

I shrugged. "Stu was a good guy. You're a woman. I don't see . . ."

"Stu was gay. My gay brother. To me, it was either incest, or else I . . ."

I held out my arms to her. "Come here," I said quietly.

She came slowly. I pulled her gently down onto my lap. She put her face against my chest. I kissed her hair. "It's not complicated at all," I said. "You are a woman, that's all. A very desirable woman."

She looked up at me, with her big dark eyes and funny nose and scraggly hair, and she said, "Prove it, then."

I smiled. "Okay. I will. Gladly."

6

Two days later, in the middle of the morning, Julie buzzed me, interrupting the current version of my favorite mid-winter daydream. This one was set on a remote Alaskan river, and the fish were Dolly Varden trout, big ones, which were taking well on bushy dry flies in the shallow riffles.

I flicked on the intercom. "Yes, Julie. Is it important? I'm pretty busy just now."

"It's Mrs. Carver. She sounds agitated."

I sighed. "Okay. I'll talk to her."

A moment later I said into the phone, "Meriam. How are you?"

"I am not at all happy, Brady. Not at all."

"I'm sorry to hear it. Time heals all."

"Oh, it's not that. It's you."

"It's me?"

"I *want* that condominium. I do not want that Semitic bitch living in our place, and I do not intend to sit by and have that happen, regardless of what you may think. Or perhaps I misunderstood Benjamin."

"No, Meriam. You didn't misunderstand him. He pays me for my best advice. My best advice here is to forget any claim on the condominium. It belongs to Heather Kriegel, whether we like it or not."

"We emphatically do not like it, Brady. And I should remind you that it's the family that pays you, not Benjamin, and if you ask me, I think we're paying you too damn much to tell us not to do anything. Now you listen to me, Brady Coyne. I want you to pursue this thing. Do you hear me?"

I took a deep breath. "Meriam, I do hear you. I can only repeat to you what I told Ben. There is no case here. If you insist on pursuing it, we will lose."

"Well, you just make a case. We employ you to do our legal business, not to sit on your fanny collecting a fat retainer. So do it." She hung up abruptly.

"Go to hell, Meriam," I said to nobody in particular, replacing the receiver on the hook.

I stared out my window, trying to recapture that scene in Alaska, when the intercom buzzed again. I picked it up. "What now?" I said.

"Oh, boy," said Julie. "Excuse me if I do my job."

"Sorry, kid. What is it?"

I heard her expel her breath quickly. I could picture her rolling her eyes in exasperation. "It's a Ms. Kriegel. It's probably not important."

"Put her on."

"She's got a sexy voice."

"Oh, really?"

"Another big case, eh, Counselor?"

"All cases are important. Justice, you know, is blind."

"Justice ain't the only one," said my secretary. "Just a sec."

There was a click in my ear, and I said, "Hi, Heather."

"That was nice the other night," she said.

"You *do* have a sexy voice."

"Beg pardon?"

"Nothing," I said. "Thank you for saying that. I wasn't sure if . . ."

"Aha. You *were* feeling guilty. I thought so, the way you snuck away so quickly. Did you really have an appointment?"

"Well, I . . ."

"I knew it," she said. I heard her laugh. "I got the picture, Brady. Sex-starved young thing, all helpless and vulnerable and on the rebound, poor baby, and along comes this brutish fellow to take carnal advantage. No better than rape, eh? Wham, bam. A tidy little seduction, and then the guilt comes on quick and hard, doesn't it?"

"I'm sorry, Heather."

"When you're done punishing yourself can we talk?"

"It was too quick," I said. "That's not the way to start a relationship."

"I personally thought it was a hell of a way to start a relationship. It was just fine. I liked it a lot. I want to do it some more."

I fumbled for a cigarette. "Look," I said, after I got it lit. "I think we should start over again."

"What did you have in mind?"

"Prime rib at Finnerty's. And there's a little place that has good jazz on Route 9 in Framingham. Do you like jazz?"

"I adore Oscar Peterson. I play his records all the time. It's not bombastic enough to accompany my exercising, though. What'll we do after the jazz?"

"By then," I said, "I'll probably have worked off most of my guilt. How's Friday night?"

"Jeez, I've got this really busy schedule. Let me check." She hesitated for about three counts. "Hey, it looks like I can squeeze it in."

"Good. I'll pick you up."

"The reason I called . . ."

"Oh. There was another reason?"

"Yes. The reason I called was that I've gone through all those notebooks of Stu's, and there seem to be several missing. I wondered if you forgot to bring them with you, or if you were keeping them for some reason."

"No, I don't have any others. What you see is what there is."

"Hm," she murmured. "It's kinda weird. One of them is completely blank. And in some of the others, there are places where Stu seems to be alluding to a diary, as if it were something different from the notebooks. Does that make any sense to you?"

"There was an old guy who used to bring me the notebooks every Monday. I figured that one time Stu just had nothing to write, but wanted to keep his friend in business. I always bought him lunch and gave him money when he brought the notebooks to my office. So Stu gave him a blank notebook."

"Altoona? Was that his name?"

"Yes."

"Stu wrote about him a lot. Brady, there's nothing at all for the last week."

"The week before he died."

"Yes. And there's this diary he talked about."

"I don't know anything about a diary."

"Oh, well." She paused. "It's just that I have a feeling he wrote lots of other stuff. I'd like to have it."

"This is the very gentlest of hints, Heather."

"I don't know what I expect you to do. But . . ."

"I could go talk with Altoona, I suppose. I think I know where to find him."

"I can't ask you to do that."

"You didn't," I said. "I should look him up anyway. He's a nice old guy who's pretty sick, and I'd like to buy him lunch again. It's something I've been meaning to do since Stu died."

"And you could ask him about the other notebooks, or the diary?"

"Sure. I could do that."

"Will you be able to do it before Friday?"

"Are you suggesting some sort of *quid pro quo* here?"

"Absolutely not. What do you think I am?"

"I really haven't figured that out yet, Heather. I'm pretty sure I know what you're not, though. And I do look forward to working on that puzzle some more."

"It might be fun, at that."

"Friday, then."

"Friday," she said.

After I hung up the phone, Julie tapped on my door and poked her head in. "Coffee, boss?"

I looked into my mug. Aside from the coating of black sludge on the bottom, it was empty. "I can get it," I said.

She came to my desk and picked up the mug. My younger son, Joey, had constructed it for me in a junior high school ceramics class several years earlier. It was a little lopsided, and there were finger marks baked into the sides. Julie looked into it and said, "Yuck!"

"Don't you dare use soap on it," I said. "It ruins the taste."

"Not a chance. You don't mind if I rinse it lightly, do you?"

"If you feel you must. I'm just getting it properly broken in. When you come back you can tell me what it is you want to tell me."

"What makes you think I want to tell you something?"

"When else do you fetch me coffee?"

"Righto," she said, and she twirled away. I noted again how marvelously well her body had withstood the rigors of childbirth.

She was back in a minute with coffee for both of us. She took the chair beside my desk. "This is the point at which you light a cigarette, I believe," she said.

I did. "I'm bracing myself," I said. "What is it? Some

Harvard Law School type offering to double your wages? Edward getting transferred to Santa Monica? My God, you're not pregnant again, are you?''

Julie raised her mug to her mouth and peered at me over the rim. "It's not me, Brady. It's you. You've done it again, haven't you?"

"Probably," I said. "Give me another hint."

"Don't play dumb with me. You haven't done any work for the past two days. You cancelled your appointment with Mrs. Bailey and then sat in here staring out the window all morning dreaming about trout. I gave you those letters to sign yesterday, and I can see them still sitting there."

I puffed on my Winston. "I've had some things on my mind," I muttered.

"Who is she, Brady?"

"Who is who?"

"The new girlie?"

"Oh," I said. "Look. It's not the way it seems."

She nodded and grinned.

"Well," I said, "I guess it *is* the way it seems. If it'll make you feel any better, I'm not particularly happy about it."

"That," she said, "is a vast relief to me. At the risk of sounding overly maternal, may I remind you that you are forty-something years old. You have two practically grown sons, an ex-wife whom you still love, if the truth were known, and who still loves you, as you know. You've got a lucrative little law practice, a devoted—and rather skilled—secretary, and clients, bless them, who actually regard you as a responsible and competent adult. You know a number of mature women with whom you share warm and hassle-free relationships."

"I know all that," I said miserably.

"I'm not an attorney," she continued. "I got a lousy BA in art history, for God's sake."

"And you've been doing all my work."

"Aw, that's not it, Brady. I just hate to see you miserable again, that's all."

"But I'm *not* miserable. I'm . . ."

"You will be."

I stubbed out my cigarette. "It usually does end up that way, doesn't it?"

"It *always* does."

"Thanks for the advice."

"I'm not giving you any advice. I don't have any advice. If I did, you wouldn't listen to me, anyway. I'm just warning you that I can't represent your clients in court."

"And you don't like to see me miserable, because you love me."

She reached across the desk and touched my cheek. "You got it, big guy. Watch yourself. Okay?"

"It's all your fault, you know."

"What sort of twisted logic allows you to say that?"

"You turned me down."

"Best thing that ever happened to either of us," she said.

"I know, I know." I blew a kiss into my hand and touched it to her face. "Thanks for your concern. I'll try to do better around here."

She nodded and stood up. "If you want to talk about it, I'm here."

"Thanks."

She headed for the door. "Her name is Heather Kriegel," I called to Julie.

"I figured that out already," she answered without turning around. "That was easy."

7

I found the St. Michael's mission on one of the narrow little side streets that connects lower Tremont with Washington, not too far from City Hospital. It was a brisk twenty-minute walk from my office in Copley Square, where Trinity and Old South Church reign benignly in the shadows of the John Hancock Tower and the Prudential Building and the new Westin Hotel.

It was, as the kids say, a walk into a whole 'nother world.

The smudged brick buildings seemed to lean in over the deserted street, casting it into perpetual shadow. Their facades were decorated with spray-painted greetings, most of them variations on the "fuck you" theme. Here and there a parked car huddled under a shroud of gray snow, plowed in for the winter. If there were sidewalks against the buildings, the city had failed to clear them.

I walked the length of the narrow street once, then doubled back and examined the buildings more closely. The second time by I found a small hand-lettered sign beside a doorway that read, "St. Michael's." I mounted the three cracked concrete steps. An index card tacked over the bell beside the solid door announced, "Clinic open 10-12 Tues. Wed. & Fri." I rang the bell.

It was two or three minutes before the door opened and a slim man with a fox face and pointed black beard peered out at me. I guessed he was in his middle thirties. He looked me up and down, decided, I supposed, that I wasn't a homeless waif, and said, "Yes?"

The clerical collar he wore under his green plaid shirt assured me I had the right man. "Father," I said, "my name is Brady Coyne. I'm an attorney. I wonder if I might speak with you for a minute."

He frowned. "Don't I . . . ?"

"Yes. I phoned you some time ago."

"Altoona, wasn't it?"

"Yes."

"Well, come on in, Mr. Coyne."

He opened the door and stepped back. I entered into a dark, narrow hallway, which opened on the right onto a long room filled with rows of rectangular tables. Several closed doors lined the hallway. A couple of men stood leaning against the wall outside the closed doors.

"You picked a good time," said the priest, gesturing me into what I figured was the dining room. "Dr. Vance is just finishing up in the clinic. He won't be needing me anymore this morning. The men'll be queueing up for lunch in an hour or so." He motioned me to take one of the mismatched chairs. It creaked and complained as I gingerly perched upon it. He pulled a folding metal chair up close to me. "Not that comfortable, is it? Salvation Army special. The price was right. I'm Joe Barrone. Call me Joe."

He leaned toward me and held out his hand, and we shook quickly. His hand was dry and bony, but his grip was firm. "Father," I said, feeling awkward about calling a priest "Joe," "I'm looking for Altoona. I haven't seen him in a while. Is he still staying here?"

He sighed and crossed his legs. I noticed for the first time that he was wearing blue jeans and cowboy boots with elevated heels. "Why? What's the problem?"

"No problem, really. We had a mutual friend—a man by the name of Stu Carver. He was killed a couple of weeks ago. I haven't seen Altoona since then. I wanted to ask him a few questions. I also wanted to see how he's doing. I got to know him pretty well, I thought, and I've been concerned about him."

The priest frowned. "Stu Carver, did you say?"

"Yes."

"Should I have known him? Was he one of our, er, patrons?"

"He went by the name Cutter, I think."

He nodded. "Oh, sure. Altoona had him in a few times. Young fellow. An outsider."

"How do you mean?"

He chuckled. "These men, they're private, cliquey types, you know. Not what you'd call sociable. Get a bunch of them in this room, you'd hardly hear a word passed in an evening. But this Cutter, he was different. He'd go around introducing himself, asking questions. Trying to be friendly, I guess. But, of course, they didn't trust him. One evening—it was one of the times he stayed the night—he sat with the Puerto Ricans chattering away in Spanish at them. They just looked at him with their stone faces. Another time it was the blacks. Same thing. Altoona, I think, tried to tell him how it was. These are troubled people who don't like themselves very much. They're defeated. Running away from life. Losing themselves in a bottle. They want to forget their past. They don't want to think about their future. All those clichés are really apt. Anyway, someone like this Cutter sticks out like a sore thumb. Makes them uncomfortable, wary. He was just too interested in things. I remember hearing about his death." He paused. "He wasn't really a bum, was he?"

"No. No, he wasn't. He was studying them."

Father Barrone nodded. "They'd know that immediately. They don't like being studied."

I shrugged. "Altoona didn't seem to mind."

"Altoona isn't typical."

I nodded. "I don't suppose he is." I noticed ashtrays spread out on the tables in the room, so I shook a Winston out of my pack and lit it. "Didn't the police question you about Carver's death?"

He shook his head. "No. I wouldn't have been able to help them."

"Still, you'd think . . ."

"Mr. Coyne, I don't know these people. I don't even pretend to know them. I provide some warmth at night for the first fifty of them that show up. I can handle eighty for meals. First come, first served. Three times a week one of the residents from City Hospital—Dr. Vance, a real saint—comes over. All these sick men, but not many take advantage. See, they don't even want a doctor getting to know them. He starts trying to get a medical history, they walk away. So I couldn't help the police. I can't help the men, either. Not really. I respect their privacy. Try to give them a little spiritual sustenance. Some of them'll come to Mass. 'Singing for supper,' they call it. They're not sincere, I know that." He sighed. "It's not what I bargained for. As a pastor to them, I'm a failure."

"Can you tell me how I might get in touch with Altoona?"

He laughed. "I can take you to him, if that's what you mean. As for getting in touch with him, that may be a bit more difficult."

"What do you mean?"

He stood up. "Come on. Follow me. You'll see."

He led me back into the hallway and then put his hand against one of the closed doors. "Altoona's a regular," he said back over his shoulder to me. "He sweeps up, does a few odds and ends—nothing very taxing. He's very sick. He needs medication. Neither Dr. Vance nor I can persuade him to accept the appropriate treatment. But I can keep him inside in the winter, usually.''

"I knew he was sick."

"He's worse now."

Father Barrone pushed on the door. It opened into an L-shaped room which was sprinkled with an eclectic collection of old straight-backed chairs and overstuffed sofas, a large television set, and faded curtains and rugs. It was what, in institutions, they called a day room. A place to sit around while waiting to heal.

I heard the whistling first, and then I saw Altoona. He had on the same red flannel shirt and baggy pants and oversized boots that he wore the first time he appeared in my office. He was standing in the alcove formed by the leg of the L, where the three walls were lined from top to bottom with books. He was miming a basketball player. He bent over, pretending to dribble an imaginary ball—behind his back, through his legs, forward and back, one hand to the other, all the while whistling. I recognized the tune. "Sweet Georgia Brown," the theme song of the Harlem Globetrotters.

Father Barrone and I stood and watched for a moment. "I don't get it," I whispered to the priest. Barrone shrugged.

Altoona looked over. "Ah. Goose Tatum," he said. "Catch, Goose."

He mimed a pass to me. I pretended to catch the ball and passed it back to him. He caught it and resumed his mock dribbling. He began to sing in a raspy monotone. The tune was "Sweet Georgia Brown." The refrain was "Sweet Georgia Brown." The rest of the lyrics were vulgar, so out of character for the gentle, refined man I had thought Altoona to be that it saddened me.

"Hey, old friend," I said softly. "Can we talk?"

He bent at the knees and pretended to take a two-handed

set shot. He watched the flight of the imaginary ball and pounded his fist into the palm of his hand when it missed. Then he looked over at me and the priest.

"Ah, it's the good Father Joe on his pastoral rounds." He struck a pose and began to sing again:

> Christianity hits the spot
> Twelve disciples, that's a lot,
> Jesus Christ and a virgin, too
> Christianity's the thing for you.
> Holy, holy, holy, holy, holy.

"Forgive us our trespasses, Father," said Altoona. "More of your opiate for the people."

"See what I mean?" whispered the priest.

I walked over to where Altoona stood. I reached to touch his arm, and he jumped away from me.

"Cutter is dead," I said.

"Alas, poor Cutter. Hey, nonny, nonny."

He sat suddenly on one of the wooden chairs and began to cough. This spasm seemed to last longer than those I had witnessed before, and I sat beside him, my arm across his shoulders, until he finished. When it was over, he turned to look at me. "Ah, dear Brady. My late lamented patron. Yes. Cutter is dead."

"Who killed him?"

"Ah. Mum's the word, my man. Keep it in your armpit. The gendarmes took their rubber hoses to me. They flayed my flesh, screwed my thumbs, stocked and pilloried these poor old limbs, but ol' 'Toona was too much of a man for them. Now here comes the good guy." He shook his forefinger in my face. "Now, now. These lips are sealed."

"Do you know something? He was your friend, you know. Others may be in danger. You know you can trust me."

He glanced toward Father Barrone, who had sat on one

of the sofas, and then he looked at me sharply. I wondered just how crazy he really was. "Cutter asked too many questions. Bound to offend. Talked too much. Not me."

"Who? Who did he offend?"

He put his hand over his mouth and squinted slyly. "Let's discuss books." He waved his hand around at the rows of old volumes against the walls. The books looked faded and dusty and unused. He hummed "Sweet Georgia Brown," and for a moment I thought he had forgotten I was there. Suddenly he jabbed at me with his forefinger. "Spinoza, for example. Do you know Spinoza, Brady Coyne, attorney at law? The good Father Barrone here knows Spinoza. Most intelligent fellow, Spinoza. Jewish boy. Died of consumption, he did. TB, that is. Foul disease. At the callow age of forty-five. You and I'd be dead by now if we died at the callow age of forty-five. At least I would. Wrote things in Latin, Spinoza did. He was a book writer. I don't think this institution carries the works of Spinoza. They have some interesting tomes here. But no Spinoza."

"I'm not familiar with Spinoza," I said.

"More's the pity."

"What about some lunch? Let's go have lunch."

"Oho! Oh, no you don't, sir."

"I'd like to buy you lunch, my friend. For old time's sake."

"You don't owe me. I don't owe you. We're even. The slate is clean. *Tabula rasa.*"

"Coffee, then, at least. What do you say?"

"I have no information to sell." He whistled a bar of "Sweet Georgia Brown."

"Dammit, I'm not trying to buy you."

He twisted his head so that his face was close to mine. "You are a good man," he said in a low voice. "We have exchanged favors. Value for value. Now we're done."

"I'm disappointed."

He shrugged. "As am I."

"Did Cutter leave any more notebooks with you?" I persisted. "Or any other notes? A diary, perhaps?"

Altoona stood up and began to dribble the imaginary basketball again. "Do you remember Cousy? Marvelous talent, Cousy." He darted back and forth among the chairs, dribbling and whistling "Sweet Georgia Brown." I sat for a few minutes, watching him. Then I got up and left the room. Father Barrone followed me out.

We went back into the dining room. The priest frowned at me. "Are you all right?"

"I'm a bit shaken, to tell you the truth," I said. "Can we talk some more?"

"Sure. Let's sit."

I lit a cigarette. "How long has he been like this?"

"Since around New Year's. Few weeks, now."

"Since Stu Carver died, then."

"Yes, just about that." He cocked his head and peered at me. "If you're reading something into that, you should know that Altoona has a history of mental disease. He was institutionalized for several years. He was released only because of Reagan's cutbacks. He was never considered cured."

"Yes, he told me that."

"He's a very sick man. In many ways."

I nodded. "That is evident. Just how sick is he?"

The priest shrugged. "You probably should talk to Dr. Vance about that."

"I'd like to," I said.

Barrone glanced at his watch. "He should be almost done. He has taken special interest in Altoona. He's quite an unusual person, Mr. Coyne. Dr. Vance, that is. Donates his services. Do you know where places like this would be without the good will of lots of skilled professional people?"

I shrugged. "I can imagine."

He looked sharply at me. "We can use all sorts of help."

"About Altoona," I said.

The priest smiled.

"You'll continue to take care of him?"

"Sure. As long as I'm here, he's got a home."

"Are you planning to leave?"

The priest grinned. "Mr. Coyne, priests don't make plans. They pray. I have been called to serve. I go where I'm sent, I serve whomever I find there."

"I admire the work you do."

His eyes glittered in a cynical smile. "Don't. I didn't choose it. I dream of a little rural parish near the sea, where there are birds and sunshine and fields, and young matrons come to me crying over their petty marital spats." He looked at me. "I trust that doesn't shock you."

"No." I smiled. "I indulge myself in daydreams, too."

"Well," he said, "I guess that's what keeps us going. These men, they don't have daydreams. Well. Let me take you to Dr. Vance now. He can fill you in on Altoona."

"Good."

I followed the priest to the end of the narrow corridor. He rapped lightly on the door and then pushed it open. The room was small and square and windowless. The walls were lined with shelves and glass cabinets holding bottles and vials and medical gear. It smelled of antiseptic.

A big bear of a man dressed in a white jacket stood beside an older man who was perched up on an examining table. The doctor had skin the color of dark tanned leather. His black beard had streaks of white in it. The hair on top of his head had receded about halfway back. The patient had skin the color of school paste, except for feverish patches of red on his cheeks and a bulbous red nose. Both men looked up when the priest and I entered.

"With you in a minute," said Dr. Vance, his voice rumbling in the fifty-gallon drum that was his chest. He turned to his patient. "Now, Charles," he murmured, "This been hurtin' you some, I 'magine." The doctor's accent was Caribbean—Jamaican, I guessed, with a British seasoning.

"Hurtin' like a sumbitch," the older man whined. "Can't sleep. Even the spirits don't help none."

"Well, then, my frien', you shouldn' worry about my takin' a li'l nick out of it, make all that pain go away."

The doctor peered at the man's neck, touching it tenderly with rubber-gloved hands, and I saw the problem. A boil the size of a silver dollar and the shape of Mt. St. Helen's threatened to erupt just at his hairline. It hurt me just to look at it.

"Don't touch it," said the man. "I don't think I could stand it. Just give me some pills."

"Pills ain't goin' help you, Charles. You let Doctor Adrian take care of you right now."

"You'll make it better?"

Vance chuckled. "All better. Promise."

He swabbed the neck with a bright orange antiseptic, then went to one of the cabinets and removed a slim surgeon's lancet from a container where, I assumed, it had been bathing in alcohol. When Charles saw it he started to climb down from the table.

"Sit still, there, Charles. It's just going to make you feel better."

"You gonna hurt me."

The doctor turned to the priest. "Give me a li'l hand, here, Father Joe," he said. "You just give Charles your hands for him to hang on to for a second, while I make him all better."

The priest stepped around so that he stood directly in front of Charles. He said, "Give me your hands, now, Charles." The other man did. "Would you like to say a little prayer?"

Charles shook his head. "He's gonna fuckin' hurt me, Father, 'scuse me."

"He's going to fix you up," said the priest, and both he and the doctor murmured soothingly. Vance held a piece of gauze in his left hand and the lancet in his right. He stood behind Charles. He placed the gauze against the boil. When he touched his neck, the old man cringed.

"Hold tight," said the priest.

"Nasty carbuncle, there, Charles," said the doctor, and as he spoke he touched the tip of the scalpel to the white center of the boil. Charles screamed, a sudden cry of pure pain. I turned my head away.

"It's done," rumbled the doctor.

"My good God," said Charles, breathing rapidly. "Oh, Christ, that hurt."

When I looked again, the doctor was swabbing the area with more antiseptic. He bandaged it tenderly. Charles had broken out in a sheen of perspiration.

"You all better, now," said Vance. He handed him a paper towel. "Wipe off your face, Charles."

Vance peeled off his rubber gloves and dropped them into a wastebasket. Then he turned to one of the cabinets and extracted a bottle, from which he took a small handful of pills. He gave two of them to Charles, then got him a paper cup of water. "Take these right now, Charles. I'm going to give you some more. You take two every eight hours until you run out. Understand, now? This is important for you. You got a li'l staph infection in you, and these pills'll take care of it. Tha's why you got that ol' boil on your neck."

Charles swallowed his pills and accepted the little bottle that Vance handed to him. "Take 'em when?" he said.

"Every eight hours. Can you remember that?"

"Yes, sir. I'll remember. Don't want to get another one of them things."

Father Barrone helped Charles down from the table and walked out the door with him while Dr. Vance went to the sink and rinsed off his hands.

The doctor glanced at me. "He's goin' try to sell those pills."

"What are they?"

"Penicillin. Don't matter. He'll try to sell 'em, and

somebody'll buy 'em, lookin' for a high or a low. Either one. Don't matter. That's how these men are."

Father Barrone came back into the room. "Poor fella's still shaking. Well. Have you met? Adrian, this is Mr. Coyne. He's an attorney, and he came by to visit Altoona."

The doctor's smile was as broad and strong as the hand he offered me. "Pleasure, sir." His voice rumbled as we shook hands. "You a frien' of ol' Altoona, eh?"

"Yes. I'm concerned about him."

Vance nodded somberly. "He's a dyin' man." He pronounced it "mahn."

"So Father Barrone told me. TB, is it?"

"Yes. Many of our patients have it. It's a plague."

"He won't accept treatment?"

"He shoul' be in the hospital. I can't treat him properly here. He won' take his medicine. Like he wants to die."

"What about his mental condition?" I said.

"I'm no expert on that, Mr. Coyne. But I can tell you this much. He's a schizophrenic, ol' Altoona. This is his syndrome. Fairly typical, I un'erstand. These periods of—what would you call it?—lunacy, I guess. Maybe only last a few hours. Maybe years." The big doctor shrugged. "Maybe forever. But the ol' man's harmless. He won't hurt nobody. He won't hurt himself, either, Mr. Coyne. He jus' needs lookin' after, he does. And, who knows? Maybe tomorrow he'll be lucid again." He shrugged. "Or maybe he never will. Better, maybe, if he never does, actually."

"What do you mean?"

"He don' know he's dyin'."

I nodded. "I see what you mean. You know, if it's a matter of money . . ."

"It's not," said the doctor. "We could find a way to take care of that." He glanced sharply at me. "Not that we can't always use money. But ol' Altoona, he's scared of hospitals. He was in one once."

"That was a mental institution, I thought."

"All the same to ol' Altoona." He nodded slowly. "All the same. He won't go." He shrugged off his white jacket, hung it on a hook, and took down an expensive looking leather coat. "Well, back to the hospital."

I held my hand out to him. "Thank you for your time, Doctor. I know you'll do your best for Altoona."

His hand engulfed mine. "I will. But he's goin' die, I'm afraid."

After Dr. Vance left, Father Barrone led me out of the doctor's little office. We paused by the front door. "If there's anything I can do for you, Mr. Coyne," he said.

"Yes, there is. Let me know if anything changes with Altoona, will you? Any change in his health, or if he should become lucid again, I'd like to know about it. Also, if you should hear anything that might shed light on Stu Carver's death, I'd like to know that, too." I took a business card from my wallet and handed it to him.

He studied it for a moment. "That's a nice address, Mr. Coyne. Sure. I'll call you."

I buttoned up my coat. "About Altoona," I said. "Do you think he's afraid? Is that why he's retreated like that?"

Father Barrone smiled. "I just think he's a crazy old man. That's all."

I nodded, shook hands with him, and walked out into the street.

"Oh, Mr. Coyne!"

I turned. Father Barrone stood in the open doorway.

"Come back and visit us, won't you?" he called. "I'd like to talk to you about our operation here."

I nodded, smiled, and waved to the priest. Then I started up the street. Groups of men, clad almost uniformly in long drab-colored topcoats, huddled outside in groups of twos and threes. The thin, cold sunlight, even at noontime, only reached halfway down the sides of the buildings on the opposite side of the street. The slush lay like a gray blanket over the ice on the pavement. I began the long walk back to my office high above Copley Square, where my own daydreams might seem a little more real to me.

8

The Harvard Faculty Club sits right next door to the Fogg Art Museum on Quincy Street, in back of the Yard. It's a pleasant brick building, more of a house than an institutional structure. Ben Woodhouse, as a Harvard alumnus and occasional lecturer on politics, used the Faculty Club now and then, when it suited his purposes. Luncheon at the Harvard Faculty Club impressed out-of-state dignitaries and certain Boston politicians, Ben would say, enough to give him whatever small edge he might need.

This time Ben wanted me to join him at the bar downstairs at twelve-thirty. There was somebody he wanted me to meet. When I got there, five minutes early, Ben was there.

The man seated at the round table with him wore a ratty old Harris tweed jacket with leather elbow patches. He was a slim, wiry guy, with a raggedy beard the color of Grade A maple syrup. The hair on top of his head was longish and curly and a few shades lighter than his beard. He had smoky gray-blue eyes and a sunburned face. He jogged, or did something to keep himself trim. I guessed he was close to fifty, even though he looked younger. He struck me as one of those guys who would always look younger than they really were. Typical professor—political science, specialty in the Middle East, author of a definitive text, just back from sabbatical. The sort of guy Ben liked to hang around with.

Ben saw me and waved me to a chair at the table. "Glad you could make it," he said, as if I'd had a choice. "Brady Coyne, I want you to meet Gus Becker."

I reached across and took the hand of the other man, who nodded and smiled pleasantly.

"Bourbon, Brady?" said Ben.

I nodded, and Ben relayed my preference to the college-aged boy who materialized at his side. I grabbed a handful of little goldfish crackers from the bowl on the table and popped them into my mouth one at a time.

"Anyway," said Ben to Becker, "this fellow—he's an Italian, mind you, and from the Back Bay, no less—he says to me, 'I paid my dues, Senator. I stood up for Goldwater, I stood up for Nixon. I said what had to be said against the colored. I worked for Ray Shamie, for Christ's sake.' " Ben's voice imitated the raspy whine of the unnamed politican he was quoting. "Know what I said to him?"

Becker grinned. "What?"

"I said, 'Go talk to Ed King.' And he looked at me and said, 'You kidding? Ed King?' And I said to him, 'Exactly. Just because I used to hunt ducks with Frank Sargent doesn't change anything. This is still Massachusetts.' "

Ben sat back with both hands flat on the table and chuckled.

Becker nodded, smiling. "It's quite a city, Boston," he said. He reached into the inside pocket of his jacket and extracted a plastic-tipped cigar. He removed the cellophane wrapper, ran his tongue over it, and lit it. I noticed that he inhaled it deeply. A reformed cigarette smoker, I guessed.

My drink arrived. The waiter hovered there until Ben looked up at him. "Another, sir?" he said.

"No," said Ben. "No, we're going up to eat now." He turned to me. "Bring that with you Brady."

Becker and I followed Ben up the second floor and down a corridor to one of the private dining rooms. The room was dominated by a large oblong table, big enough to seat twenty comfortably. It was set at one corner for three. The single window looked out onto a curving concrete piece of the Fogg. Ben gestured for Becker and me to sit on either side of him, and we waited in silence while a middle-aged waitress presented us with bowls of thick potato and leek soup, served hot.

We bent to the soup. If there was to be any business transacted, it would be after the meal, over coffee. Ben Woodhouse felt that it was uncivilized to discuss business while eating.

The soup was followed by a plain salad with bottled dressing, and then an open-faced roast beef sandwich on toast tips with mushroom sauce. The meat was nice and rare and sliced wafer-thin. The sauce was a little heavy on the sherry. Our meal was supervised by a row of dour old men in oil paintings, who appeared to take offense at our pleasure.

While we ate, the Senator told Becker anecdotes about Boston politicians—not cruel stories, really, not tales that were intended to demean anybody, because that wouldn't have been consistent with Ben's nature. They were stories that illustrated the convoluted, Machiavellian character of the city's politics, the legacy of James Michael Curley and Calvin Coolidge and Honey Fitz and Kevin White and all the ambitious Irish and Italian School Committee and City Council people from Eastie and Southie and Dorchester who never seemed to get any farther, despite their unbounded ambitions.

When we were done, and the waitress had cleared away the plates and brought Gus Becker and me coffee, Ben stood up abruptly and said, "Well, I'll leave you two. Brady, cooperate with the man, please. And I'd like a report as soon as possible on how you're proceeding with Stu's estate."

Becker stood and shook hands with Ben. After the Senator was gone, Becker resumed his seat and smiled at me.

"Ben says you're a first-rate attorney."

"I am, although Ben and I seem to be having somewhat different views of what that entails lately. I am also curious to know what this mysterious little get-together is all about."

"Ben says you dot the i's and cross the t's with the very best of them. He says there are damn few lawyers in town who can keep important and sensitive business out of the papers—and out of the courtrooms—any better than you. He's awfully pleased with the job you're doing on his nephew's death. Keeping the lid on, I mean."

I lit a cigarette and waited for him to continue.

"Discreet. That's the word he used. He says you're discreet as hell. A master of the telephone. A virtuoso at the two-Manhattan luncheon. You keep things quiet. You settle things. You get things done."

"You're pretty good at what you do, too," I said.

"What's that?"

"Irritating people. I assume that's what you're trying to do now."

Becker grinned. "Ben also tells me that you like to fool around with police work. A regular crime-buster. This does not please him. He suspects that you just might be sleuthing around on the Stu Carver case. That right?"

"Just who the hell are you, anyway?" I said.

He stared at me. I stared back into his smoke-colored eyes. It was an old schoolboy game. This time I won. Becker dropped his eyes, smiled, then looked up at me again. "Okay. All right. There's no sense fooling around. Ben wants you to stay out of the investigation, such as it is. Just do the legal work, and leave the sleuthing to others.''

"Like you?''

Becker shrugged. "Ben asked you to cooperate.''

"Ben Woodhouse is my client, not my boss. He doesn't tell me what to do.'' It sounded prissy, even to my own ears. "Look,'' I said, spreading my hands, "why don't you just tell me what you're after?''

He gazed at the ceiling for a minute, as if seeking patience there. Then he said, "I really can't tell you. You'll have to trust me.''

"Top secret stuff, eh?''

"You might say that.''

"I'm familiar with that ploy,'' I said. "I use it myself. Sometimes it works. Other times people tell me to fuck off.'' I grinned at him. "Fuck off,'' I said.

He glared at me for a moment. Then he nodded. "You're right. Let's start over again. You can't blame me for trying, can you?''

I shrugged. "I could. But, okay. Start again.''

He took his time. He fished out another plastic-tipped cigar, fired it up, puffed on it, sipped his coffee, studied the old oils lined up on the wall. "You've got to understand, Mr. Coyne, this *is* top secret,'' he began. "It involves something very big. Much bigger than the murder of Stuart Carver.'' He puffed, stared, sipped, then leaned toward me. "I'm with the Drug Enforcement Administration,'' he said finally. "Boston. It's a battleground. It's a territory, and there are armies fighting to control it, armies from Detroit and New York and Miami. It's a real war, and soldiers are dying. Civilians, too. All to see who gets to sell the cocaine in your city. Ben has been educating me a little. But it's a hell of a lot deeper than the petty stuff the politicians are into—although some of them have their fingers in this pie, too.''

"You think Stu was dealing drugs?''

Becker shrugged. "That's a big step. There are certain

connections I can't make yet. I hope you can help me. I'll tell you this, though. I don't think that boy's death was a random, meaningless thing, the way the police do. Just how it's related I can't tell you. Maybe he stumbled onto something. Maybe he was involved in some way. Maybe he bought drugs, or sold them, or carried them. I don't know. That's what I'm trying to figure out.''

I thought for a moment. It made some sense, I realized. I had never been comfortable with Al Santis's assumption that Stu's death ought to be passed of as the work of teenage hoodlums or some perverted thrill-killer. On the other hand, I couldn't imagine Stu being involved in drug traffic, either.

''So what do you want from me?''

Becker's eyes were as cold and gray as the slush on the sidewalks outside. ''Stu Carver was working on a book,'' he said.

I nodded. ''That was no secret.''

''You were his agent.''

I nodded. ''So?''

''I figure,'' said Becker slowly, ''he must've been keeping some sort of journal. A diary, maybe. Something for when he went to write the book.'' His eyes stared impassively into mine.

I shrugged. ''That would make sense.''

He suddenly grinned. ''You're not bad, Mr. Coyne. Not bad at all.''

I nodded and stood up. ''Why don't you give me a call tomorrow morning. Maybe by then I can think of some way to help you. Okay?''

Becker stood and held out his hand. ''That's just the way I'd do it. And I've already got your number.''

''That,'' I said, ''doesn't surprise me.''

When I got back to my desk I called Charlie McDevitt. ''Mr. McDevitt's line,'' answered Shirley, his secretary.

"Oh, be still, my heart," I said.

I heard her giggle. "Oh, *you*, Mr. Coyne. You're going to get in trouble someday, you talk to the ladies the way you do. Did you call to talk to me? Do you want to take me dancing?"

Shirley was a chubby old gal about sixty years old. She wore her gray hair in a tight bun. She had a mole on her chin with several curly black hairs growing out of it. She had eleven grandchildren, whose pictures I exclaimed over every time I went to Charlie's office.

Charlie McDevitt was an attorney with the United States Justice Department's Boston office. I had roomed with him in New Haven when we were both at Yale Law School. He was still my best friend, as well as my golfing and fishing partner. From time to time we found ways to help each other out.

"Shirley, sweetheart, would that I dared take you dancing. But I know I couldn't keep my hands off you. One thing would lead to another. Alas, I must live with a broken heart."

"Oh, you rascal," she said. "Hang on. Charlie's right here."

"Hey, you wanna go ice fishin'?" Charlie's voice boomed into the phone. "They're taking big brown trout out of Walden, I hear."

"I can think of easier ways to freeze my ass off," said. "I want to try out a name on you."

"What sort of a name?"

"Guy with the DEA"

"We should be able to pop that up on the computer. What's the name?"

"Becker, Gus."

"Hold on. I'll give it to Freddy." I heard Charlie speak to somebody, then he came back to the phone. "It'll take just a minute. Damn computers. Make everything too easy."

"Julie's been after me to get one."

"We were talking here the other day," said Charlie. "Freddy, our computer whiz, was saying how he thought the computer was the best thing ever invented. Jimmy Duckworth was there, and he said that, in terms of the total impact on civilization and all, he'd vote for the gasoline engine as man's number one invention. What do you think, Brady?"

"Shit, I don't know. How about the condom?"

"No, I'm serious, Brady. Lou, the Chinese guy, he said gunpowder, for the way it changed around warfare."

"Gunpowder was very good," I said.

"Another fella in here said electricity. Somebody pointed out that, strictly speaking, electricity was a discovery, not an invention. Right?"

"Sure. You're absolutely right, Charlie."

"Anyway, I told the guys that they were all wrong, if they'd only think about it. It's really pretty obvious. The greatest thing ever invented has to be the Thermos bottle."

"The Thermos bottle," I said.

"Easy. Hands down. No contest."

"Okay, Charlie. How do you figure the Thermos bottle?"

"Look," he said. "You put soup in it, the Thermos bottle keeps it hot. You put martinis in it, it keeps them cold."

I sighed. "So what, Charlie?"

"Well, shit, man. How does it *know*?"

I groaned.

"Hang on," said Charlie. "Freddy's got a printout here for us. Let's see. Okay. Becker, Augustus. Born December nine, nineteen thirty-eight, Des Moines, Iowa. BA University of Iowa nineteen fifty-nine, blah, blah. What do you want to know, anyway?"

"He's with the DEA, then?"

"Sure. Just like you said. Been all over. Europe, Middle East, South America. Working out of Washington right now."

"He's here. In Boston."

"Well, sure. That would make sense. Anybody working the east coast would be working out of Washington."

"That's all I wanted, I guess," I said.

"That's it, huh?"

"Yup."

"Well, you wanna try some ice fishing, let me know. I'll bring the Thermos bottle, keep our coffee hot."

"How would it *know*?" I said, and hung up.

Gus Becker called me the next morning. I told him to come on over. He arrived in less than an hour.

Julie showed him into my office. He sat on the same sofa that Altoona always took. He crossed his ankle over his knee, hooked his elbows over the back of the sofa, and grinned. "Your secretary's got a nice ass."

I nodded without smiling. "I will help you," I said.

He nodded. "I figured that's why you invited me over. What've you got for me?"

I picked up the stack of papers that I had left sitting on the corner of my desk and handed it to him. He held it in his hands and narrowed his eyes at me. "What's this?"

"Stu's notebooks. You guessed right. He left them with me."

Becker grinned. "What's in 'em?"

"I don't know. Stu's handwriting is terrible. I haven't tried to decipher them."

Becker looked down and started to riffle through the pages. "These are photocopies," he said.

"Yes. Does it matter?"

He picked up one random page and held it close to his face. "Hard as hell to read."

"It's the best I can do for you."

"Where's the originals?"

"Stu's roommate has them. She's thinking of doing some sort of book."

He glanced up at me. "No kidding?"

I shrugged.

He put the stack of papers back onto his lap. "You going to sit down, Mr. Coyne, or are you trying to tell me that I should leave?"

I sat on the chair across from him and lit a cigarette. He studied me with those narrow smoke-colored eyes. "So," he said after a moment. "What else can you tell me?"

"I checked up on you," I said.

"I figured you were going to. Glad you did."

"If you really are who I guess you are, then there's no reason for me not to do all I can to help you."

"No reason whatsoever."

"Do you really think Stu's murder was purposeful?"

"If you mean not random, yes, I believe that," said Becker. "I think it was drug connected."

"Stu was assassinated, then?"

Becker shrugged. "Call it what you will. The police are off base, I can tell you that."

"Well, there is one other thing," I said.

Becker showed no eagerness. He just gazed at me.

"Stu was gay."

Becker nodded. He didn't seem particularly surprised. "That might fit," he said after a moment. "It might mean something. Was he a flirt, do you know?"

"You mean did he pick up guys?"

He nodded impatiently. "Yeah."

"I don't know. I don't think so. I think he had a lover."

"Who?"

"I don't know."

"Can you find out?"

"I suppose I could try."

"Did Carver do drugs, Mr. Coyne? That you know of, I mean."

"I don't know."

He shrugged, then patted the stack of papers on his lap. "I hope you won't be needing these right away."

"Just so that I get them back eventually," I said.

"Sure. No problem." He took a small notebook from his jacket pocket, tore out a page, and scribbled onto it. Then he handed it to me. "Here's a couple of phone numbers where I can be reached. If you hear anything, or think of anything, please call me."

I took the paper from him. Then he stood up and moved toward the door. I followed him. He put his hand on the knob, then turned to face me.

"Sorry about jerking you around yesterday, Mr. Coyne. Reflex, I guess."

I shrugged. "I hadn't noticed."

He laughed and clapped me on my shoulder. He opened the door. "Don't forget," he said. "If anything comes up, give me a buzz."

Later that afternoon I punched my fist into my palm and muttered, "God damn it," and called Ben Woodhouse at home.

"How'd it go with Becker?" he said.

"Fine. I cooperated."

"Good. That's good, Brady. Now, I expect you called to tell me how we're going to handle that business with Stu's condominium."

"There's only one way to handle it," I said. "Drop it."

I heard Ben clear his throat. Ben cleared his throat when he was angry. "I want this case handled, not dropped, Brady."

"I am not going to handle it, Ben."

"Well, now, I thought we discussed that. Meriam is quite adamant, you know. She wants the girl out of there."

"And I gave her my best advice."

"Well, yes, I know you did. However, that's not the way we're going to go with this one, Brady. The family has decided."

"I understand that," I said. "If you'd like, I'll recommend an attorney for you."

"What do you mean?"

"Count me out, Ben."

He was silent for a moment. "What exactly are you saying, Brady?"

"I quit."

"What the hell do you mean, you quit?"

"I mean what I said. I quit. Get yourself and Meriam another attorney."

"Hell, man . . ."

I hung up before I could hear the rest of it.

9

"You know," said Heather, reaching across the small table to touch my hand, "we haven't talked about Stu all evening. That's been kinda nice."

I smiled and nodded. My knee was bouncing in rhythm to the good jazz of the group that called itself "IUD"—a private joke of theirs, I assumed. They had a bass and a piano and a sax and percussion, and their sound was good New Orleans blues, with hints of Ellington and Garner and Getz melded in, and I liked it. The place was dark and intimate and not very crowded. Heather and I had a table close enough to the four black musicians so that we could smile and nod our approval to them and they could bow toward us in reply. The drinks were cheap and generous.

I feared the place would go out of business soon, the same way that the Jazz Workshop and Paul's Mall in Copley Square had a decade or so ago. Unamplified music in Boston was not big business these days, and this little spot on the edge of the sticks on Route 9 didn't have much of a chance.

Earlier, Heather and I had had big slabs of prime rib at Finnerty's. We had agreed not to bore each other with our life stories. Our decision to avoid talking about Stu Carver had been tacit.

"Actually," I said to her, "you are quite a beautiful woman."

"I love that 'actually,' " she said. "Clearly you are attempting to refute an obvious piece of conventional wisdom. Very obvious, what with this big turnip for nose and this mouthful of crooked teeth." But she smiled, and it all fit together, as I thought she realized. She had the kind of look that sneaks up on you—not striking or dramatic, like lanky blondes with Farrah Fawcett hair. But her warm good nature shone through. "Ah, I'm just this dumpy Jewish kid," she added, and crossed her eyes at me.

"I'll bet you'd like me to elaborate," I said.

"No. I know when to leave well enough alone."

"Like the music?"

"Very much. It's been a nice evening. Good food, good music. Company hasn't been all that bad, either."

I squeezed her hand and then let it go. I picked up my drink. "There are some things we need to talk about," I said.

She nodded. "Here it comes."

"First, just for your information, I no longer call the Woodhouse clan my clients."

"Because of me, huh?"

"Not really. Because they do not accept the legal counsel they pay me for. It happened to come to a head over your condominium."

"Brady, I'm sorry."

"Don't be. I feel rather good about it, actually. Anyway, I won't go hungry. The point is, they seem fixed on pursuing the case in court. I'm certain they'll get nowhere with it. Still, make sure you talk it over with Zerk."

She nodded. "What else? Was there something else?"

I lit a cigarette. "I met this guy the other day. Friend of Ben Woodhouse who's some kind of federal agent. He's with the Drug Enforcement Administration, and he's interested in Stu's death."

"Interested," she said. "Interested how? I don't get it."

"Did Stu do drugs?"

She scowled. "I still don't get it."

I explained Gus Becker's hypothesis to her—that Stu might have been murdered because he had become involved in, or had learned something about, the cocaine war in Boston. I took it slow and careful with her, watching her face for a reaction. Throughout my recitation Heather's eyes never left mine, and the frown never left her face.

When I had finished, she said, "Oh, wow! That is wild."

I nodded. "You haven't answered my question."

"Did Stu do drugs? That's some question. Really. I mean, everybody does drugs. But everybody doesn't get an icepick stuck into their head. Jesus! Yeah, sure, Stu would do a couple lines of coke once in a while. That's no big deal. We'd do a little grass occasionally. But nothing heavy, Brady. Listen. I know about big drug use. I've seen it. I know about cocaine, what it can do, how people can get ruined by it. It was nothing like that with Stu. He cared about his body. He took care of it. He ate well and exercised. If anything, I suppose he drank too much. But he wasn't crazy. You tell me about drug wars and South American dealers and people killing each other and all I can say is that I knew Stuart Carver and he would never never get involved in something like that."

"But if he used coke, even just occasionally, he had to buy it somewhere," I persisted.

"He had a friend. Definitely not a dealer or anything."

"Was this friend by any chance also his lover?"

Heather made her eyes go wide. "My, aren't we the shrewd attorney, now."

"Okay," I went on, "and if this friend had drug connections, then Stu might have known about them. Q.E.D."

"Oh, Q.E-bullshit," she snorted. "You're on the wrong track. You're way off, believe me. Hey, maybe he found out about something, I don't know about that. Although there's nothing in the notebooks to suggest it, as far as I can tell. But I am absolutely positive that Stu was not involved in anything. That is really far out."

"Tell me about his friend."

She let her shoulders sag. Then she reached again for my hand. "I can't, Brady. I can't violate their trust. Either of them. I am the only person on earth who knew about them."

"Maybe not."

She cocked her head. "What do you mean?"

"Think about it."

She shifted her eyes to watch the musicians. They were doing something slow and syncopated that might have had its roots in Bach, the pianist and the guy on the sax taking cues from each other. It was compelling, and I assumed Heather was absorbed in it.

When it was over she clapped politely and turned to me. "He teaches math. He's a very nice guy. He and Stu were friends since Harvard. He's a gay math teacher and nobody knows it and he doesn't want anybody to know it. He's quite poor and quite dedicated to his students. He coaches soccer, heads up the computer program, and he emphatically does not fool around with the boys, and I don't want to say anything else about him."

"Yeah, I understand that," I said. "But he might be in danger, you know."

"You think . . . ?"

"I don't know what the hell is going on, but I can't help feeling that if what happened to Stu was related to drugs—or his being gay, for that matter—then this guy ought to be warned."

"I never thought of that," she said. She frowned and

then leaned across the table toward me. "Hey, Brady?" she said in a low voice.

"Yes."

"C'mere," she whispered.

I leaned toward her. She touched my face. "Please kiss me."

I complied, intending a brief touching of lips. But she held it, her hand against my jaw, with an urgency that I didn't reciprocate.

She pulled her face back and looked into my eyes. "I'm sorry," she said. "I guess you're not into PDA's, huh?"

"What's a PDA?"

"Public display of affection, dummy." She sat back. "I still need a hug."

"Soon," I said. "After they finish this set. Then, in private."

"A deal," she replied. After a moment, she said, "Okay. His name is David Lee. He teaches at Lincoln Prep, which is, surprise, in Lincoln, just outside what passes for the center of town there, not far from the Audubon place. If you feel you have to talk to him, please be sure to tell him that it was me who told you about him, because otherwise he'd be paranoid as hell about it. If you can make it so that he understands why I told you, without scaring the wee-wee out of him, I'd really appreciate it."

I nodded. "I'll be sure to do that."

"I feel rotten for telling you."

"I hope you feel you can trust me," I said. "By the way, I did try to do you a favor the other day."

"Yeah? What?"

"I went to see Altoona."

"Who? Oh, yeah. The guy in Stu's notebooks. What'd he have to say? Did he know anything about the diary?"

"He didn't have anything to say. He's had some kind of schizophrenic episode, and I couldn't get through to him. Very sad. When I saw him before—as I did weekly for a couple of months—he was very sharp and smart and good company. Now he's off in his own world somewhere. If Stu kept a diary, or if there were other notebooks, I couldn't learn it from Altoona. But I did try for you."

"Appreciate it. Too bad about the old guy. From what Stu wrote, he was really close to him."

"What else did you find in the notebooks?"

"Oh, you know Stu. Trying to be a sociologist. He was really fascinated with the types of people he met, those poor street people. He seemed quite taken with the fact that so many of them were young. A lot of women, too. And he really got into the way they grouped themselves. Almost exclusively by their ethnic identity. Puerto Ricans and blacks and Arabs. The stereotyped old winos—maybe like your Altoona man—they stuck to themselves, too. From what Stu wrote in the notebooks, there were little clusters of Greeks and Poles and Lithuanians, and just about anything else you can imagine, and they all liked to talk their own language and keep to themselves. It'd be fun to try to photograph them, to capture their differences, their poor old pride, to see if you couldn't get a feel for the sadness and hopelessness of it." She shook her head. "It would beat the hell out of doing portraits of snotty suburban toddlers and high school graduates, I can tell you that."

The sax player announced that the group was going to take a short break. I lifted my eyebrows at Heather. "Let's get out of here," she said.

It was about a twenty-minute ride back to her condominium. Heather rested her hand lightly against the back of my neck as we drove, and we didn't talk much. Neither of us had said anything about it, but we both knew that we were heading back to go to bed together, and I sensed a kind of distance between us, a mutual shyness, and an apprehension, too.

When we got inside, she bustled about, turning on lights, moving pillows around on the sofa, lining up the edges on a stack of magazines. "Oh, the place is a mess," she muttered. "Do you want to put on some music? Help yourself.

Listen. Just make yourself comfortable, okay? I just want to—''

"Heather," I said.

She turned to look at me. "What?"

I held out a hand. "Come here."

She smiled. "What for?"

"That hug."

She regarded me solemnly. "Yes. All right, then."

She came to me slowly and put her arms around my waist. I held her carefully, standing there in the middle of her living room, my face in her hair, breathing in her good clean smell. After a moment she shuddered and adjusted herself against me. "Thanks," she mumbled into my chest. "I needed that."

"Me, too," I said.

She stepped away from me. "At the risk of committing a cliché, I think I'd like to slip into something more comfortable. Want to find something to drink?"

"Sure," I said.

She was back downstairs in a few minutes, barefoot and wearing jeans and a man's shirt with its tails flapping. "Oh, that's better," she sighed. "I still can't get used to pantyhose."

I had found two bottles of beer in her refrigerator. I handed her one. "I haven't seen any of your work," I said. "Don't you do anything except department store portraits? Most photographers hang their stuff on their walls."

"My photographs are kind of like music to me," she said. "I'm not always in the mood for them. When I am, I take them out. Wanna see?"

"Very much."

She went over to her desk and came back with a stack of matted, unframed eight-by-ten glossy black-and-white photos. "These are my favorites," she said, handing them to me.

We sat side by side on the sofa. She lay her head against my shoulder as I flipped through the dozen photographs.

Each was a study in contrast of line, shape, and texture—something soft, irregular, rounded, and natural juxtaposed with something sharp, angular, and manmade. There was an oak leaf caught on a sewer grate, a cloud formation shot into the sun through the struts of a suspension bridge, tall weeds with tiny round blossoms growing up through a rusting hunk of farm machinery. Each photo, at first glance, struck me as simply a snapshot. But each one compelled me to look twice, and when I did I discovered the composition and point of view that gave it a kind of completeness and unity. The pieces fit together.

"I showed these once," she said. "I called the set 'The Machine in the Garden.' Not very original. A man offered me five hundred dollars for the set. I turned him down."

"What were you asking?"

"Oh, I got what I wanted. I wanted someone to offer to buy them. I wanted someone to say that they were worth money, that these creations out of my own mind's eye were actually of value. Five hundred dollars was probably a very generous price for a dozen photographs by a complete unknown. But right then, it was absolutely fulfilling to get the offer. It made me love these pictures too much to sell them. Do you understand?"

She looked up at me and I kissed her forehead. "I think so," I said. "I like your pictures very much. There's a tension in them, a war going on there between the forces of nature and progress, or civilization, or mankind. You can't tell who's winning, but they're kind of ominous. That's what you mean, I guess, by machines and gardens, huh?"

"Something like that, yes."

She snuggled against me while I riffled through the stack of pictures again. I put the one of the bridge and clouds on top and studied it. "Like that one?" Heather said.

"Especially, yes. It's my favorite."

"It's yours."

"Oh I wouldn't want to break up the set. Hey, if you wouldn't even sell it . . ."

"Don't you want it?"

"I'd love to have it."

"Take it, then. Please."

"I accept." She looked up at me and smiled, and I kissed her on the mouth. She moved against me for an instant, and then she touched my face with her fingertips and drew back.

"Hey, Brady," she murmured.

"Yes?"

"Do you know how to play gin?"

I smiled. "I think I can remember the rudiments."

She sat sideways on the sofa and folded her arms. "Penny a point. What do you say?"

"You're on."

She went looking for cards and sent me to the kitchen for more beer. When I returned to the living room she was seated crosslegged on the floor. She had put a Chuck Berry tape on, and we hummed and sang when we knew the words, and when we didn't we made them up. Heather dealt the cards deftly, making them click as she flicked them out. She played fiercely, frowning a lot and chewing on her tongue and offering a running commentary on the progress of the game.

When we were done, she announced that I owed her four dollars and seventy-one cents. "Pay up," she said.

"Sure," I said. "I will."

"Now."

"Don't you trust me?"

"That's not the point," she said.

I counted out the bills and change for her. "Where'd you learn to play like that?" I said.

"My Daddy taught me. He was a real *maven* on cards, Daddy was." She grinned at me. "He tried to teach me a lot of other stuff, too, but except for the cards, my Daddy wasn't so smart, so I don't pay that much attention to the other stuff.''

"What sort of other stuff?" I said.

"Aw," she said, waving her hand vaguely around, "Just his ideas about what was fun and what wasn't. Know what I mean?"

"Nope. Haven't the foggiest."

She put her hands on her hips and sighed. "Well, come on, then. I suppose I'll just have to show you."

She took my hand and led me toward the stairs. She paid absolutely no attention to my cries of protest.

10

"So this is getting serious, huh?" remarked Julie a couple of days later.

She was seated beside me at my desk waiting for me to sign a stack of letters and documents she had typed up. She cupped her chin in her hand, her elbow propped up on the corner of the desk, and she was staring at me as if she could read secrets from my face.

"I like your hair that way," I said, as I scanned one of the letters and then scrawled my name at the bottom.

"It's the same way it's been for months, and don't try to change the subject."

"It looks different. Sort of windblown."

"All the blather around here, it's no wonder. The Kriegel dame, is it?"

"No one says 'dame' anymore, Julie. You've been reading too much Mickey Spillane."

"You've got a real thing for photographers."

"You noticed my new picture, eh?"

"Yes. It's swell. I suppose that's why you've given it a position of such prominence. On the wall right across from my desk."

I shrugged elaborately. "It was a place that needed something."

"One of the shots Gloria did of your boys would have looked just fine there. This one is so depressing."

"It *is* powerful, isn't it?"

"I said depressing, not powerful. Look, Brady. If you're so hung up on women who can take pictures, why don't you just go back to Gloria?"

I put down my pen. "Because she won't have me, for one reason. Now why don't you lay off my private life, huh?"

"You know why."

"Hey. I've been hurt before, I'll be hurt again. That's part of the fun of it. I like this girl."

"Next thing, you'll be saying you're in love with her."

"I would never say that."

"Already I can see it. You've become a quivering mass of chocolate pudding. No. Vanilla. Vanilla pudding has less character than chocolate."

"Yeah, I know, and my practice is suffering and you're doing all my work for me. We've talked about that before."

She didn't smile. "We talk about that all the time. Look. I'm not complaining." She knitted her brows and turned down the corners of her mouth.

"You could have fooled me." I patted her hand in what I hoped was an avuncular manner. "You're beautiful when you pout," I said, which produced the desired effect. She stuck her tongue out at me. "I'm headed out to Lincoln this afternoon," I said. "Don't wait for me."

"Gonna stop off in Sudbury afterwards?"

"No, smartass, I'm not. I'm going to come back and catch up on my paperwork in peace, without people distracting me with dire predictions and suffocating concern. Besides," I smiled, "Heather is tied up all evening."

Julie gathered the stack of letters together, tapping the

edges even before she picked them up. Then she stood and frowned down at me. "It's just that you're such a baby. You're so easily hurt."

"Oh," I said with a wave of my hand, "I guess I can take care of myself."

"That," she said, pivoting toward the door, "is the most ridiculous thing I've ever heard."

Lincoln Prep was a cluster of old brick buildings tucked against a piney hillside on one of the winding country roads in Lincoln, near the DeCordova Museum. Across the street endless acres of meadow and woodland rolled downhill toward a low horizon. The Lincoln town mothers and fathers, with excellent foresight and apparently limitless funds, had purchased and preserved all of this beautiful New England countryside as consevation land. It has always seemed to me that most of Lincoln consisted of conservation land. They conserved meadows and marshes, bogs and fens, hills and dales, to the delight of cross-country skiers, cyclists, hikers, picnickers, and wildflower pickers—out-of-towners, most of them, whose presence, I suspected, was barely tolerated by the residents of Lincoln, who, if the truth were known, wanted it all to themselves. It wasn't the ecology they wanted to conserve, so much as it was the buffer between themselves and the hoi polloi surrounding them.

As I strolled from the parking lot toward the nearest school building, I half expected to see deer grazing on the brown grass that stuck up here and there through the crusty snow that sheeted the meadow. I saw no deer, but as I watched, a wedge of geese cruised over on its way to the open water at the Great Meadow in Concord.

A blond boy in a designer jogging suit directed me to David Lee's room. Classes had evidently ended for the day, because the campus was virtually deserted. Inside the classroom building, the corridors echoed my footsteps. Down the hall I heard voices. I stopped outside the open doorway and peered in. Seated side by side at two student desks were a dark-haired boy with a bad case of acne and a dumpy middle-aged man wearing thick glasses and thinning grayblond hair.

I stood there uncertainly for a moment, and then the man looked up. "Help you, sir?" he said.

"I'm looking for Mr. Lee."

"I am he. What can I do for you?"

"I'd like to talk with you."

He nodded, as if that was what he assumed. "On what subject?"

"Private," I said. "I can wait."

He frowned for a moment, then shrugged. "Okay. We'll only be a few minutes."

He returned his attention to the boy with the unfortunate complexion, and I wandered up and down the corridor. I tried to match up my first impression of David Lee with the suspicion that had been nagging at me since Heather had mentioned him to me. Given their relationship, I had no trouble abstracting the teacher as Stu's killer. I supposed there was a twisted sort of motive in there somewhere. But try as I might, I could not visualize this David Lee slipping an icepick into Stu Carver's ear, and even though I also knew that appearances made a most unreliable basis for judging character, I still felt vaguely disappointed that Lee had not turned out to be a hulking, sneering, drooling monster.

I stopped to read the notices on the bulletin board at the end of the hall. Baseball tryouts were coming up soon. A foreign film festival was scheduled for the weekend, featuring Ingmar Bergman. An assistant dean from Bowdoin was coming to address the student body on the subject, "How to Get the Edge in College Admissions."

After perhaps ten minutes, the pimpled boy left Lee's classroom and the teacher poked his head out of the door and called to me. "You may come in now, sir."

I went into the classroom. It felt as if I had been there a million times before. The heating pipes along the outside wall still clanked and farted, the round clock at the rear of the room ticked loudly just as I remembered. It smelled faintly of chalk dust and old sweat and Lysol. The blackboard—actually, this blackboard was green—was covered with messy hieroglyphics intended, I gathered, to uncover the identities of such mysteries as x, and $a + b$, and the volume of a cone. The one-piece desks were neatly aligned in rows facing the institutional metal teacher's desk up front, as they always had been. An American flag and a replica of Gilbert Stuart's George Washington hung on the side wall opposite the windows.

David Lee stood behind his desk, leaning forward on it, propped up on both of his hands. He wore a blue buttoned-down shirt with the cuffs rolled halfway up his surprisingly ropey and thickly veined forearms. His striped tie was loosened at his throat. His eyebrows were raised in inquiry behind his thick glasses.

It gave me a strange sense of *déjà vu*, right down to the vague tension in my gut that reminded me of how much trouble I used to have with the volume of cones.

Lee smiled uncertainly at me and gestured toward one of the student desks.

"Please have a seat. If you can squeeze yourself in."

I folded myself in, and he moved around to sit beside me. "Now, Mr . . . ?"

"Coyne. Brady Coyne."

He frowned.

"I am Stu Carver's attorney."

He ran his fingers through his hair. "I assumed you were one of my students' fathers. Whose attorney did you say?"

"Stu Carver."

He shook his head slowly. "Is he a student here?"

I sighed. "Mr. Lee," I said, "let us not bullshit each other. I know you were friends with Stu Carver. I know about your relationship with him. I am not here to make trouble for you. There are some things that I need to know.

I think you would be well advised to cooperate with me. What do you say?'' I showed him my teeth.

He stood up and wandered over to the window. He stood there for a long minute, staring out onto the wooded hillside. Then he turned, sighed, and came back and sat down. ''What exactly do you know about me and Stu?''

''Do you want me to spell it out?''

He smiled thinly. ''I guess you don't have to. Do you mind my asking how you found out about me?''

''Heather Kriegel told me.''

''Ah, Heather. I'm surprised.''

''She did it for your sake, Mr. Lee. She has told nobody else except me. Your secret is still safe.''

He paused for a moment, then said, ''I can believe that. She's an honorable person. I guess you better explain yourself.''

''I assume you know Stu is dead.''

He nodded. ''Heather phoned me.''

''And that he was murdered under rather confusing circumstances. That his killer has not been apprehended. That the motive for the murder remains a mystery.''

Lee was staring at me through his glasses. With his thinning hair and round, shapeless body, he was not a conventionally attractive man. But he had an open, pleasant face and a quiet demeanor that I thought would wear well. ''Why are you telling me this?'' he said.

''Mainly, I like to see the guys in white hats win, and the bad guys get their due. It has also occurred to me that you could be in danger.''

''Why me?''

''You are, er, gay, if that's the word you prefer. You also use cocaine. One or both of those factors may explain Stu's murder. There's at least one federal policeman who thinks so.''

He stood up abruptly and moved to close the door. When he came back he remained standing. ''Mr. Coyne,'' he said, "I assume you realize that I would lose my job in about one minute if this ever got out."

I nodded.

"I'm good at my work. I love it, and I need it. I don't hurt anybody. Yes, okay, I'm gay. And, no, it's not the word I prefer. There is nothing particularly light-hearted about people with my sexual predisposition, in spite of what some believe to be the increased enlightenment of our time. Queer is more like it, don't you think? Or faggot. That tells it straight, if you'll pardon the expression. Homosexual is too clinical." He placed both hands on the desk I was sitting at and leaned toward me. "Why do we need to be called anything? I'm a man. I'm a teacher and a coach and a chess player. I'm a bad poet and a good son. I've got bursitis in my shoulder and a partial plate in my mouth. Define a heterosexual person, and the first thing you say about him won't be that he's straight. Right?"

I nodded. "You're right. Of course."

He straightened up and sighed. "I sound paranoid, I guess. I don't really think I am. I'm sorry to lecture you."

I shrugged. "I'm sorry I had to mention it. But it seems relevant, in this case."

"Here's the relevant question," he said. "Can you tell me why people think that so-called gays are so much more dangerous to young people than heterosexuals? Some of the men on this staff—women, too, for that matter—are absolute rabbits, utterly promiscuous. This is not perceived as a problem. But I, who mind my business and keep my private life private, would be heaved out on my poor fat bottom if there was the remotest suspicion of what they like to call a perversion. No questions asked. No due process, not in private schools. And as for drugs, okay, another no-no. This is the biggest hypocrisy in the school. The kids are totally open—even blatant—about it. But teachers? Corrupters of the youth, all of us. Okay. Yes. Stu and I were lovers. And now and then we smoked a marijuana cigarette and used a little cocaine. In the privacy of our own homes. We hurt nobody. I don't see how any of this could get Stu murdered, or pose a danger to me."

"Where did you get your drugs?"

He shook his head. "I'd hate to have to tell anybody."

"You may not have a choice."

"Are you threatening me, Mr. Coyne?"

"No. I'm simply telling you that a policeman could come by with questions for you, and he might not care as much as I do about discretion."

Lee sighed. "I see," he said. "All right, then. I see how it is. He's a professor of physics at Harvard. Living in Cambridge, he has what he calls sources. I never inquired about them. He is emphatically not what you'd call a pusher, or a dealer, or any kind of criminal. He gets stuff occasionally. When he does, he's good enough to share it. That's all."

I nodded. "Has this professor ever had a problem with it? Been arrested, or threatened, or extorted? Anything like that?"

"Not to my knowledge. He's a highly regarded member of the faculty, fully tenured, the author of a definitive textbook. I'm certain he's extremely careful. He has too much to lose."

"Stu Carver went to Harvard."

"So did I."

"Did Stu and this professor know each other?"

"No. This man has only been at the University for seven years. Stu graduated something like twelve years ago. Anyway, Stu had no idea where I got the stuff."

"I'd like to know his name."

"I suppose you would."

"Well?"

"No. I don't think I'll tell you. I'm certain it would do no good, and it could do much harm to a good man."

"Mr. Lee—"

"The answer, Mr. Coyne, is no. Emphatically, finally, definitively no."

I shrugged. "Okay. Let me ask you about Stu, then. Can you think of anything that would indicate he was in danger? Did he say anything to you, or did you notice anything in his behavior? Anything to do with his being threatened, or in some financial difficulty? Any new acquaintances?"

He frowned for a minute, then slowly shook his head. "No. Nothing like that, no."

"When was the last time you saw Stu?"

He hesitated, then said, "Well, it must have been late September, early October. Just before he donned his rags and went to live on the streets."

"You knew about his project, then."

"Yes. I tried to discourage him from it, but he was adamant."

"Why did you try to discourage him?"

Lee smiled. "Because I knew I would miss him terribly."

I nodded. "And you had no communication with him after that?"

"None. When I heard he was dead . . ." He took off his glasses and pinched the bridge of his nose. "I still miss him terribly."

I thought for a moment, then stood up. I held out my hand to Lee. "I appreciate your time," I said. "I'm sorry if I have upset you."

He grasped my hand. "I understand what you feel you have to do, and I hope you catch the son of a bitch who murdered Stu. I'm afraid I haven't helped you."

I grinned. "Well, no, you really haven't. Perhaps you'll think of something. Let me give you my card. Call me if anything occurs to you, will you?" I took a business card from my wallet and handed it to him.

"I will," he said. "I'll call you."

I started to leave, then turned to face him. "One more thing, Mr. Lee."

"Yes?"

"Is the physics professor by any chance gay?"

"That word again." He laughed. "Mr. Coyne, if you'll excuse my saying so, that is the sort of question that is produced by a stereotyped mind."

"You're excused," I said. "Whatever. Is he?"

"As a matter of fact, I have no idea."

By the time I got back to my office, Julie had already left. The coffee was unplugged, the answering machine was turned on, and a thick stack of memoes sat in the exact center of my desk. These were arranged according to Julie's usual system—in descending order of her definition of urgency, from top to bottom. I glanced through them, finding, as I expected, according to my own standards of importance, the most urgent to be the least interesting.

On top was the message that old Doc Segrue, who was embroiled in a dispute with the IRS over some investment property, had called. I made a note to phone Doc's accountant first thing in the morning. Eileen Benson was concerned about the claim her deceased husband's son by one of his previous marriages was making against the estate. I could smooth her feathers at my leisure. Frank Paradise had an emergency which he refused, as usual, to explain over the phone—to Julie, or to me, for that matter. I'd have to drive down to Brewster to visit him sometime soon.

Meriam Carver had called. I knew what that one was all about. I had no intention of returning her call.

Near the top of the stack was a note that Gloria had called. Julie considered all my messages from my former wife urgent. If Julie had her way, I would marry Gloria again. On the memo, Julie had noted, redundantly, "Something personal," and, editorially, "sounds important." Gloria's phone calls were always personal, and, in her mind (as well as in Julie's imagination), always important. She and I harbored no significant grudges against each other. We had no disputes over alimony (generous but fair), nor did we exchange recriminations over the issues that had led to the dissolution of our marriage a decade earlier (mutual agreement, spiced with a pinch of incompatibility).

In fact, Gloria and I got along considerably better once the marital bond had been broken, so that now our communications tended to focus on the growing-up crises of our two boys—young men, actually—Billy and Joey. Gloria and I weren't that much different from any middle-aged married couple, except for the fact that we were no longer married.

We even loved each other.

Perhaps *that* made us different.

Often, we called each other just to say hello. When Gloria called me to say hello, however, she usually had an afterthought to share—which, of course, wasn't really an afterthought at all.

She'd say, "Oh, by the way, the guy at the Ford agency is trying to rip me off."

Or, "That reminds me, I'm sure I smelled booze on Billy's breath last night."

I put Julie's memo aside. I would call Gloria back. I was sure I could handle that one.

I riffled through the rest of the memos. The one on the very bottom of the stack said, "Al Santis (the cop??) wants you to call him." That Julie would bury that particular message didn't surprise me. She didn't approve of my involvement in police matters. I had done it before and ended up with my jaw wired shut for a month. Another time it got me a raised red scar on the back of my leg. I also suspected that Julie didn't think it was dignified of me.

I picked up the phone immediately and tapped out the number Julie had jotted down for me.

"Yeah, Santis," he answered.

"This is Brady Coyne, returning your call."

"Oh, right. Hang on a second, can you?"

"Okay," I said, sensing that he had already put the phone down on his desk by the time I got out the word.

I lit a cigarette, and Santis came back on the line in a moment. "Sorry about that. There was a guy here I had to get rid of. Reason I called was, a couple weeks ago we were talking about the kid that got killed with the icepick, right?''

"Yes. Did you catch somebody?"

"Nope. Listen, do you remember I said I bet we'd find another stiff, killed the same way?"

"Yes, I remember."

"Well, we did."

"You did."

"Yup. Same MO. We found this old wino in a parking garage down of Washington Street. Same wound, in the left ear."

"Have you identified him?"

"Not exactly. That's why I'm calling. We checked around. The priest who runs the St. Michael's mission house there knew the guy. He also mentioned you. I think it might be a good idea if you could come over and we could have a little conversation."

"Oh, Jesus . . ."

"The priest says the dead guy went by the name of Altoona.''

11

Al Santis had a square of waxed paper spread out on his desk. It was splattered with the droppings from his half-eaten Italian sub, which he waved at me when I entered, pointing with it to the chair beside his desk.

I took the seat. He put the sandwich down on the waxed paper, wiped both hands on his shirt, and drew his forearm across his mouth. He nodded his head twice, as if he were confirming something we both knew. "Another friend of yours, huh?"

"Yes," I said.

"Well, I'm sorry." He gazed up at the ceiling. He was embarrassed, I realized. He was not comfortable expressing sympathy. I liked him that much more for trying. "You don't really get used to it," he said, still focused on some spot over my head. "Listen. Let me tell you about this one we had last winter."

I opened my mouth to tell him that he didn't have to bother trying to make me feel better, but he wasn't looking at me. "Got a call from the T cop down at the car yard, where they store all the trains. Big maze of tracks there, and all them cars either waiting to be repaired or beyond repair. Those they cannibalize. Use 'em for parts. Very popular place with the bums. They try to get into the cars to stay warm. There's a big chain link fence around it, and they have a patrolman on duty. But, to tell the truth, nobody minds too much if the bums get in."

Santis picked up his sandwich, regarded it with distaste, and put it back down. "Anyway, this must've been around five or six in the morning. It was just getting light. Cold as a bitch, I remember. The T cop had found this stiff laying on the tracks. Frozen, he was, just like your friend there . . ."

"Stu Carver."

"Right. Carver. Well, this one wasn't that old, either. Dressed up like a Marine, he was. Had the khaki coat, pants, and the high boots. Even had that olive drab underwear the Marines wear. Reason we knew that right off was that his pants were down around his knees, and so were his shorts. Laying right there on the tracks, bare-ass. So we stand around staring at the stiff and freezing our own asses off, wishing we had some hot coffee, until the ME gets there. It didn't look like any homicide to me, and I wasn't that happy about being there at all. On the other hand, it didn't look like the Marine had just pulled down his drawers so he could lay down on the tracks to take a nap. Hard to figure just what did happen. Anyways, the ME finally gets there. He's a grouchy old bastard. Who wouldn't be, you have to get up at that hour to run down to the car yard to look at a dead body? He scootches down beside the body and puts his face up real close to the dead Marine's poor shriveled-up cock, then he chuckles, which he hardly ever does, and stands up. He says to us, 'Guess what happened?' "

Santis cocked his head and moved his eyes from the ceiling to my face. "Well, guess what happened?"

"I don't have any idea," I said.

"What happened was, the Marine, probably half crocked on wine, lets down his drawers to take a leak. Sends off a big stream of piss—right onto the third rail. Zap! About a billion volts of live electricity shoot up his urine to his pecker. The ME said the poor bastard never knew what hit him. Deader'n a mackerel—fried mackerel, I guess—before he hit the ground."

Santis grinned expectantly at me, and I nodded my dubious appreciation. "Anyway, the thing is, a lot of these old people—and some of them not so old—die in Boston in the winter. That's all I'm trying to say. So if I don't come across, well, sympathetic, see . . ."

"I understand. Thank you."

He seemed relieved. He broke a piece of cheese off his sandwich and shoved it into his mouth. "So, Mr. Coyne. Whaddya think, anyway? About this new one, I mean."

I shrugged. "I guess I think that the person who killed Stu Carver probably killed Altoona. I imagine you already had that thought."

He curled his lip back and picked at his teeth with his thumbnail. "Yup. I already had that thought. We gotta try and figure out if there's some other connection, know what I mean?"

"A motive."

"Right. Now, since you knew both of them, I guess they knew each other. True?"

"Yes. They did."

"Just from being bums together, or what?"

"They were special friends," I said. "As a matter of fact, they were special men. They weren't just your average, run-of-the-mill bums."

"I'm a slow learner, Mr. Coyne, so you're going to have to run that past me slowly."

So I did. I explained to Santis about Stu Carver's project, and how Altoona delivered the notebooks to me every week, and how I had gotten to know the old man. I told him of my recent visit to the mission and described Altoona's bizarre behavior.

"What'd you go there for, anyway?" he interrupted. "Just a social call?"

"Well, partly. I hadn't seen him since Stu's death. I wanted to see how he was."

"And?"

"Like I told you, not good. He'd had some sort of psychotic episode. He was out of touch. Not the same man at all."

"Why else did you go there?"

"To see if he knew anything about more notebooks, or any other material Stu had written that we didn't have."

"For the girl's project, huh?"

"Right."

"Did he seem afraid? Any reason to think he felt endangered?"

I flapped my hands. "He was just too crazy for me to tell."

"What about common acquaintances?"

"You mean someone who knew them both? I expect the priest, Father Barrone, could help you more there."

"Yeah, I asked him. He mentioned you. Anybody else?"

I shrugged. "Just the priest, and the doctor, there, Dr. Vance. And whoever else might have hung around the mission."

"And you." Santis picked up a stray piece of lettuce from the waxed paper and pushed it into his mouth with his forefinger.

"Well, we already said that. Sure. And me. Does that make me a suspect or something?"

"I haven't got any suspects right now. That makes everybody a suspect. Don't worry about it."

"I mean," I said, "are you interrogating me, or are we just discussing this thing? Either one is okay with me, I guess, but I would like to know."

"We're discussing it, that's all. I don't think you killed these guys with an icepick, Mr. Coyne. I mean, you could have. Stranger things have happened, you know? But you can probably account for yourself on New Year's Eve, not to mention two nights ago, and I don't see any sense of even asking you about it right now." He grinned at me. "Do you?"

"Is that a question?"

He shrugged. "Well, okay, then. It's a question."

"No. There's no sense of even asking me."

He smiled broadly. "See?"

"Well, good," I said. I tapped a Winston from my pack and lit it. "What can you tell me about Altoona's death?"

"More than you can tell me, I guess. There's a parking garage down there near the hospital. You know, you can walk in right off the street. Lots of nooks and crannies where the junkies like to go to get a hit, and the kids sometimes sneak in looking for unlocked cars to climb into so they can get laid. The winos go in there, too. Good place to get out of the wind, curl up on a back seat with their bottle. That's where they found him."

"In a car?"

"No. He was lying there under the front bumper of a parked car. Guy saw him when he backed out of his parking space, told the attendant, who phoned us." He rubbed his forehead with his fist. "We got nothing on either of these, Mr. Coyne. I'm willing to bet that it was the same guy, using the same weapon. But that don't take much brains. Otherwise, we're right back where we were with the first one."

"Are you aware that there's a federal agent looking into Stu Carver's death?"

Santis nodded. "Yeah. Whatsisname. Becker, there. Yeah, we talked a while ago. I dunno. He didn't seem all that interested, tell you the truth. I got the idea it was just a loose end or something, like he was going through the motions. Those Feds, they got bigger fish to fry."

"Do you think this second murder changes that?"

He scratched his chest. "If anything, it seems to me I've been on the right track."

"You mean a serial killer."

"Well, yeah. That's what those newspaper people like Mickey Gillis call 'em, don't they? Somebody who gets their jollies out of sticking icepicks into the brains of old drunks. So they keep doing it. Yeah."

"And the fact that the two victims knew each other is just a coincidence, then."

"Well, it's not exactly a coincidence. They both hung around the same part of town, they both went out alone, they both tended to get loaded, they both looked like bums."

I nodded. "I see what you mean. Have you been able to identify Altoona?"

"You mean get his real name, next of kin, that sort of thing? Not yet. We sent his prints to Washington. See what they come up with. Meantime, his body's with Welfare."

"He once told me he had been in a state mental hospital."

"What state?"

I smiled. "He didn't say. Pennsylvania, maybe. He came from Altoona, he told me."

"That's where he got his name. Makes sense. We could try down there. Can't do everything, though. You gotta understand, there's a limit."

"Sure."

"We get lots of unidentified bodies. There's only so much we can do."

"I understand." I stubbed out my cigarette. "You didn't find anything on him?"

"You mean to identify him with? No. There wasn't anything. The preliminary report from the ME said, you know, male Caucasian about sixty years old, etcetera, etcetera, apparent cause of death—puncture wound in left ear. He had nothing in his pockets, I know."

"Would you mind if we went over what you found on Stu Carver again?"

"Why?"

"Don't you have his file handy?"

Santis sighed. "Why not? Hang on."

He pushed himself away from his desk, stood up, then reached down to pick up the remains of his sandwich. He took a big two-fisted bite, put it back down, wiped his hands on his pants, and left the room.

He returned in a minute. "You got something in mind?" he said, easing himself back into his chair.

"Not really. I'm still interested in trying to find out if there were other notebooks. And I guess I'm just curious."

"You mean, us cops ain't doing our job?"

"I didn't say that."

He peered at me. "We ain't, you know. There's practically zero priority on this case. I dunno, maybe now that there's another one . . ."

"I would think that might get people mobilized."

He laughed. "Mobilized. Yeah. That's the word for it. That's what Mickey Gillis keeps saying. We ain't mobilized to fight street crime. So we ain't mobilized, and you're gonna solve the mystery for us, huh, Mr. Coyne? Hey, let me tell you something."

I held up both hands. "You don't have to."

"I'm gonna anyway. The Carver case was dead. I admit it. We had nothing to go on. Now maybe it won't be dead anymore. That's not a promise, mind you. More like a prediction. But we still got people like the Gillis broad breathing down our neck on that assassination thing. You see the paper yesterday?"

"Sure."

"You see that broad's column? Just thinking about it makes me want to puke my sandwich all over my desk. Big chunks of salami and provolone and onions and hot peppers . . . ."

"Hey!" I said.

Santis cocked his head and grinned at me. "Gillis is blaming us, for Christ's sake. For letting the spic get close to whatsisname, the State Department guy, Lampley, and for the little spic getting killed so we couldn't figure out who hired him. Like that. I figure about once a month for the next year or so she's gonna write a column about that one. Shit, that ain't even our jurisdiction. Don't make no difference to her. I sure as hell don't want her hearing about this one."

"What about that file?"

"Yeah. I'm not supposed to let you see it. Want me to read it to you?"

"I imagine it's pretty technical."

"Oh, absolutely. Uses words like 'alleged' and 'perpetrator,' shit like that." He lifted his eyebrows.

"Maybe you can just answer a couple questions."

"Maybe."

"There's an autopsy report, right?"

He nodded.

"And the wound in the ear, did the Medical Examiner specifically say it was an icepick?"

He grinned. "Not exactly. They don't talk that way. Hang on. Okay. 'Thin, round, rigid, pointed instrument approximately ten centimeters in length'—that's a little over four inches, Mr. Coyne—'consistent with an icepick.' That's how MEs write, see. We'll just call it an icepick. Caused massive hemorrhaging in the brain. Similar to a stroke. Quick, painless, actually. He describes the route the thing took going into his brain. Wanna hear?"

"No, that's all right," I said quickly. "Did they verify that Stu had been drinking?"

"Yup. Right here. It says, 'BAC point-two-four. Residue of Scotch whiskey in stomach lining.' "

"Scotch, huh? They can tell that sort of thing?"

Santis shrugged.

"Do those men, those bums, generally drink Scotch?"

"How the hell should I know?"

"What's BAC mean?" I said.

"BAC. Blood alcohol content. A point-two-four means falling down, throwing up, passing out drunk, or close to it. Put it this way, Mr. Coyne: a point-one is legally drunk. In Maine, a teenager with a point-oh-five can be charged with drunk driving. A point-four is a coma. Point-five is dead. A guy the size of your friend Carver—he was what, about one-forty?—he'd have to take eight or ten shots in the space of an hour or so to get that loaded."

"He could do that," I said. "I don't suppose they can tell what brand of Scotch someone's been drinking, can they?"

"Maybe they can. This one didn't."

"Okay. They found a matchbook on him, I recall."

"So?"

"Well, was it old or new? Had it been used? Did it have anything written on it?"

He stared at me for a moment. "Those ain't bad questions, you know that?"

I shrugged.

He peered at the papers in the file. "Here we go. Hm. It doesn't say whether it was old or new, or if any matches were missing. I assume if something was written on it, it would say so here. I suppose I could try to find out. It was from a place called the Sow's Ear. You ever hear of it?"

"No. Sounds tacky."

"It's a dive, all right. Uptown a ways, on Washington Street, a little bit this side of the Combat Zone. You thinking Carver was there?"

"He might've been, huh?"

Santis thrust out his lower lip and nodded. "Yup. He might've." Then he took another bite of his sandwich. "Not that it matters much," he mumbled, his mouth full. "Though we shoulda checked it out, I guess," he added. "If we weren't so goddam tied up around here."

I nodded and smiled.

"Aw, now, Mr. Coyne, you don't wanna go messing

around in something you can't handle. Maybe I'll send a couple boys over there to ask around.''

"Think they'll learn anything?"

He stared at me. "Nope," he said finally. "They won't talk to cops. But, look. They won't talk to you, either, so don't go doing something stupid."

"No harm in having a drink, now, is there?"

"At the Sow's Ear? Yep. There just might be harm in it. Take my advice . . . . Ah, forget it. I don't imagine you take advice very good. Listen. Let me know anything you hear, willya?"

"Sure. I'll do that." I stood up. "I haven't had my supper yet, and between that delicious looking sandwich of yours and this uplifting conversation, my stomach's starting to growl. So if you don't mind, I'd like to get going."

"You find out what you wanted?"

"I guess so," I said. "Did you?"

He grinned. "You were a big help."

He reached across his desk without standing, and we shook hands.

"The Marine corpse," Santis said suddenly.

"What?"

"That's what the ME called that stiff we found last winter. The one who pissed on the third rail. The Marine corpse. Closest I've ever seen that doctor come to smiling, when he came out with that one. Thing is, we checked the dead guy's fingerprints, like we always do. Guess what?"

"He wasn't a Marine at all," I said.

"Jeez," said Santis. "You're right."

I had my hand on the doorknob when Santis said, "Hey, Mr. Coyne, do me a favor, will you?"

"What's that?"

"Don't let that Mickey Gillis get ahold of this story, huh? She's a fuckin' vulture, know what I mean?"

"I know what you mean," I said. "Her column's the first thing I read in the paper."

I didn't bother telling him that Mickey Gillis was an old friend of mine.

When we were seniors in high school together, Maureen Sadowski was voted "Class Athletic Supporter." This sophomoric play on words was meant to convey, for one thing, that Mickey was a jock such as girls' sports had rarely seen, in those days when they were not allowed to cross the midcourt line in basketball, and seemed to pride themselves on their inability to throw a ball like a boy. Mickey Sadowski roamed centerfield like the Yankee centerfielder of the same era—from whom she derived her nickname. She hit slashing line drives, slid into bases, and often as not came up swinging her fists at startled, ponytailed shortstops. She could dribble a basketball with both hands, drive the baseline, and she was considered a genuine freak because she could shoot a jump shot.

She had a hard little athletic body and a wide mouth that usually wore an expression that could have been either a sneer or a grin—and, as I got to know her, I realized it was usually a little of each. She had the best legs in school, and in an era when skirts were generally worn ankle-length over layers of petticoats, Mickey favored tight skirts with a hemline at the knee.

Mickey Sadowski was also an athletic supporter of a different kind. It was no secret that at one time or another she had supported most of the members of the high school football team from a supine position—including a big, awkward tight end named Brady Coyne.

Mickey Sadowski, in the locker-room parlance of the day, "put out."

I thought I was in love with her for a while, and one starry summer night when we lay beside each other on an Army blanket spread over the pine needles up on Granny Hill, she having just finished supporting me with more finesse than I had reciprocated, I said to her, "Doesn't it bother you? Your reputation, I mean?"

"Does it bother *you*?" she asked.

"Well, yes," I said. "I really like you, Mickey."

"I like you, too," she said. "I can talk with you. The others, they don't like to talk. They just grunt and groan and then when they're done they just want to take me home."

"Why do you do it then?"

"Same reason you do. I like it. It's fun. It feels good. You think boys are the only ones who like to fuck?"

It was typical of Mickey to use words that boys thought belonged exclusively to them. It was also, I learned, typical that she perceived no significant difference between herself and us members of the other gender.

I visited Mickey a few times while she was at Smith College. We'd go drinking at Rahar's and then drive down a dirt road alongside a tobacco field near the Connecticut River and make imaginative love in the back seat of my Volkswagen. I had, by then, accepted Mickey's understanding that she and I were good friends who shared several common interests—sports, Buddy Holly songs, and sex.

She ended up marrying an engineer from MIT named Brendan Gillis, a young man with a large Adam's apple and terrific prospects. They moved to Charleston, South Carolina, where Brendan made a lot of money and Mickey had two miscarriages. I hung around Boston, got married, and lost track of her until her byline began to turn up in the *Globe*. She started as a reporter on the City Hall beat, but within a year they gave her a three-times-a-week column. She wrote about cops and dope peddlers, old folks in the projects whose welfare checks were getting stolen from their mailboxes, delinquents who managed to slither through the judicial cracks, and Red Sox pitchers who threw too many gopher balls.

She wrote, she liked to say, the same way she played ball: like a man.

I ran into her now and then around the city. Her hair, which in her youth had been long and silky black, was now cut short and flecked with gray. Her vanilla skin had coarsened and her voice rasped from cigarettes and booze. She still had great legs and, from what she said to me, I gathered that her interest in sports and sex had not waned over the years.

Her reputation as a vulture was well earned and widely repeated. Al Santis had not made it up. Mickey Gillis could smell the rotting carcass of a political coverup or high level incompetence with uncanny acuity, and she would swoop down on it and begin to peck at it, and nobody could drive her off.

It was no wonder that Santis feared her. Everybody did.

Hard little kernels of sleet were rattling against the sliding glass doors that opened onto my balcony over the harbor six floors up. Outside my apartment, the purple of the ocean was about three shades darker than the sky, and here and there against the darkness the running lights of big ocean-going tankers and the landing lights of airliners homing in on Logan by instrument blinked and winked through the storm.

It didn't seem all that much cozier inside.

I kicked off my shoes, tossed my topcoat and jacket and tie in the direction of the sofa, and rinsed out two tumblers that had spent the past few days in the sink. I set them on the dining table by the sliders and poured each half full of Jack Daniel's. Then I set myself down, lifted one of the tumblers, clicked it against the other, and held it aloft toward the ocean outside.

"To you, Altoona, old friend," I said. "And to beautiful women." I downed the contents.

I put it down, raised the other one, and tossed it off, too.

When you live alone, as I do, you had better enjoy your own companionship. I do. I have interesting discussions with myself from time to time, and that evening as I sat staring out at the darkness and feeling the loss of another friend, I debated what I should do about it.

On the one hand, I was a middle-aged lawyer with no particular talent—or stomach—for the investigation of violent crimes.

On the other hand, I had lost two friends whom I cared about, and it pissed me off.

On the first hand, it was clearly a police matter.

On the second hand, Al Santis had not encouraged me that they were pursuing it with diligence.

On the first hand, again, I could hurt myself. I did not like pain.

On the other hand, in this case it just might be worth the risk.

It went on for a while, oiled by two more tumblers of Black Jack—these sipped slowly, savored pensively—and when the debate was over, the other hand was declared a winner by unanimous decision. I would do what I could, and if it turned out not to be much, at least I would have tried. And if I got hurt—well, sometimes debate judges make mistakes.

I put the tumblers back into the sink, pried the top off a can of chili, and dumped it into a pot. I sprinkled a heaping tablespoon each of chili powder and paprika on top, because they never make the canned stuff hot enough, and put it on low heat. Then I went to the telephone.

Gus Becker answered on the second ring.

"This is Brady Coyne," I said.

"Oh. Oh, sure. How are you?"

"I'm fine. I want to help."

"Help?"

"With the investigation."

He was silent for a minute. "Yes," he said slowly. "Stuart Carver. Right. You want to help."

"I do. Yes."

"Well. Hm. Listen, I appreciate that, Mr. Coyne. But,

to tell you the truth, I'm not sure there's much you can really do."

"I know. I'm not either. But another man has been killed the same way Stu Carver was, and he was a friend of mine, too, and I feel like I need to do something. So I want to help."

"Another man?"

"Yes," I said, and I summarized for him what I had learned from Al Santis.

"Sounds to me like maybe the police are right and I'm wrong," Becker observed. "It was a long shot anyway. It could very well be some nut out there. And if it is, you better leave it to the proper authorities. I seem to be drawing a blank with the drug connection in any case. Listen, you haven't happened to come up with any more notebooks, have you?"

"No. I don't think there are any more."

"Maybe. But in what you gave me there are these references, hints, like, that seem to suggest there's more. Look. If you really want to help out with this thing, the best way would be for you to come up with those other notebooks, if there are any."

"There are a few things you should know," I said.

"Such as?"

"One, Stu Carver did do a little drugs. His roommate insists it was only recreational, as they say. Two, he had a boyfriend, and he was the one who had the stuff. Three, this boyfriend got it from a physics professor at Harvard."

"And his roommate being the girl."

"Right."

"Think she's telling the truth?"

"Yes," I said. "I'm sure she's telling me what she thinks is the truth."

"That's not exactly the same thing."

"Granted."

"What about the boyfriend?"

"I talked to him. I don't know. He's a teacher and he's

pretty petrified of being found out. Both on the drugs and on the homosexuality.''

"Understandable.'' Becker paused. ''None of this exactly fits with what I'm investigating.''

"Well, you're investigating a drug thing and I'm interested in two murders. I don't see why we can't try to help each other.''

"I'm not sure that would be equitable,'' he said. "Look, Mr. Coyne. I don't want to sound unkind, or ungrateful, but I really do think that you ought to leave the detective work to the detectives, just the way your client, Senator Woodhouse, wants you to.''

"Ben Woodhouse isn't my client anymore,'' I said.

"Well, whatever. I still think you ought not to get involved. Don't you?''

"No, not really. But thanks for the advice.''

"Was there something else?''

"No,'' I said. "Anyway, my chili's bubbling. Gotta go.''

"I hope you'll keep in touch. I'm still interested in those notebooks.''

"Sure,'' I said.

"I mean it,'' he said. "About letting the police do their thing.''

"Right,'' I said, and I hung up.

I took the chili to the table and ate it out of the pot, alternating hot spoonfuls with cold swigs of Molson's ale. Becker's indifferent response to the information I had given him confused me at first. But as I thought it through, I realized that Altoona's murder, identical to Stu's, diminished the likelihood of a drug connection. And Stu's casual use of drugs, assuming that's what it was, didn't fit into Becker's hypothesis, either. From what he said, he didn't find anything in the notebooks to implicate Stu. I understood that Carver's death was just a secondary piece of Becker's investigation. He wasn't interested in the murder at all, really—only where its resolution might lead him. If a crackpot killed Stu—and Altoona—then it was of no interest whatsoever to Gus Becker.

But it was still of interest to me.

I timed it so that I'd follow the last spoonful of chili with the last swig of the second bottle of ale. Then I lit a cigarette and went back to the phone.

12

Joey, younger son, answered the phone, "Hullo?"

"You shouldn't talk with your mouth full," I said.

"Oh, hi there, Pop. Eatin' a piece of pie. Sorry."

"Your mother's chocolate cream, I'll bet."

"Lemon meringue."

"Yum. So. What else are you up to?"

"Just watching the tube, pigging out. The usual."

"School?"

"Senior slump time. You wanna talk to Mom?"

"Please. But listen. It's been great engaging in meaningful discourse with you. We'll have to do it again sometime."

"Sure. Hang on a sec."

I heard him yell, "Hey Ma. It's the old man."

A moment later Gloria picked up the extension. "You can hang up now, dear," she said.

Joey said, "Okay. Bye, Pop."

"The old man," I said.

She chuckled. "And I've become the old lady. So what do you expect?"

"Whatever happened to honoring thy father and thy mother? What about civility?"

"We never did give them much religious training."

"What's that got to do with it?

"They're teenagers. That's it." She sighed. "Anyway, how are you, Brady?"

"I'm okay. Returning your call. What's up?"

"Why does something have to be up?"

"You called."

"Can't I call you without something being up?"

"How long do you want to do this, Gloria?"

"Do what?"

"Sparring. Thrusting and parrying. Come on. When you do that, it's because there's something unpleasant you have to say to me, and you're afraid I'll be angry or upset, but you know you have to say it anyway. So out with it."

"Well," she said. Then she hesitated. "Well, okay." She paused again. "You really do know me, don't you?"

"All too well. Come on, Gloria. What's wrong?"

"It's Billy."

"That's no surprise."

She sighed. "He wants to quit school."

"And?"

"And? What do you mean, 'and'? That's it. Our number one son, the kid with that one-hundred-forty-something IQ who could've gone to Harvard or any place but decided to go to UMass because he didn't want his friends to think he was a snob, and who refused to apply for scholarships because his old man was loaded, and who started growing a beard and used his first shot at the franchise to vote Socialist Labor—he says college isn't real. That's what he's saying, Brady. 'College isn't real.' Actually, if you can believe it, he said, 'College *ain't* real.' " Gloria took a deep breath. "I thought you'd be furious," she finished in a small voice.

"Hmm," I observed.

"You think I'm overreacting?"

"I didn't say that."

"But you do, don't you?"

"Come on, Gloria."

"You think I should say to him 'Well that's just fine, dear. That's your decision, and we respect your decision. You're a big boy. It's your life.' You think I should say that?"

"Exactly," I said.

I heard her snort, an abrupt, mirthless laugh. "Well, it's too late."

"That's not what you said to him."

"No."

"Funny, but that doesn't surprise me. So what *did* you say to him?"

"I said, 'Your father will be furious.' "

I laughed. "You are truly a piece of work, Gloria."

"We make a good pair, don't we?"

"We did."

"We still do, you know."

I found myself smiling and nodding as I sat there in my apartment staring out into the night. "Okay, Gloria. I'll talk to him."

"What will you say?"

"I'll be furious."

"I'll bet."

"Hey, I'll give it my best shot."

"Look, if you don't think . . ."

"Hey, I'll work on conjuring up some fury. I can do it."

"He shouldn't quit, Brady. You always taught the boys never to quit. Remember when Joey was playing Little League?"

"Okay. I'm getting furious. I think I've got a handle on it now."

"The way that awful man never put him into the games,

- **143** -

and yelled at the kids when they made errors? Remember? And you told Joey to tough it out, to prove who was the best man? Tough it out, you said.''

"Sure, I remember. You were all for slicing off the guy's testicles with something dull and rusty, as I recall. Not that this is the same thing.''

"Close enough," she said. "Listen. You interested in home-made lemon meringue pie sometime?''

"Sounds like a bribe to me.''

"It is a bribe, and you know it," she said softly.

"Yes, I do know that.''

"Let's get together.''

"We should do that," I said. And we said good-bye and disconnected, leaving it that way, with a vague promise that fell short of a commitment.

Snowflakes the size of dimes sifted and swirled in my headlights the next night when I picked up Zerk at his place in North Cambridge and pointed my BMW toward the city.

"Lookin' like a big storm," he observed.

"Big flakes, little storm," I said. "Old Yankee adage.''

I took the Mass Ave bridge across the Charles. When we passed Symphony Hall a few minutes later, Zerk said, "Where you takin' me?''

"For a drink, like I said.''

"I figured the Ritz, or Copley Plaza. Something befitting two successful young attorneys with business to transact. *I'm* young, anyway. And you do have business you want to transact, I assume?''

"More or less.''

"We gonna iron out Ms. Kriegel's condominium? Your client prepared to submit an offer? A buyout, maybe? 'Cause if that's the case, you can ply me with good booze till I pee my pants and it won't change a thing. She ain't movin', man.''

"Is that your negotiating posture, Zerk?''

"Hey, I learned how to do all this shit from you, my man. But, just because it's you, old mentor, I'll tell you straight ou   the lady has every right to keep her pad, and the only way she'll lose it is if I fuck up. Which I ain't gonna do."

"The fact is, I quit the case. Thought Heather might've told you."

"You quit? Damn! I was lookin' forward to some good hardass headknocking."

"That's a fascinating mixture of metaphors, Zerk."

"Ms. Kriegel didn't mention anything to me about you quitting."

"And the Woodhouse clan hasn't had their new attorney rapping on your window?"

"Nope. Maybe they decided to drop it."

"That," I said, "I doubt. That was my advice. They didn't like it. That's why I quit."

"So you're off the case."

"Actually, I'm off all Woodhouse cases."

"Hey, no shit! Good for you. I didn't think you had that much integrity, my man."

"I often wondered, myself," I said.

I had taken several back roads I knew, and we now were on Washington Street, headed intown toward the Combat Zone. It had stopped snowing. I slowed down and began studying the signs over the establishments along the way.

"Look for the Sow's Ear," I told Zerk.

"You're shitting me."

"Nope."

"That's where I'm getting my drink? The Sow's Ear? You know what that place is?"

"A dive," I answered, quoting Al Santis.

"That's a quaint way to put it."

"You've been there, then?"

"I've heard of it, that's all," said Zerk. "It's got a certain reputation. Unsavory."

"There it is," I said. The sign, in winking red and blue

neon, spelled out "The Sow's Ear." It had a blank brick front decorated with peeling old posters and spraypainted graffiti. It was flanked by Buddy's on the left, and the Midnight Lounge on the right.

"We have arrived at the very cultural hub of the universe," I said.

A block up the street I found a parking lot. I gave the attendant a twenty-dollar bill and asked him to keep an eye on my BMW. Then Zerk and I headed back towards the Sow's Ear. "This is probably a wild goose chase," I told him. "Stu Carver had a matchbook from this place on him when he died. Maybe he was here that night."

"You're still into crime-bustin', I see," grinned Zerk. "Woulda been thoughtful of old Stu to have gone to Locke Ober's if he was gonna leave these clues around when he got himself killed."

"I got a photo of him from Heather. Let's see if anyone recognizes it."

"A long shot."

"Granted."

"And you need me for protection?" Zerk's face broke into a broad smile.

I tapped him on the shoulder with my fist. "You're my main man."

"You bring your weapon?" His smile widened.

"I've learned some lessons. The weapon is locked in my safe. Where it shall remain."

We pushed open the door and went inside. An L-shaped bar extended along the left and rear walls. On the right was a low stage where five scruffy guys and one definitely unscruffy girl were singing and sawing, plunking, and strumming at a variety of stringed instruments, making country and western noises. The male musicians all wore dirty blue jeans, flannel shirts, and baseball caps bearing the logos of breweries and heavy farm equipment manufacturers. The girl was young and blonde. She had a wholesome smile, a tight little leather skirt that stopped halfway down her thighs, and a surprisingly good singing voice.

Her lyrics were filthy.

In front of the band was a small open area where a skinny black man wearing a red bandanna around his head clutched a much larger white girl. They swayed back and forth, more or less in sync with the music. Each of the man's hands had a firm grip on one of the girl's ample buttocks.

The rest of the floor was cluttered with small tables and chairs. Across the other wall was a row of high-backed booths.

The lights in the place were dim and pink, the music loud, and the few patrons clad mostly in denim and leather. When the band finished its number, no one bothered to applaud. The girl said into the microphone, "Well, thank y'all very much. Thank you very kindly. I know you wanna hear more, but we're gonna take a little break here, so y'all just sit tight." She gave a mock curtsy, and one of the band members gave the finger to the sparse audience.

Zerk and I sat at the bar.

"Man," he said, "if I'd known you were takin' me to a real fancy place I woulda dressed for the occasion."

I surveyed his natty gray three-piece suit. "You look fine to me," I said.

"Fine for the Ritz. Fine for the Copley Plaza. Not good enough for the Sow's Ear."

"Loosen your tie. You'll fit right in."

The bartender was a red-headed woman whose stained white blouse was tolerating considerable stress as it stretched across her ample front. The red smear of lipstick on her mouth clashed with the orange of her hair.

She made a pass in front of us with her rag. "Help ya, boys?"

"Beer," said Zerk.

"We got Miller's on tap, Bud, and Löwenbräu . . ."

"What've you got in bottles?"

She cocked her head at him. "Why dontcha tell me what you want, I'll tell you if we got it."

"Beck's."

"Try again."

"Heineken."

"You want fancy beer, you came to the wrong place, mister."

"Schlitz, then."

"Two Schlitz?"

"I don't—" I began.

"Two. Yes," interrupted Zerk.

She turned away, and I said to Zerk, "I don't want beer. It's cold outside and I want bourbon. What'd you do that for?"

"You come to a place like this," he said, "you want something out of a bottle. Then you know what you're getting. Hey, if you took me to the Ritz you could have had Wild Turkey."

"I don't want beer," I mumbled.

The redhead slid our beers in front of us, each bottle with a glass overturned on top. "Twelve bucks," she said.

"Jesus," I said, reaching for my wallet.

"Look," she said, "we got no cover, no minimum here, so you just sip away, take your time, look around, see what you like, okay? Just don't piss and moan about the prices."

I took two twenty-dollar bills from my wallet and laid them on the bar. She picked up one of them. "I'll get your change."

"Take them both. Keep the change."

"A big-timer, huh?"

"Wonder if you might be able to help me out?"

She put her thick forearms on the bar and leaned toward me, grinning and nodding her head. "I thought when you first came in. Then I said, 'Nah. They'd know better than to dress that way.' Then I figured maybe private eyes, not cops. So, one or the other, anyway. Probably not cops. Cops don't like to pay. Anyway, don't tell me. Let me guess. You're gonna show me a picture. A girl, probably, right? Young one. Runaway. See if I ever saw her before, maybe a few nights ago. Right? Am I right?''

"Well . . ."

"Forget it," she said. "I'll get your change." She pivoted around, leaving one of the twenties on the bar.

"Wait a minute," I said. I glanced at Zerk, who was smiling and drinking his beer from the bottle. "We're not police or private investigators. You're right, though. I do have a photo." I took out the picture of Stu Carver and put it on the bar. "Please look at it."

She turned back to face us. "What the hell are you, then, anyway?"

"Just private citizens like you, ma'am," I said.

"Private citizens," she said, as if it were a curse.

"New Year's Eve," I said. "Was this man in here? That's all I want to know."

She barely glanced at the picture. "I didn't work New Year's. I was home New Year's."

"Is there anybody here who might've worked that night?"

She stared at me for a moment, then glanced down the bar. I followed her gaze to a black-haired girl who was smoking a cigarette and studying the row of bottles lined up behind the bar.

"Her?" I said.

"Maybe."

"Would you ask her if I could buy her a drink?"

She shrugged. "Sure. You're the guy who's giving me the big tip."

She moved to where the girl was sitting. I saw them exchange a few words.

"It ain't gonna work," said Zerk.

"Why not?"

"Watch," he said.

The bartender came back. "Trixie says no thank you."

"Trixie?" said Zerk. "That her name?"

- **149** -

The redhead smirked. "Trix. Yeah."

She took the two twenties and walked away.

"Wait here," said Zerk.

He took his beer bottle with him. He strolled down to where the black-haired girl was sitting, leaned over, and spoke into her ear. She glanced up at him, hesitated, shrugged, and shook her head. Zerk settled onto the stool beside her. A moment later he gestured to the bartender, who smiled and produced a bottle of champagne. Zerk and the girl huddled together, their heads close. Now and then I could see them laughing and smiling and rubbing shoulders. Zerk kept filling the girl's champagne glass.

The band returned to the stage and began to play. The place was slowly filling up. It was a middle-aged crowd, more men than women. They slouched in wearing heavy shapeless coats and bland, defeated faces. They sat by themselves, most of them. They drank shots with draft beer chasers and drummed their fingertips on the tabletops to the beat of the music. A few of them danced. They didn't seem to be having much fun. The Sow's Ear didn't appear to be the sort of place you brought a date to.

"You want another, or what?"

"Huh?" I spun around on my barstool. The bartender was going through the motions with her rag. "Okay. Sure. Another bottle of Schlitz."

"Your friend's makin' out okay, huh?"

Zerk and Trixie were sitting facing each other, their knees touching. She was holding her champagne glass for him to drink from. "He's got a way with women," I said.

"There are plenty of other girls in here, you know."

"That's all right," I said.

She fetched my beer for me, and I put a ten on the counter. "Where does a place like this get a name like the Sow's Ear?" I said.

"Fella who owns it is lookin' to get a fancy place down in Quincy Market. Wants to attract the tourists and the rich

- 150 -

folks from the suburbs. That's what he wants. This is what he's got." She shrugged. "Not real fancy, you know?"

I nodded.

"If he gets that fancy place he wants, he's got the name all picked out for it."

"Don't tell me," I said.

"The Silk Purse," she said. "The owner says you can't make a silk purse out of this dump, see?"

"So it's the Sow's Ear."

"Cute, huh?"

I thought of the fatal wounds Stu and Altoona had received, and wondered idly whether the owner of the Sow's Ear had some sort of ear fetish. "Where's the owner?" I said.

"Vegas," she said. "Been there all winter. He's got half interest in a joint down there. He don't like the cold."

So much for that theory.

The bartender wandered off with my ten dollar bill, and a minute later Zerk and Trixie came over and sat on either side of me.

"Darlin'," he said, his dark face solemn, "this is my good friend, Mr. Coyne."

She extended her hand. I held it briefly. "Pleased to meet you," I said.

"The pleasure is mine, I'm sure," she said in a low husky voice.

"Trixie was here on New Year's Eve," said Zerk. "She says she might be willing to look at that photograph."

I took it from my pocket and handed it to her. She picked it up and squinted myopically at it. The pink tip of her tongue showed between her teeth. She nodded slowly. "Yeah," she murmured. "Yeah. I remember this guy."

"He was here New Year's Eve?"

She gave the picture back to me. "Yeah. He and the other guy were sitting right over there. In that booth."

She pointed across the room toward the corner booth.

"Are you sure?"

"Sure I'm sure. He was wearin' a beard, but it was him. The eyes. I recognize his eyes. I sat with them for a few minutes." She grinned. "Shoulda known, though. Pair of fairies."

"What do you mean?"

"Oh, they were nice enough. Even bought me a drink. But I could see there was no future in it. Like, I was interrupting them, you know?"

"Interrupting?"

"Xerxes, honey, would you pour me another glass of champagne, please?" Zerk did, and she downed it. "A lover's quarrel, you'd call it. Not screaming and pulling hair, understand. But the other one—not this one here in the picture, but the other fella—wanted this one here to leave with him, and he wouldn't. Something like that. That's all I got out of it, really. I left them. Waste of my time."

"What did the other one look like?"

"Older. Pudgy. Glasses. Not all that good-looking."

"So you sat with them, and they were arguing. Can you remember anything they said?"

She bit on her thumbnail and frowned. "Not exactly. The fat one kept saying how he missed this guy, he wanted him to come home. And the guy in the picture was saying how he couldn't, he was into something—yeah, that was it. He kept saying how he was into something—or maybe he said he was *onto* something—something important. He couldn't leave it, he said. The fat one wasn't buying it, but, see, they were trying to be polite, I guess because I was sitting right there. When I got up to leave they didn't ask me to stay. I guess they wanted to be left alone."

"What were they drinking, do you remember?"

She frowned. "Scotch, I think. Yeah, it was Scotch. They ordered a round while I was there. The young one, he was getting pretty sloshed, actually. Really puttin' 'em away. The other guy was nursing his." She nodded several times, as if to emphasize the accuracy of her recollection.

"Can you remember anything else?" I said.

"Well, the fat one was dressed nice. Too nice for this place. Like you boys. The other one fit right in. Grubby, that beard, kinda rough looking. Good-looking, though. I wouldn't of pegged him as a queer."

I nodded, encouraging her to go on.

She shrugged. "So, that was it. I left them. Few minutes later I remember looking over and the fat one was gone. The younger one stayed a little longer. Left after midnight, I remember, because everybody yelled and stuff when midnight came. You know, the new year and all, and I remember seeing him, still sitting there by himself, not looking real happy. Pretty drunk, is what he was."

I smiled at her. "I appreciate your help, Trixie."

"Oh, that's okay." She turned to Zerk. "You ready, sweetie?"

He reached across in front of me to touch her hand. "I don't think tonight, Trixie."

She frowned. "Something wrong?"

"No. Another time, okay?"

"But . . . ?"

He got up and moved to the empty stool on the other side of her, kissed her cheek, then whispered something into her ear. She pulled her face back and smiled at him. "Okay, honey. See ya, Mr. Coyne."

She moved back to her stool at the far end of the bar.

"Nice kid," observed Zerk.

"She seems to be."

"Barmadam," he called. "Another Schlitz, if you please."

"I'll be damned," I muttered.

"That help you any?" he said.

"Yes. Yes, it did. How the hell did you do that, anyway?"
Zerk widened his eyes. "Trick of the trade."

"I never taught you anything like that."

"Not *that* trade, man. Trixie's a hooker, been around a bit, and she assumed we were cops. Naturally. I mean, a white guy and a black guy in suits come into a place like this, we gotta be cops, right? So if you're a hooker, you don't want to talk to us. You sure as hell don't want to get yourself into a position where you might be soliciting. So you steer clear of cops. However, if one of those cops should proposition a girl, then she's in the clear, dig? Matter of fact, she's got him right by the short hairs, since the last thing a cop wants to get caught doing is propositioning a hooker.''

"So you propositioned her?"

"Even better. I paid her in advance. Forty bucks. Which I assume will be reimbursed."

I nodded. "Sure. I'll reimburse you. Business expense."

Zerk's beer arrived. I paid for it, too.

"Any idea who the other guy was?" he said.

"Yes," I said. "I have a very good idea who it was. Listen. I have to go to the men's room. Be right back."

I maneuvered my way among the tables to the back corner of the place, where I found a door labeled "Men." I pushed it open. There were two urinals, a stall with the door missing, and a sink. The empty frame of what had once been a mirror hung over the sink. I eased myself into position in front of one of the urinals, trying to avoid breathing through my nose. The urinal had not been flushed for some time, and the sharp odor of stale vomit hung in the air.

I heard the door open and close behind me. Then I felt a prick of pain over my right kidney. "You just keep on doing what you're doing, friend," whispered a harsh voice in my ear, so close that I could smell the whiskey on his breath. "You just keep your hands full, there, and don't turn around."

The sharp pain in my back increased a notch. It was penetrating my skin, and it hurt. A sharp, pointed instrument. A switchblade. Or maybe an icepick.

"That hurts," I said.

"You just keep ahold of your pecker, there, or you'll lose it."

He found my wallet in my hip pocket and removed it deftly. Then he patted my jacket pockets. "Put your hands up in the air," he said.

I did, feeling vulnerable and exposed.

"Take off the watch."

I did, and he took it from me.

"Thank you very much," he whispered.

Then the lights went out.

It was probably only a few seconds later that I found myself sitting on the damp floor of the men's room, trying to decide whether the back of my neck hurt worse than the wound over my kidney. I decided it was the neck, and I wondered if he had hit me with his bare hand, or had used something heavy and hard. I rubbed it until the pain began to subside into an ache. I pulled myself to my feet, brushed of my jacket and pants, zipped up my fly, washed my hands and face, and went back to join Zerk.

When I sat beside him, he looked at me and said, "You lookin' a bit rumpled, my man." He noticed that I was rubbing the back of my neck. "Hey," he said. "You okay?"

"You didn't happen to notice anyone go into the men's room right after me, did you?"

"No. Why?"

"I just got mugged is all. Guy stuck a knife or something into my back while I was taking a leak, took my wallet and my new watch, and slugged me on the back of my neck."

"It's these threads, man. I told you. We're dressed all wrong for this place. Might as well wear a sign. Rob Me."

"Your sympathy is touching," I said. "Take a look at this wound, will you?"

"Swivel around this way," said Zerk. "Gimme a peek."

I rotated so that my back was to him. He hoisted up my jacket and pulled up my shirt. "Hmm," he mumbled.

"What's it look like?"

He let go of my clothes. "Just a scratch. Stop whining. It's a clean little incision, not a round puncture. In case you were thinking about icepicks."

"That's the thought that occurred to me, yes."

13

Zerk and I were back in my apartment. He had me draped over the back of my sofa like a blanket over a clothesline. He was swabbing the little wound on my back with a wad of cotton batting soaked with cheap vodka. I had told him I couldn't spare any good bourbon. He seemed to be enjoying the poking and prodding.

"How's it look, Doctor?"

"Hmm," he said. "Merely a flesh wound. Fortunately, you have an abundance of flesh there. It could do with a couple sutures." He whacked my fanny. "However, I stuck a Band-Aid on it. You can pull your pants up." I did. "Interesting, wasn't it, old Trixie placing Stu Carver right there at the Sow's Ear on New Year's Eve? And you think you know who was with him. I'll bet the same thing occurred to you that occurred to me."

"Probably," I said, tucking in my shirt. "That the guy with Stu was the one that killed him. And if he wasn't the one who actually icepicked him, that Stu said something to him that would help." I went over to the cabinet where I kept my bottles. "I'm going to have a shot of Jack Daniel's and a cigarette. I figure I earned them. Join me?"

"Scotch. Hold the cigarette."

I poured our drinks and we sat at my kitchen table. I lit a cigarette. "I think I'll invite David Lee to my office for a little chat."

"David Lee. That the guy who was with Stu?"

"I'm pretty sure."

"What about getting mugged and robbed? What're you going to do about that?"

"I don't know. That was a new Rolex he got. Not to mention my credit cards. Plus the humiliation of it all. Any suggestions?"

Zerk sipped his Scotch and frowned. "Nope. Guess not. Something occurs to me, though."

"What's that?"

"Pretty easy for a guy to get himself killed, sometimes. Happens a lot. In alleys, men's rooms."

"You mean Santis might be right? Just a random act with no logical explanation?"

"After what happened to you, I'm beginning to think it makes sense."

I nodded. "Me too. I'm still going to talk to Lee."

"Don't you think you ought to inform the authorities?"

"I probably should give Gus Becker a call," I said. "Think I'll talk to Lee first, though."

After Zerk left, I snapped on the eleven o'clock news and sprawled on the sofa. The lead story reported that "sources close to the White House" had released a trial balloon hinting that the President was contemplating sending "military advisors" into Haiti. A member of the Senate Foreign Relations Committee, known to be close to the Administration, commented to an interviewer that the American people should be wary of drawing close parallels between Haiti and Vietnam. Haiti, he declared solemnly, was different. He invoked the Monroe Doctrine, the Cuban Missile Crisis, Franklin Roosevelt, Winston Churchill, and, in what I could only interpret as a telling slip of the tongue, the Tonkin Gulf Resolution. He refrained from mentioning the attempted assassination of Thurmond Lampley in Boston a month earlier.

Scary stuff, I thought.

There had been a big drug bust in Revere. The television camera lingered on a tabletop in police headquarters, where glassine bags of white powder, sets of scales, assorted firearms, and stacks of high denomination bills were displayed. I wondered if Gus Becker had finally hit the jackpot.

A giant blizzard had paralyzed Chicago, and was heading our way. The Celtics won. The Bruins lost.

Nothing, I decided, snapping off the set, was new.

I showered, letting the hot water splash against the back of my neck, where a hard little knot had formed. The incision over my right hip stung. I remembered my feelings when the knife had pricked my skin. Humiliation, I had told Zerk. That, yes. But fear, too. I had been acutely aware that a quick, easy thrust of that razor-sharp weapon could have killed me. I wondered if Stu Carver and Altoona had felt the same sphincter-tightening fear the moment that icepick touched the skin inside their ears. Perhaps they had been too drunk to contemplate clearly the imminence of death. I hoped so.

I toweled myself dry and slipped into my ratty old flannel pajamas. I poured two final fingers of bourbon into my glass and brought it to bed with me. I was drinking too much, I thought idly. Smoking too much, too. Somehow, the thought of sudden, unexpected death in a dirty men's room put Surgeon Generals' warnings and actuarial charts into perspective.

That thought led me to the next one. I picked up the

phone beside my bed and tapped out Heather Kriegel's number.

"Hmm," she answered after two rings. "Whozit?"

"You were sleeping. Sorry."

"Mmm. S'okay." She yawned. It sounded like a moan of pleasure. I imagined her springy muscles stretching and flexing, her hair tousled, her bedclothes rumpled. "Wha's up, friend?"

I resisted the impulse to answer, "Me."

"Wanted to say hi is all," I said.

"Miss me?"

"Yup. Guess I do."

"Hey, now," she said. "Don't go getting all mushy and sentimental with me. Hang on a sec. Let me sit up." A moment later she said, "There. I've been trying to reach you.

"You have?"

"It's—annoying, is what it is, I guess. Kinda scary, in a way, too. It's Meriam. She called me this afternoon."

"What did she want?"

"She wants Stu's notebooks. She stopped a little short of calling me a whore and a thief, but the implication was clear enough. She practically accused me of killing Stu."

"Don't worry about Meriam, Heather. She's harmless."

"She didn't sound harmless."

"Hey, she's an old lady whose only son got murdered."

"So what about the notebooks? What do I do about them?"

"Nothing. Ignore the whole thing."

"Is this a legal opinion, Brady?"

"It is. If she wants to take you to court for the notebooks, it'll be about five years before anything happens. Then you can get a couple of continuations . . ."

"I get it."

"Did you tell Zerk about this?"

"No. I will."

"He's your lawyer. He's the one you should be talking to, not me."

"I wanted to talk to you."

I said nothing. Heather couldn't see me smile.

"You there, Brady?"

"I'm here."

"Am I going to see you sometime?"

"You name it."

"Now?"

"Well . . ."

"Just kidding," she said. "You're not all that big on spontaneity, are you?"

"Let's make a date, Heather."

"Okay." She sighed. "Let's see. Tomorrow's no good. Ted Kennedy's taking me to the opera. Just kidding. How about the next night? Tell you what. I'll broil us a couple of steaks. You bring a bottle of expensive wine. I've got a new Miles Davis tape you'll really love, and we can play a few hands of gin. How's that sound?"

"Perfect. How's seven?"

"Seven is good. I've got a session in the afternoon. That'll give me a chance to shower and unwind. Maybe even grab a quick nap." She yawned again. " 'Scuse me. Listen. I'm still deciphering Stu's notebooks. There's some funny stuff in them. Funny strange, I mean. References that I can't figure out. Maybe you can take a look at them when you're here."

"What kind of references?"

"If I read it accurately, he jotted down thoughts on Haiti and Cuba."

"Well, that's been on the news a lot, of course," I said. "Tonight, as a matter of fact."

"I know. Can you believe that guy? What I don't get is why Stu would mention that in these notes."

"What was the context?"

"No context that I can figure out. It's as if he were trying to write reminders for himself that no one else would understand. Purposely ambiguous, almost. And anyway, his handwriting was so lousy that I'm not sure I've even got the words right. Anyhow, maybe you can help."

"Sure. I'll try. You didn't come across any references to drug dealing, did you?"

"Are you still on that kick?"

"It's not a kick, Heather. It's a hypothesis that the police are pursuing."

"Nothing on drugs. Nothing on David Lee, either, in case you were wondering."

"Matter of fact, I was, yes."

"Well, nothing on that."

"Hey, don't get angry with me," I said. "That's not why I called at all."

She sighed. "I'm not mad. I'm sorry. I don't mean to be a *kvetch*. It's just that . . ."

She was silent for a moment.

"I know," I said. "I know how you feel about Stu. I do, too. Also his friend Altoona. I'm just trying to resolve it all."

"Oh, when you told me about that poor old man . . ."

"I considered not telling you."

"No, I'm glad you told me. But it's just so sad. Stu was really fond of him, I can tell from what he wrote."

"Yes. I was, too. And that's what I want to understand."

"I know, Brady. You don't have to explain." She paused. "I miss you," she said in a small voice.

"Me, too."

"There you go, getting all syrupy again. Look. Bring one of those hugs with you when you come over, will you?"

"I'll bring several."

We exchanged soft good-byes and hung up. I picked up the copy of the *Yale Law Review* that I kept on the floor beside my bed. It was full of important stuff that an up-to-date attorney was truly obligated to know. But my eyelids kept falling down. "*Mañana*," I muttered to myself, and the last thought I had before I fell asleep was the translation of that word that I had heard from an Hispanic attorney I knew. *Mañana* doesn't mean "tomorrow," he told me. It means "not today."

It was, I thought, an important distinction.

At five minutes of four the following afternoon, Julie buzzed me and said, "Mr. Lee is here for his appointment."

I swiveled my desk chair around to look out the window at the end of another gray winter day in Boston. "Let him wait," I said.

"But . . ."

"I want him to stew in his own juices for a little while, okay?"

"Certainly, sir," she said. She did not approve.

I gave him twenty minutes before I went to the door and said, "Mr. Lee, won't you come in, now?"

I went back behind my desk. David Lee entered, paused in the doorway, then came and took the straight-backed chair across from my desk. I didn't stand for him or offer him my hand.

He leaned toward me. "I really don't appreciate being summoned like this, Mr. Coyne. I hope you understand that it's damned inconvenient."

"Then why did you come?"

He looked startled. "I—I thought I owed you the courtesy."

I lit a cigarette and stared at him for a moment. "You do, Mr. Lee. You do owe me the courtesy, as you put it. And I thought I would extend to you the courtesy of this meeting before I speak to the authorities."

"What the hell is that supposed to mean?" He tried to convey outrage. He fell just short of succeeding.

"You lied to me, Mr. Lee. It changes everything."

"Now, just a minute—"

"No," I said. "You wait a minute. You were with Stu

Carver the night he died. The night an icepick slid into his brain. You told me you hadn't seen him since October. That was a lie. There is only one reason why you would lie about that.''

"Now, listen," he said, placing both fists on my desk. "I wasn't lying. I never saw Stu."

I shrugged. "Have it your way, then." I buzzed Julie.

"Yes?" she answered.

"Get Detective Santis for me, please."

"Certainly."

I sat back and stared at David Lee. He returned my gaze for about five seconds, then dropped his eyes. "Okay, Mr. Coyne. I'm not going to call your bluff. Will you listen to me?"

"Why bother? You can talk to the police."

"Please."

I nodded. "Okay." I buzzed Julie again. "Cancel it," I told her.

"Playing games, are we?" she said sweetly into the phone.

"Yes, that's right," I said. I turned to Lee. "Okay, then. Go ahead."

He sighed. "It was the afternoon before New Year's Eve. Stu called me at home. I was correcting a set of exams. He sounded quite agitated. He said he wanted to see me, he had to talk to somebody. I said that of course I'd meet him. I missed him terribly, and I told him so. I hoped he had decided to come home. He told me to meet him at this awful place . . .''

"The Sow's Ear," I said.

Lee grimaced. "Yes, that's right. Stu was there before me. He had already had several drinks. I didn't think too much about it. He did that sometimes. But this was different, I quickly realized. He was in a corner booth, sitting back in the shadows. As if he were hiding, you see. His eyes kept darting around, as if he were afraid he had been followed, or someone might have followed me. I sat down across from him and touched his hand. He snatched it away from me. 'Jesus Christ,' I remember him saying. 'Not here.' Well, I took encouragement from that. If not here, I thought, then someplace else. But that wasn't what Stu wanted. Matter of fact, it wasn't at all clear what he *did* want, because he started mumbling about how he shouldn't have called me, he didn't want to get me involved, and the more I asked him what the hell he was talking about, the more he said I should just leave. I told him I wasn't going to leave until he told me what the trouble was. He said it wouldn't be fair to tell me. It went on like that for a while. He had some more drinks. I kept begging him to tell me about it." Lee paused. "Mr. Coyne, may I have a drink of water, please?"

"How about Scotch? That's what you prefer, isn't it?"

He looked startled. "Why, yes. Yes it is. Scotch would be fine. And water, if that's all right."

I went to the cabinet and poured each of us a drink. He took his and sipped at it. "I told him I really meant it, I just wouldn't leave him until he told me what was on his mind. I'd never seen him so excited. Upset and excited both. Finally he leaned across the table and whispered to me. 'I'm really onto something,' he said. 'Something big.' Then he said he shouldn't tell me. It was too dangerous."

"Dangerous," I said. "Was that his word?"

"Yes. He said dangerous. But then he started to tell me this story when a girl came and sat with us. We tried to be polite with her. She was a prostitute. I tried to suggest that we weren't interested. All the while, Stu is mumbling about being onto something big. Once he got started, he couldn't seem to stop. At last the girl went away. I said to Stu, 'What is it? Tell me what this is all about.' He was pretty drunk, Mr. Coyne, but I gathered it had something to do with that business in Haiti, and the assassination attempt back in December. Remember?"

"I remember," I said. "Felix Guerrero. The Happy

Warrior, as Mickey Gillis called him. Thurmond Lampley. Sure, I remember. What about it?''

Lee shook his head. ''I don't exactly know. Stu was not coherent. I begged him to come with me. We'd talk to the police, I told him. He said, no, he was already dealing with it.''

''What did he mean by that?''

Lee sighed. ''I wish I knew. He might still be alive if he had told me. But he got very sly. Paranoid, almost. He told me to go away, mind my own business, as if it were I who had called him up rather than the other way around. I think he was trying to protect me, do you see? Anyway, he wouldn't budge. He just got abusive.'' He sipped at his Scotch and shrugged. ''So, after a while, I left.''

''What time did you leave?''

''It must've been around eleven. I got home just in time to see the New Year being ushered in on the television. You know how that big ball comes down . . . ?''

''Yes,'' I said. ''Is that it?''

''Yes. That's all of it.''

''Did he mention any names?''

''No. I would remember if he did.''

''What about Father Barrone. Joe Barrone.''

''No.''

''How about a Dr. Adrian Vance?''

He shook his head. ''No.''

''Did he mention Altoona?''

Lee frowned. ''That's in Pennsylvania. No, I don't think so.''

''Altoona was a person. A friend of his. Who has also been killed.''

''He didn't mention anybody by that name, no. He mentioned no names.''

''Any reference to his notebooks, or a diary, or a journal?''

He shook his head.

''Did he say anything about meeting somebody that night?''

He thought for a minute. "Well," he said slowly, "not in so many words, no. But now that I think of it, he did look at my watch a few times, as if he had an appointment. I remember thinking that he acted as if he had a date, and wanted to get rid of me before a certain time."

"Did he say anything about a date specifically?"

"No. I think I'd remember if he did."

I leaned back in my chair. "What else, Mr. Lee?"

"What do you mean?"

"What haven't you told me?"

"I've told you everything."

"That's what you said last time."

"Mr. Coyne, you've got to try to understand. Nothing I can do or say can bring Stu back to me. But it can ruin me. I explained that to you before. I didn't kill Stu. I hope you know that. I don't know any more about it than I've told you. But if my relationship with him ever became public knowledge . . ."

"I'm an officer of the court, Mr. Lee," I said. "And you have withheld information relevant to the investigation of a felony. Do you understand?"

"I understand that you don't seem to want to believe me. But it's the truth. If you want to wreck my life, you have it in your power."

"Your career is not relevant here."

"It is to me." He shook his head. "I'm not going to beg you. I told you everything. I do not want to be involved. As much as I loved Stu, I do not want to be connected to his death. It would do nobody any good."

"How do I know you're telling me the truth now?"

He shrugged. "I guess you don't."

"What are you hiding?"

"I'm hiding nothing from you. From the world, I'm hiding a great deal." His shoulders slumped, but he held my gaze with his eyes. "I've told you all I know."

"You understand I'll have to talk to the police."

"Will you have to give them my name?"

"They can be more effective than I in getting at the truth."

"For God's sake, Mr. Coyne! I've told you absolutely everything."

"Have it your way, then," I said.

He stood up. "I hope you have a conscience," he said. "Good day, sir."

He started for the door. "Mr. Lee," I said.

He stopped and turned to face me. "Yes?"

"I'll try to keep your name out of it."

He nodded slowly. "I would appreciate it," he said. Then he left.

I poured a little more bourbon into my glass. Then I called Gus Becker. I told him what I had learned from my visit to the Sow's Ear. I included the information David Lee had given me, but I made it sound as if Trixie had overheard all of it. I left my interview with Lee out of it. For the time being, I thought I could justify that.

I told Becker about getting mugged. I had the impression that he thought it was funny.

But he seemed interested in what I had to say. "Now we're getting somewhere," he said. I told him that I failed to see the connection with the cocaine wars, and he said, "It's very complicated." He asked again about Stu's notebooks, and I told him I had nothing new on that subject. He asked if Heather had started her book yet, and I said I didn't know. He told me I should stop butting into police business. It sounded perfunctory. He suggested we get together for a drink sometime. I said I'd like that, and we left it there.

Al Santis did not seem interested. "So he went to a bar, shot the shit with a hooker, and got drunk," he said. "Then he went outside and passed out in an alley. That don't get us any closer to whoever stuck an icepick into his ear, now, does it?"

"You don't think his talking about Haiti and Thurmond Lampley's assassination attempt makes a difference?"

"Maybe you can explain it to me. You're the lawyer. You've got all the brains. You understand confusing things."

"I can't," I said. "It makes no sense to me, either. It just seemed pertinent."

Santis and I did not talk about having a drink together.

14

I was nursing a beer at a corner table at Marie's when Billy walked in. I didn't recognize my son at first. Somehow, I still expected to see the pre-pubescent eleven-year-old who smiles at me from the photos in my office, rather than the twenty-year-old man he'd become, largely in my absence. I missed most of my two sons' adolescences, which makes me an object of envy among those of my contemporaries who had the full benefit of the experience.

Billy has my gray eyes and longish nose. From Gloria he got his fair complexion and good teeth. Most of it all was hidden from view behind a bushy blond beard, which he got from neither of us.

He came to the table and lifted a long leg over the back of a chair to sit down. I reached my hand across the table to him.

"Hi, Son," I said.

"How ya doin', Dad?" he answered, grasping my hand firmly and looking into my eyes the way I taught him.

"I'm fine. Want a beer?"

He grinned. "I don't drink, remember?"

"I remember last time you didn't. Last time you were still shaving, as I recall."

"Like it?"

"Does it matter?"

"Nope. Guess not. Mom hates it."

"Are you trying to make some kind of statement?"

"What, growing a beard? Naw. Just thought I'd try it out. See how it looks." He shrugged. "No big deal."

I took out my pack of Winstons and held it to him. "Smoke?"

"Don't smoke, either. At least, not those things."

Our waitress, a college kid from B.U. clad in tight faded jeans and a white blouse, stopped beside our table. She looked down at Billy. "Can I get you something, sir?" she said to him.

He barely glanced at her. "Food. Feed me."

"Mr. Coyne? Another beer?"

"Bring menus, I guess, Gwen."

She bobbed her head and gave us her slightly lopsided smile. "Right back," she said.

I watched her walk away. "Good-looking girl," I observed.

"Didn't notice particularly," said Billy. But the sly grin that peeped out from the hair on his face gave him away.

"So," I said with elaborate casualness. "How have you been?"

"Aha. Here it comes. In most cultures, you know, they postpone the business until after the eating. It's considered polite. Refined. Civilized. Especially when the business is unpleasant." He looked down and tinkered with the silverware. "You wanna talk about me quitting school, right?"

I nodded. "Right."

"Okay. Go ahead."

I shrugged. "Fine. So what the hell are you quitting school for, then?"

His eyes twinkled. He was actually enjoying it. "I've gotta find myself," he said, making it clear that we both knew he was parroting a cliché, and that I shouldn't take it too seriously.

I decided to play along with him. "Where do you plan to start looking?"

Gwen appeared bearing menus. "The specials are on the blackboard, as you know," she said. "I'll bring salads and bread and you can order in a minute."

"Gwen," I said, "this is my son Bill. He's a sophomore at UMass."

She smiled crookedly at him. "Hi."

"How ya doin'?" he said.

She cocked her head. "Well, I'll be right back."

"She's in the nursing program," I told Billy. "Smart kid. Works hard to keep herself in school."

"I hear you, Pop," he said. "As for me, I'm in the business program and I hate it and I'm not working very hard at all. So I thought I'd go looking for myself. I figure I'll start in Florida. Try the canals where the snook and tarpon live, maybe the flats off the keys for bonefish, prowl the mangrove swamps where there are largemouth bass. If I don't find myself there, I'll take a peek in Montana and Wyoming where the trout live." He shrugged. "Like that. I'll look around, see what I can find by way of an identity for myself. You understand?"

"You're not playing fair, you know," I said. "Putting the fishing into it, I mean. You got that from me. No wonder your mother's pissed off."

He grinned.

"Anyhow, at this point I'm supposed to summon up righteous parental indignation. Ready?"

"Ready," he said. "Shoot."

"Okay. So. You plan to throw away your future, give up your education, waste my money, and break your mother's heart, just so you can go bumming around, fishing and generally squandering your abundant talents so you can have a good time while you wait for your identity magically to appear. Is that it? Do I have it right?"

He smirked. "You're doing fine, Dad. Keep it up."

"You don't think *I'd* like to chuck it all and go fishing?"

"Sure you would. Hell, Dad, you *do*."

"I do sometimes. I also work. Everything in its place. Balance. Equilibrium. Moderation. For everything there is a season. The golden mean. Aristotle."

"Look," he said, his face turning serious. "I know Mom put you up to this. I'll tell her you were really pissed off, okay? You don't have to go through the whole drill. Let's eat and relax."

I shook my head. "It's not that simple. You're right, of course. Your mother did call me, and she is upset, and she assumes I am. And you're right that I'm not. Not really. But I think I should be, and I think your mother is a better parent than I am because she *is* disappointed. She wants the best for you." I sighed. "Oh, I do too, naturally. I'm just not sure what it is."

"That's just it," he said, with an eagerness that reminded me of what he had been like many years earlier. "I don't know, either. School doesn't feel right. I don't love it. It's work, and it's hard, and it doesn't make much sense. The only thing I've learned is that I don't want to be a businessman."

"So why don't you switch majors?"

"That's not the point."

"You've got to be something."

"Hey, I don't see why this has to be a big life or death thing. I can take a leave of absence. A sabbatical, like. A furlough. R and R. I've got a good record. They'll take me back. I just need space. Time."

"I couldn't let it happen without talking to you. I know you understand that."

"Sure. I understand."

"And I did need to tell you how concerned your mother is."

"I knew that already." He leaned across the table toward me. "Look, Dad. If you want me to stay in school, if you tell me to, I will. Okay?"

"You will?"

He nodded. "Yes."

"It's tempting."

"Well?"

"No," I said. "No. I'm not going to make that decision for you. You have a lot of things to think about. All I ask is that you think about them. Then make your decision. Make *your* decision. Not Mom's, not mine. Do what you think best. But, dammit, *think*, okay?"

"You're not going to let me cop out, then," he said.

"Nope."

"Well. Thanks."

We talked about other things while we ate, fishing and the Celtics and politics. It was man talk, and it was good, and I realized I hadn't done enough of it with my sons. Maybe it still wasn't too late.

I paid the bill, and we started to leave. Then Billy said, "Wait a minute, will you?"

I stood by the door while he went back into the restaurant. I saw him talking to Gwen. She watched his face, her eyes solemn, while he bent to speak to her. Then she smiled and nodded and he rejoined me.

"Well?" I said.

"Well, yeah," he answered, grinning.

We buttoned up against the cold. When we got to the subway entrance we shook hands. "Keep in touch," I said.

"I will. I'll let you know."

I watched him go down the steps. My son was a man, now. For some reason, I found it depressing.

* * *

I got to Heather's condominium a few minutes before seven, bearing the fourteen-dollar bottle of Burgundy that the guy at the package store guaranteed would go well with medium-rare steak, and a bunch of greenhouse daisies from the Puerto Rican lady on the corner. I rang the doorbell a couple of times, and when Heather didn't answer I put my ear to the door. I could hear music playing inside. She was probably upstairs showering or changing her clothes and couldn't hear the bell over the music.

I shifted back and forth from one foot to the other for a minute, and then I remembered that she hid a spare key outside. I found the loose shingle and the key was there. I unlocked the door, returned the key to its hiding place, and went inside.

She had the radio tuned to a Boston FM station that liked to play what they called "non-stop rock." It was very loud and not especially tuneful. It served to remind me that Heather and I were of different generations.

I went to the foot of the stairs. I could hear the shower running, but I called, "I'm here," anyway, and took the wine and the flowers into the kitchen. I found her corkscrew and opened the Burgundy to let it breathe. I filled a tumbler with water and dunked in the daisies. Heather had left some peeled potatoes in the sink. A big wooden salad bowl sat on the butcher-block sideboard. She had already rubbed the inside of it with olive oil.

I opened the refrigerator to see if I could find a beer. There were two thick T-bone steaks in a shallow pan marinating in a mixture that included crushed garlic and thyme. She had left half a dozen bottles of Beck's dark to chill. I took one back into the living room with me.

I went back to the stairs and yelled again, "Hey! Did you hear me? I'm here and I'm starving, and I'm going to change the radio station and I think you're clean enough by now."

I found some light symphonic music on WCRB, adjusted the volume to my taste, and slouched on the sofa with my beer. I was eager to tell Heather about my session with

Billy. She would, I suspected, sympathize with his urge to "find himself."

I allowed my mind to drift on the music while I sipped my beer. The piece, which I recognized as something by Debussy, ended at the same time that I drained the bottle. I heaved myself up from the sofa and went to the stairs. She was still in the shower. I muttered a few generalizations about the female gender and stalked up the stairway.

The bathroom was at the head of the stairs. The door was ajar, and steam oozed out through the crack. I tapped on the door. "Come on, Heather. I'm hungry. Let's go." She didn't answer.

I pushed open the door and waved at the thick, hot mist in the room. "Want me to dry your back?" I said. Then I realized that she wasn't behind the opaque glass shower door. I turned off the shower.

She was in her bedroom, snuggled down under a blanket, sound asleep. The light from the hallway cast a beam across the mound of her rump. She was sleeping on her stomach, facing away from me. I deduced that she had gone into the bathroom and turned on the shower, then returned to her bedroom to take off her clothes. I could imagine her, after a long day of boring work, yawning, lying on her bed just for a moment, pulling a blanket over herself, and letting her eyes fall shut.

I went in and sat beside her on the edge of the bed. I put my hand lightly on her hip. "Hey," I said softly. "You want company in there? I don't know whether I should be flattered or offended. It's plain enough that you're not exactly excited about our date tonight." I put my mouth to her ear. "Uncle Brady's here," I whispered. "You gonna wake up?" I prodded her shoulder gently. She didn't move. I pushed at her hip. "Come on, Heather," I said more loudly. "Let's go."

Then I realized that her body wasn't lifting and falling in the soft rhythms of sleep.

Her breathing was too shallow to detect.

I rolled her onto her back and her head lolled loosely. I touched her face. "Heather!" I said. "Hey, wake up!" She didn't wake up.

I felt for the pulse against the side of her throat.

And then I knew that she wasn't going to wake up.

I yanked the covers off her. She was dressed in a loose-fitting pink turtleneck jersey and blue jeans. I got up and turned on the light in the room. Then I went back to the bed and looked down at Heather's body. That's when I saw the dime-sized rust-colored stain on the pillow where the side of her face had rested.

I moved her head to look at her left ear. The little streak of dried blood in it had turned dark and scabby.

I sat beside her for perhaps five minutes, stroking her hair. Then I stood up, drew the sheet over her face, and went downstairs. I picked up the telephone and told the operator to get me the Sudbury police emergency number.

I gave my name and Heather's address to the officer who answered, and told him that I was reporting a homicide. He wanted to know if I was sure that the victim was dead. I told him I was sure. He asked me if I had done it, and I told him that it wasn't me. He told me to wait there, and I told him that I had no intention of leaving. I disconnected and then rang Gus Becker.

"Yes?" he answered.

"It's Brady Coyne. I think you should know. I'm at Heather Kriegel's place in Sudbury. She's been murdered. I think someone stuck an icepick into her ear."

"Jesus!" he said. "How do I get there?"

I gave him directions.

"It'll take me half an hour," he said. "Sit tight."

Then I called Al Santis's number. An officer at the desk answered and told me that Santis was off duty, was it an emergency, was there someone else I wanted to talk to. I thought about it for a moment and then told him to forget it, I'd try to get back to him later.

The police arrived in five minutes, heralded by screaming sirens. There were two uniformed officers, a guy in a suit who appeared to be in charge, and two ambulance attendants.

The plainclothes cop introduced himself as Lieutenant Carlson. "Where's the body?" he said.

"Upstairs. In the bedroom."

He jerked his head at one of the other cops, who led the two ambulance men up the stairs.

"So, what happened, Mr. Coyne?"

"We had a date. I got here a little before seven. The date was for seven, see, but I'm always early. It's just a thing . . ."

"How'd you get in?"

"The key. She keeps—she kept—a key hidden outside. She showed it to me the first time I was here. She was dead when I got here."

"A key, huh. Hm." He pursed his lips. "I wonder who else knows about that key."

I shrugged. I felt cold.

"Come on, Mr. Coyne. Think. What about friends? Other boyfriends, maybe. People she worked with. Relatives."

I shook my head. "I don't know. She never talked about them. I can't help you there."

"Because there's no sign of forced entry here, see. So whoever killed her either let himself in, or else she let him in herself. Either way, it wasn't a stranger. So it would help us a lot if we knew who she knew."

"I just don't think I can help you there," I repeated. And I felt a pang of sadness, because it was true. There was much about Heather Kriegel that I hadn't had the chance to learn.

"What was your relationship with her?"

"We were friends."

"Friends, huh?"

"Friends. Yes."

"Tell me everything from the time you came in the door."

I did, as well as I could. There wasn't that much to tell, except that images of Heather kept intruding, so that my recitation lacked coherence, even to me.

"So you hung around downstairs for ten or fifteen minutes while she was dead upstairs, is that it?" said Carlson.

"Yes. Like I said, I thought she was getting ready. I am always early for things. She tends to be late."

"But you didn't think it was a little strange that she didn't answer when you called upstairs to her?"

"I figured she was in the shower. I assumed she didn't hear me."

"Any idea who'd want to kill her?"

I shook my head. "No."

Carlson stood up. "You sit right there, Mr. Coyne, and try to relax. I'm going to go upstairs to take a look. The Medical Examiner should be here in a minute." He glanced meaningfully at the other policeman, who had posted himself by the front door, then he went up the stairs. I looked at the cop by the door, who stood at attention and stared at the wall across the room. I said to him, "I'm going to get myself a beer, okay?"

"No, sir," he said, without looking at me. "You're supposed to stay here."

I shrugged and sat back.

A few minutes later the doorbell rang. The cop opened the door and conversed for a moment with somebody. Then he came back into the room, followed by a bulky man wearing a topcoat over a suit and carrying a black bag. He scowled down at me as he walked past on his way to the stairs. I could hear him wheezing loudly. I wondered if he'd survive the climb to the second floor.

"That's the ME," said the policeman to me.

"I figured," I said. "Hey, look. I'd really like a beer, or at least a glass of water, you know? I really don't feel too hot."

"You'll have to wait 'til the Lieutenant comes down."

"You want me to puke on the rug here?"

"Please don't move, sir."

I stood up. "I'm going to get a beer. Shoot me, if you want."

I went into the kitchen and took another Beck's from the refrigerator. When I turned, the policeman was standing behind me. "Want one?" I said.

He smiled briefly. "No, thank you."

We went back into the living room and resumed our places, he by the door and I on the sofa. I lit a cigarette. A moment later Lieutenant Carlson came downstairs with the Medical Examiner. They walked over to the door, talking in low voices. Then the doctor left and Carlson went to the phone. I noticed that he held it with his handkerchief, just like in the movies. He spoke into it, hung up, and came over and sat beside me.

"A photographer and the forensics boys will be over in a minute. While we're waiting, maybe you've thought of something else you can tell me about this."

"I called a guy named Gus Becker after I called you," I said. "He's with the DEA. Maybe he can help you. I don't know what else I can tell you."

"What's the DEA got to do with this?"

"Ask Becker. I don't know if it has anything to do with it, but I think he can explain it all better than me."

"How well did you know Miss Kriegel?"

"I told you. We were friends. I met her about a month ago."

"Anything missing in here that you noticed?"

"No. Not that I noticed."

"What about these beer bottles?"

"They're mine."

"The cigarette butts?"

"Mine, also."

"And I suppose you've touched everything in here?"

I sighed. "I got a corkscrew from a drawer in the kitchen. I went into the refrigerator a couple of times. I adjusted the volume and changed the station on the stereo.

I probably touched the knobs on the bathroom and bedroom doors. I turned on the light in the bedroom. I called you guys on the telephone." I shrugged. "I probably touched other things, too. I don't know."

Carlson sat back. "Mr. Coyne, I'm not accusing you of this, you understand. So you don't need to feel defensive. You'll notice I didn't read your rights to you or anything, so you should take it easy. But you're the closest thing we've got to a witness right now, and I want to make sure we don't miss anything. So if you don't mind, when we're done here you and I will go down to the station and you can give us a statement."

"And if I do mind?"

"You're an attorney, right?"

"Yes."

"All right, then."

I nodded. "I know. Sorry. I wasn't being defensive. I'm upset. She was—I cared very much for her."

He nodded. "Sure."

We sat in silence for a few minutes, and then four more police officers arrived. One of them carried a camera with a flash attachment and a big bag over his shoulder. One of the others was a woman with frizzy hair who appeared to be in charge of the crew. They all conferred in low tones with Carlson and then dispersed. The girl and the photographer headed upstairs.

Gus Becker arrived a short time later. He spoke briefly with Carlson and then came over and sat beside me on the sofa. He put his hand on my arm.

"How ya doin'?"

"Not that great."

He nodded. "Understandable. What'd you tell Carlson?"

"Just what happened when I got here."

"According to Carlson, the ME says she's been dead two hours at the most. He suspects a drug OD."

"For God's sake, there was blood in her ear," I said.

"Well, I know. Evidently there was so little blood the

doctor didn't make the connection. We know what we think they'll find when they do a real examination. Matter of selective perception. You find a young woman dead in her bed, no obvious signs of physical violence or anything, you make certain assumptions.''

"I told Carlson about her ear."

"I gather that the ME's not the type who listens."

"I've been thinking about something," I said. "Something I didn't tell you."

"What is it?"

"Remember I told you that the hooker at the Sow's Ear talked with Stu Carver the night he was killed?"

Becker nodded.

"And that she said he was babbling about Haiti and the Lampley assassination attempt?"

"Yeah? So?"

"Well, what I left out was that Stu was with somebody else at that place, and they were arguing."

"Somebody else. You mean—"

I nodded. "A man. Stu's lover."

"Well, for Christ's sake, Brady . . ."

"Listen, I blew it. I know. If I'd told you right away, maybe Heather . . ."

He put his hand on my shoulder. "That kind of shit is not productive. Come on, now. What do you want to tell me? What are you thinking?"

"I know who might've done it. Who might've killed Stu and Altoona. And Heather."

"Well, for God's sake, what's his name?"

"David Lee. Like I said, Stu's lover. He was with Stu that night, New Year's Eve. They argued because Stu wouldn't go with him. I don't know why the hell he had to kill Altoona, unless he thought Stu and the old guy were lovers or something. Maybe Stu told him that, I don't know. But he used an icepick on both of them."

"Why would he kill Miss Kriegel?"

"That's clearer. She was the one who gave me Lee's

name. And I told him it was Heather who told me. I thought that would make him feel better, knowing it was Heather, I mean. The guy is probably crazy. That's what Al Santis has been saying all along. That would explain it, wouldn't it? That David Lee was jealous and crazy and out of control?"

Becker nodded. "Yes. That might explain it. I'll tell Carlson, have Lee picked up. Do you know where he lives?"

I shrugged. "No, but he teaches at Lincoln Prep. They'd know."

"Okay," said Becker. "One good thing, anyway."

"What's that?"

"The girl wasn't abused, according to the doctor. No sign of rape or anything."

"Well, that's not surprising," I said.

"How's that?"

"It's fairly obvious," I said. "After all, David Lee is a homosexual."

"Good point," said Becker. "Of course," he added, "there's something else to think about."

"What?"

"It could have been a woman. A woman wouldn't rape her, either."

15

I was still there when the two ambulance attendants came down the stairs lugging the black plastic zippered body bag. They maneuvered it with casual efficiency. It was something they had done before. They didn't drop her or bump her on the stairs. But they managed to convey that what they carried was inert.

Then Carlson drove Gus Becker and me to the Sudbury police station. He questioned each of us separately, and it was after eleven o'clock when he let us go. A uniformed policeman drove us back to Heather's place where our cars were.

It was a frigid, clear winter night. A million stars glittered in the black sky. The moon was waxing toward full. Becker and I stood in the parking area, our breaths coming in steamy little puffs.

"You want to go get a drink or something?" he said to me.

"I don't think so. I want to go home."

"Carlson said he was going to talk to Santis. They'll pick up Lee tonight."

"Yeah. That's good."

"I imagine forensics will find something solid to link up Lee. Fingerprints at the girl's place, murder weapon, something."

I nodded.

"Of course, this doesn't help me that much," said Becker.

"Huh?"

"I mean, the drug connection. That's my business. I guess I was off the mark on that."

"Oh. Sure. It looks that way."

"Still, it's good to have it settled."

"If I hadn't been so goddam soft, we could have settled it a long time ago."

Becker put his hand on my shoulder. "Don't do this to yourself, Brady."

"Well, it's true. The bastard kept saying how his career would be ruined if anyone found out he was gay, and I bought it."

"It was reasonable. You had nothing to go on."

"Yeah, but I *knew*. I mean, I just felt something was off-center, you know? Maybe the first time I talked with him, okay. But then when I found out he was with Stu—hell, he was so pitiful, so scared. And yet dignified, too. He seemed innocent to me. A victim. I just couldn't imagine him shoving an icepick into somebody's ear." I shook my head. "I still can't. When I try to visualize it, try to see in my mind's eye David Lee doing that—the picture isn't there. I just can't see it."

"You never can," said Becker.

I nodded and held out my hand to him. "I guess that about does it for us, then, huh?"

He took my hand. "I guess so. I'll see you around."

"Do you think so?"

He grinned. "Actually, no. Probably not."

By the time I got back to my apartment, and had kicked off my shoes and poured myself half a hand of Jack Daniel's, more or less, it was after midnight. I figured Zerk would be sleeping, but I called him anyway.

"You awake?" I said when he answered.

"Always on the job, Counselor," he said. "Just like you taught me. Hustle, hustle, hustle."

"I never taught you that."

"No, you didn't. But you taught me good. What's up?"

"Heather Kriegel was murdered tonight."

"Oh, man . . ."

"An icepick, Zerk. In her ear. I found her body."

He was silent for a long moment. I lit a cigarette shakily. "That fuckin' faggot: Lee. That's who did it. Damn!"

"That's how I figure it," I said.

"They should have picked him up as soon as you told them about him."

"I didn't tell anybody. Not until tonight."

"You mean," he said slowly, "after what Trixie told us, you didn't go to the cops? You didn't tell them Lee was with Carver that night?"

I sighed. "No. I talked with Lee myself. His story was—plausible. He admitted he was with Stu. But he said he left before Stu did. I believed him."

"You believed him," said Zerk, irony dripping from his voice.

I puffed on my cigarette. "Yeah. I believed him. He just didn't seem the type. He still doesn't."

"You dumb honkie." His voice was not gentle. "You could have spared a life, you realize that?"

"I'm glad I didn't call you so you could make me feel better."

"You don't deserve to feel better, man. Shit." He paused. "You think Heather was involved in some drug thing with them?"

"With Stu and Lee, you mean? No. No, I don't. I think I knew her well enough. But, hell, what do I know?"

"That," said Zerk, "is an excellent question. So did you tell your buddy Becker about Heather?"

"Yes. He was good. He came right out, stayed with me, talked to the police. I appreciated having him there. He doesn't seem to think these murders are related to his drug investigation. It doesn't fit together."

"I don't know," said Zerk. "Maybe it does. Let's say Lee, there, is a middle man of some kind, okay? Carver would know about it, for sure. And if he did, then Heather would, too. So maybe Carver panicked, or somebody got to him. Maybe he was even involved in distributing. Skimming some profits, say. Whatever. Lee finds himself in a bind with the big boys. Gets his orders: Clean things up, or you'll find yourself feeding the lobsters at the bottom of the harbor. Lee goes to Carver, talks to him at the Sow's Ear. Carver lets on that Heather and the old guy, whatsisname . . ."

"Altoona."

"Yeah. Him. Those two know about it. So Lee cleans up his mess. Kills all three of them."

I stubbed out my cigarette. My head hurt. "Well," I said, "Becker didn't seem to make that kind of connection."

"He probably did, but didn't share it with you. I wouldn't tell you anything if I was him, that's for sure."

"I do seem to have a penchant for fouling things up."

"A penchant. That you do."

"I was very fond of all three of them, Zerk."

"You were sleeping with Heather, weren't you?"

"Yes."

"Well, I'm sorry, man. Really."

"I know," I said. "I'd like to have a chance at Lee with an icepick," I added.

"Let's not get melodramatic, my man. You're the same guy who puts back all his trout, and picks up spiders and takes them outside, right?"

"This is different."

"Leave it to the cops."

"I am. I will."

"You all right?"

"I'll get by."

"If you need anything . . ."

"Like spiritual counseling? You're a master at that."

"I know," said Zerk.

I didn't sleep much that night, and I made it through the next morning because, after I told her what had happened, Julie pushed me unmercifully to catch up on my paperwork.

In the afternoon Al Santis came into the office.

"Just happened to be in the neighborhood," he said when Julie showed him in.

"I'll bet," I said. "Coffee?"

"Yeah. Good."

"I'll get it," said Julie. "My turn."

"I think it's mine," I said.

"You can owe me, then," she said.

When she left, Santis said, "You take turns getting coffee?"

"Sure. It's only fair."

"If I had a secretary, she'd always get the coffee."

"Not if you had Julie for a secretary you wouldn't."

"Ah," he said, nodding. We sat on the soft furniture in the informal corner of my office. He ran his hand over the blood-red Moroccan leather upholstery of the armchair he had chosen. "Nice. Very nice."

Julie came in with two mugs of coffee. Santis accepted his with a grunt, spooned in two helpings of sugar, and sipped it, watching Julie over the rim of his mug as she bent to give me mine. When she left, he said, "That's nice, too."

"The coffee, you mean."

He squinted at me, to see if I were joking. I smiled perfunctorily to let him know I was.

"So," I said, "you just happened to be in the neighborhood. This is a social call, then."

"Naw. 'Course not. Thought you might like to fill me in on what happened last night."

"You heard."

"Oh, sure. We're getting all coordinated and organized and mobilized and everything, now. Something happens out in the ritzy suburbs, all of a sudden it's a big deal. We got the State cops in on it now, and that Fed, Becker, he's right in the middle of things. I understand it was you who found the body."

I nodded, and told Santis what had happened. While I talked, he sipped his coffee and allowed his eyes to wander around my office. He grunted a few times to let me know he was still listening.

When I finished, he said, "Well, we picked up David Lee this morning."

"And?"

"And we let him go."

I set my mug down on the coffee table. "You *what*?"

"We let him go. We had him in there for three hours. We had four different guys interrogate him. He told everybody exactly the same story. The same one he told you. So far, we've got no evidence, nothing to hold him on."

"What about last night? Where was he last night?"

Santis shrugged. "Home correcting papers, he says. He can't prove it. But the burden of proof isn't on him."

I shook my head. "God," I muttered. "What do you think? How did he seem to you?"

Santis scowled. "I don't think anymore, Mr. Coyne. I'm not some kind of headshrinker. I always assume a guy's lying. I always assume he's guilty. That's the way I hafta do my job. But think? What I think is, we've got no evidence to hold this guy."

"He's got motive, he's got opportunity . . ."

"Maybe. Maybe not."

"What about the forensics? Can't they come up with something?"

"A murder weapon would help a lot. A bloody shirt. Fingerprints at Kriegel's house. His skin under her fingernails. All that shit they find on TV that we hardly ever manage to come up with. Hey, maybe we will. But so far, zilch."

"So David Lee is free."

"Yup. Oh, we'll keep an eye on him, as well as we can. Something comes up, we can always invite him back in for more conversation. But right now, that's it. You know," he said, cocking his head at me, "you might want to take care of yourself."

"What do you mean?"

"Well, you're kinda involved in this thing."

"You mean, Lee might come after me?"

Santis shrugged. "Lee. Or whoever did it. Yeah, I think it's worth keeping in mind."

I laughed. "You're joking. It's one thing to kill a comatose drunk or an old derelict who's already dying of tuberculosis. Or an unsuspecting woman, even. But David Lee doesn't scare me. I hardly think I need to worry."

"If it was Lee."

"Who else could it have been?"

He shrugged. "Even so, be careful."

"Is that what you came to tell me? To be careful?"

He grinned. "That was one thing, yeah."

"Your concern," I said, "is touching. Unnecessary, but touching."

That evening promised to pass slowly. I heated up a frozen pizza and took it and a bottle of Molson's to the sofa in front of the television. The seven o'clock news failed to cheer me up, and my mind kept wandering back to the previous night, when I had put my hand on the slope where Heather's hip dipped to her waist. I had felt a twinge of desire, not realizing that the body under the covers in her darkened bedroom was not alive. The fact of her death seemed more dramatic to me than other deaths I had known. Because, I supposed, she had been especially alive—vivid, energized—and because we had made love, and because I had felt in my own body all the life that was in hers.

And because I had maybe loved her.

I snapped off the tube at seven-thirty, and if anyone had asked me what the big stories of the day were, I couldn't have told them. Heather's death was not news, that much had registered.

When the phone rang, I felt an unexpected surge of gratitude. I didn't care if it was an insurance salesman. I would engage him in conversation, ask after his health and that of his family, and tell him it was good to hear his voice.

It was Gloria. "How are you, Brady?" she said, with that huskiness in her tone that still stirred me.

"Oh, okay."

"You are an absolute magician, do you know that?"

"A veritable Houdini, that's me."

"Well, that goes to show what a father can do. Oh, I think you'll have to admit that I've done a pretty good job with the boys, and, let's face it, you weren't always there when they needed you. When *I* needed you. I always felt that there were some things—and I'm as liberated as the next woman, as you know, but still—some things that, especially with sons, a man, a father just had to do."

"Fishing, camping, baseball, the dangers of venereal disease. Like that," I said, still trying to figure out what she was talking about.

"Oh, you know what I mean."

"Sure." I cleared my throat. "Well, you've done a fine job with Billy and Joey, Gloria."

"Yes, I know. But I've got to admit it. This time, when I needed you, you really came through."

"Well, I try."

"It's a big relief, believe me."

"Oh, well," I mumbled.

"It's one of the things I always loved about you, Brady. You were firm in your convictions. You were never a wimp, never wishy-washy. You said what you believed. You knew right from wrong, and you were never afraid to say so."

"Well, that's what legal training does for you."

"The amazing thing," she went on, "is that he doesn't even seem to resent it. It's almost as if it were his own idea."

"Billy," I said. "You mean Billy."

"Of course. Not only is he finishing up the semester, but he seems committed to the next two years, too. He even mentioned graduate school. Amazing."

"Well, we did have a little conversation."

"I'll say you did. I wish I'd been a fly on the wall."

"It's probably just as well that you weren't."

"Pretty rough, huh? Well, I do appreciate it, anyway. They talk about a woman's fury, but I guess a father's fury is something else."

"Oh, yes," I said. "It can be."

"Anyway, thanks."

"I left it up to him," I said.

She laughed. "Oh, sure. I can imagine. An offer he couldn't refuse. Listen. I feel like celebrating. Suppose we meet somewhere for a drink? I'll pay, how's that?"

"Sounds great, Gloria. Really. A good idea. Ordinarily, I'd say let's do it. But I'm kinda tied up this evening. Another time. Okay? Let's do it soon."

"Sure," she said. "Understood." She forced a laugh. "Anyway, I'm glad you read the riot act to Billy. He's still a kid, you know. He still needs to be told what to do."

"It was his decision," I said.

"Right," she said, chuckling. "Thanks, anyway."

"It was the least I could do."

"That," she said, "is true."

After we hung up, I sat there in the gloomy, empty silence of my overpriced apartment cell and wondered why I had refused Gloria's offer. Moments earlier I had been eager to talk to telephone salesmen. It's not that I don't like my former wife. I do. I continue to love her, in fact. But I didn't want to see her, not that evening. Heather was on my mind, I realized, and it seemed that I'd feel better if I suffered a little, if I felt some loneliness, some emptiness of my own. It would be nothing compared to Heather's.

I pulled on a heavy coat and went out onto the little balcony that hung on the side of the building. The winter air was clear and sharp. It bit at my face like a mouthful of tiny, pointed teeth. The moon and the stars lit up the water, which was as shiny and inky-black as Heather's plastic body bag. I slouched on one of the aluminum folding chairs I kept out there, staring without focus at the point where the ocean's curve disappeared over the horizon. I stayed there long after the chill had invaded the last layers of insulation on my body, and the skin on my face had become taut and numb. Then I went inside and stripped for a steamy shower.

And by the time I was toweling myself dry, I found myself humming an old Chuck Berry tune, one that Heather and I had sung together not that long ago in her living room. The memory of her bawdy interpolations made me smile. Coyne's balcony and shower therapy. Cheaper than a shrink's sofa, safer than drugs, and, for Coyne, damn reliable. The big empty sky and the boundless sea never failed to pull unraveling strands back into some kind of logical pattern.

Heather was dead, and I had cared for her, and now I missed her. But I knew I would soon be ready to hum our tunes and remember her well.

When the phone rang, I mumbled, "Now what?" before I picked it up.

Al Santis's voice was decidedly not cheerful. "Mr. Coyne. Some bad news."

"Christ! What now?"

"Your friend David Lee. He shot himself this afternoon."

16

I felt as if someone had rammed his elbow into my solar plexus. I sat down heavily. "What happened?" I said.

"It was around suppertime tonight. He was in his classroom there at the school. Custodian heard the shot. The door was locked from the inside. The janitor had enough sense not to go inside. He just took one look through the window in the door and called the local cops. They eventually called me, and I went out to take a look. Quite a mess."

"I can imagine," I said quickly, fumbling for a cigarette and trying *not* to imagine the scene, which worked about as well as when somebody tells you not to think about elephants. "You're sure it was suicide, though?"

"Like I said, the door was locked from the inside. He ate his gun. A .38, snub-nose, registered to him. Makes a neat little hole going in and a great big mess coming out. All over the blackboard."

"Spare me, please," I said. "Was there a note or anything?"

"Of sorts. He wrote something on the board.

"What?"

" 'You win,' is what it said."

"That's it?"

"That was all. The janitor had washed the boards that afternoon, after all the kids had left, so it's pretty certain that Lee wrote that. It's all there was. 'You win.' What do you suppose it means?"

"I think the 'you' refers to me," I said.

"Ah, I don't think you should worry about that," said Santis. "We were pretty rough on him today. I think it's simpler than that."

"Oh?"

"Yeah. I think it means that David Lee was guilty as hell. A bona fide wacko, just like I always thought."

"I hope you're right."

"Me, too," said Santis.

A few days later Al Santis called me again. The Medical Examiner's reports on both Heather and David Lee had been completed. All the forensics had been done. The police were satisfied that David Lee had been responsible for both deaths—Heather's and his own—as well as those of Stu Carver and Altoona. The cases were closed, wrapped up and knotted into a tidy package and filed away. They had not recovered an icepick from Lee's home, but otherwise, according to Santis, the evidence was compelling.

Circumstantial, but compelling.

I tried to sketch out scenarios in my own mind to help me understand it all. I liked the drug story less than the jealous lover script. I saw David Lee as a desperate, insecure, paranoid man, whose personal and professional life had been shattered. Neither murder nor suicide would be unthinkable for such a man.

I tried to persuade myself that Lee was a murderer. Because if he wasn't, then his suicide was my fault.

As the days passed, it became easier to tranquilize the little jerks and tugs at the edges of my conscience. I just had to remind myself that it was David Lee, after all, not I, who had committed murder. And gradually it became easier to believe.

Oh, there was a twitch now and then, usually at night when I was alone in my apartment and the sky and the ocean outside were black and cold and vast and the world seemed especially empty. Then I would see David Lee's face, and it wouldn't be the face of a murderer. I missed Heather then, too, and a little rodent of doubt—or guilt—would nip at the back of my neck. What if I had just minded my own business right from the beginning? What if I had never insisted that Heather tell me about Lee? What if I had refused to tell Lee how I had gotten his name? What if I had showed up at Heather's house an hour earlier the night she was killed?

What if David Lee had killed nobody except himself?

But I knew that history, both cosmic and personal, is etched mainly by forces beyond our control. It is a surging river, moving too fast, and it carries us all in its eddies and currents. The best we can do is splash and flutter in it for the few moments that we have. It tumbles us downstream, through time, whether we like it or not. And eventually we drown in it. All of us. No choice.

No, there was no purpose to be served by what-ifs, and whenever I doubted that, I only had to go sit on my balcony for a few minutes and see how the moon and the stars and the planets splashed puddles of light onto the surface of the Atlantic Ocean. You could look back a million years out there. A million years forward, too.

It put things into perspective.

Julie buzzed me in my office one afternoon in the second week of March, about six weeks after David Lee's suicide.

"A Joe Barrone for you?" she said, with that rising

inflection that demanded to know who this Joe Barrone might be.

"The priest," I told her. "Put him on."

"Mr. Coyne," he said, after I had said hello, "how have you been?"

"Pretty good. You?"

"Still here, ministering to the lame and the halt."

"They haven't given you your little parish by the sea, then, eh?" I said.

He chuckled. "No. I'm still waiting."

"What can I do for you?"

"I've got something here. I guess you're the logical person to have it. Old Altoona's personal effects. There's not much, just a shopping bag full, but you're the closest thing to next of kin he had, and I thought you might like to have them."

"There's nobody else?"

"The Welfare people checked it out as well as they could. I guess they got nothing out of the computers in Washington or the records of the Commonwealth. As far as they know, Altoona never existed. No idea what his real name was, even. Anyway, I've had this stuff sitting here all this time gathering dust."

"If it's clothes, why don't you just give them to your men?"

"I already gave away the clothes. There's some other things. Couple wood carvings, a pen knife, some paperback books, a transistor radio."

"Nothing anybody wants?"

"I suppose one of the men might like to have the radio and the knife."

"I'd like the carvings," I said, remembering the wooden hand Altoona had crafted for me. "And, just for the sentiment of it, the books. Give the other stuff away. I'll drop by sometime."

"I'll be right here, Mr. Coyne. Doesn't look like I'm going anywhere."

A few mornings later I started to head to Marie's for lunch. It reminded me of the old Monday ritual, when I used to collect Stu's notebooks and feed Altoona vermicelli and we'd talk current events. It was one of those warm late winter days when little rivulets of melting snow ran from the bottom of the gray piles and formed puddles on the sidewalks. The kind of day that reminded a right-thinking man that the trout season was only a few weeks away. A good day to be outside. So instead of heading back for Marie's, I pointed myself in the direction of Father Barrone's mission.

I got there twenty minutes later. The front door of the narrow building was ajar, so I stepped inside. Five or six raggedy old men were lounging in the dimly lit hallway. They glanced at me briefly, without interest, and then looked away. I touched the arm of the man nearest to me. He turned his head slowly and lifted his eyebrows, as if to say, "I've already looked at you, sized you up. What now?"

"Excuse me," I said. "I'm looking for Father Barrone."

He ran his hand over the white stubble on his cheeks. "Joe's up there," he said, jerking his head toward the end of the hallway.

I nodded. "Thanks," I said, and shouldered my way around the men. I walked down the hallway to the clinic door and rapped on it lightly. A moment later Joe Barrone stuck out his fox face and said, "I told you, you'll just have to . . . Oh, Mr. Coyne. Sorry."

He stepped out and closed the door behind him. "I'm trying to help the doctor get some medical history in there. Some of the men will talk with me a little. You came for Altoona's things, right?"

"Yes. If you're busy . . ."

"No. It's all right. Come on."

I followed him out through the empty dining room to a tiny office. There was a desk littered with papers, a tall file

cabinet, a wall of bookshelves that contained stacks of manila envelopes, loose papers, and a few books. The room
had a single dirty window that looked across an airshaft to
another brick building. There was a Girl Scout calendar on
the wall, along with a framed photograph of Father Barrone
shaking hands with Mayor Flynn. The room, from what I
could see of it, was completely devoid of religious arti-
facts. No artist's rendering of Jesus, no crosses, no photographs of the Pope or the Cardinal. I didn't even see a
Bible on the bookshelves.

The priest moved behind his desk, bent over, and came
up with a shopping bag, the kind with twine handles. He
handed it to me. "Altoona's stuff," he said. "There was
a cap and scarf in there, which I forgot to mention to you
on the phone. I gave them to a poor fellow who was as
bald as Altoona."

"Good," I said. "I gave that cap and scarf to him for
Christmas."

"Oh. Maybe I shouldn't have given them away."

"No. That's fine. I'm glad you did."

He smiled. "Thank you."

We left the office and walked back toward the front door,
where two men were still waiting for their turn in Dr.
Vance's clinic. "Well, thank you for thinking of me," I
said to the priest. "I was very fond of Altoona, as you
know."

"Are you in a hurry, Mr. Coyne?"

I glanced at my new watch, a cheap Timex that I
wouldn't mind having stolen off my wrist. It was a couple
of minutes after twelve. "No, not really. Why?"

"Would you like to talk?"

I shrugged. "Sure, if you want."

"Good. Look, I've got to get back to the clinic for a
minute. The fellow in there's in really bad shape. Looks
like advanced liver disease. Dr. Vance wants to get him
admitted to the hospital, but he needs to pry some data out
of him. We're almost done. Those other fellows are just

waiting for their medication, so he doesn't need me for them. I'll just be a few minutes. Okay?''

I nodded and took the paper bag that contained all of Altoona's earthly possessions into the dayroom. I put the bag on a table and peered inside. There were three wood carvings. One had been completed, a miniature decoy, a teal, so exquisitely carved that it looked feather-soft. The other two were roughed out but recognizable—a female torso, and the head and shoulders of what looked like a German shepherd. Both struck my untrained eye as perfectly proportioned. The man had had a talent.

I glanced through the books. They were mostly old, tattered, and evidently well-read paperbacks. In addition to several novels by authors I had never heard of, there was a pocket dictionary, Edith Hamilton's *The Greek Way*, and John Stuart Mill's *On Liberty*. The single hardcover volume was rather new looking, a book called *The Harlem Globetrotters* minus its dust jacket. It explained Altoona's basketball pantomime. He must have been reading the book at the time of that strange performance.

I lit a cigarette and wandered into the library nook. I glanced idly at the rows of books on the shelves and wondered how many of the St. Michael's patrons other than Altoona had sampled them. One of them caught my eye. *The Harlem Globetrotters* was printed in bold red letters on the spine of the dust jacket. I slid it from the shelf, assuming it was a duplicate of the book in the shopping bag.

This was a thin volume, and the jacket was too big for it. When I opened it I understood that the old saw about not judging a book by its cover could actually apply to books.

"Sampling our library, eh, Mr. Coyne?''

I closed the book hastily and turned.

"Not many of our men are readers,'' said the priest. "It's too bad. Books are one thing that people are willing to donate.''

I nodded. "Do you mind if I borrow this one?"

"There's no waiting list. Help yourself."

I put the book into the shopping bag that contained Altoona's things. "There was something you wanted to talk about?"

He touched my arm. "Come on." He steered me out of the dayroom. I brought the shopping bag with me. "What happened to poor old Altoona points up a real problem our men have. Many of them, as you may imagine, are veterans, and should be receiving benefits. A lot of them are entitled to Social Security, or food stamps, or various other forms of welfare. Most of them don't get it, for the simple reason that they don't know how, or are unwilling, to negotiate the bureaucracies. They slip through the cracks. They are nonpersons. I try to help. But I'm a priest." He shrugged.

"You're not a lawyer," I said.

He grinned. "I'm not a lawyer. Sometimes I wish I were." We had moved down the hallway, now empty of men, and he pushed on the door that led into the clinic. "Ah, here we are."

Dr. Vance stood when I entered and offered me that big snowshoe of a hand. "Ah, Mr. Coyne, indeed a pleasure to see you again, sir," he said. His toothy grin gleamed in his dark face.

"Mr. Coyne was a friend of Altoona, you remember," said the priest. "He's an attorney."

"A nice mahn, ol' Altoona," said the doctor. "On the rare occasions when he would come down here, before he got crazy, he'd only talk politics. 'Adrian,' he'd say, 'what you think about the Caribbean? Next battleground, don' you think?' He was a sick ol' man, refused medication. 'I'm goin' die,' he'd say. 'I'm goin' die anyway. Nothin' you can do about it.' "

"It didn't happen the way he expected," I observed.

Vance shrugged his great shoulders. "Better this way, maybe."

"Adrian donates his time to the clinic," said Barrone, emphasizing the word "donates."

The big doctor grinned. "Since the President decided to spend his money on sending guns and boats into Haiti instead of on poor ol' folks like Altoona, public health funds been drying up." He shook his head. "I do what I can. Bring medicine samples from the hospital. Come over a few hours, three times a week. People should do what they can."

"I get the picture," I said, smiling at the two of them. "You've ganged up on me. What is it you think *I* can do?"

The priest said promptly, "They need an ombudsman. They need an advocate on Beacon Hill. They need legislation. They need somebody to cut through the red tape." He stared at me.

"You're trying to shame me," I said.

"Right," he said. "I am."

"You're very good at it, both of you."

They both smiled. "Give it some thought, Mr. Coyne," said the priest.

I nodded. "Okay. I will. Let me think about it. I'll call you."

"If you don't," said Barrone, "I'll call you. Count on it."

"What've I got this afternoon?" I said to Julie when I got back to the office.

"Where've you been? You said you'd be gone for an hour. You've had a million calls."

"Sorry, Mother," I said. "You can unfold your arms and stop tapping your foot. I went over to St. Michael's and then I stopped by Marie's for a big bowl of potato gnocchi, with her special meat sauce, Italian sausages, hot bread . . ."

"You're supposed to meet Mr. Boynton at his office at four-thirty. The Bruner estate?"

"Oh, right." I glanced at my Timex. It was a little after three. "Okay. Hold any calls, please. And have a cab come by for me about four-fifteen."

"My goodness, we're suddenly businesslike. I suppose when one grows accustomed to four-hour lunch hours—"

"I said I was sorry," I said, and I went into my office.

I put the shopping bag on top of my desk and removed the volume with *The Harlem Globetrotters* on the dust jacket. It was not a book about the basketball team. This dust jacket had been taken from the book it originally covered, and it was used to disguise this one.

This one wasn't a book at all.

It was a diary. Stu Carver's diary.

Altoona hadn't been as crazy as he had seemed. It occurred to me that he hadn't been crazy at all. His miming Bob Cousy and his singing the Globetrotters' theme song had been intended to convey a message to me. He had given me too much credit. I had accepted the opinions of Father Barrone and Dr. Vance and the superficial evidence of Altoona's behavior. I had thought he was just crazy. It was nothing but good luck that I had happened to find the diary.

I wondered why he had gone through the elaborate charade. Maybe it was simply paranoia.

On the other hand, he *had* ended up getting killed.

Fear, when it's justified, isn't paranoia at all.

Who, then, did old Altoona fear so much that he felt compelled to disguise Stu's diary, and hide it, like Poe's purloined letter, in such an obvious place, and then direct me to it with his weird theatrics?

Father Joe Barrone was the first name I came up with. The priest could have been Stu's enemy, and Altoona's, too, for that matter. But I didn't see how Heather fit in. One thing was clear: Altoona hadn't trusted Father Barrone. Otherwise he logically would have turned Stu's diary over to him.

Dr. Adrian Vance was the second name I came up with.

I remembered how confidently the big doctor had wielded his surgical lancet. Might he handle an icepick with similar deftness? And if there were a drug connection, might his power to write prescriptions, and his access to hospital medicines, somehow explain Vance's apparent commitment to the poor and downtrodden at St. Michael's?

What had Stu Carver written in that diary that provoked such fear in old Altoona, and that made the little volume so valuable that someone had been willing to kill three times for it?

I would find out. I sat down to read it.

17

"She was funny about doing a will," said Zerk. "She kept saying, 'Do you think something's going to happen to me?' I assured her that it was simply a good policy for anybody with any kind of estate to have a will. She said she didn't want to think about it. Anyway, we did one."

"And I'm the executor," I said. "I was flattered that she asked me. We laughed about it. Some joke."

Zerk and I were driving out through the suburbs to Heather's condo in Sudbury. A soft, misty rain was falling, and fog drifted up from the rapidly shrinking patches of snow in the shady corners and along the roadside. The countryside was March brown, all the mud and dead leaves and winter trash along the roadside newly unveiled where the snow had melted away. In the marshlands and along the swollen streams, pale patches of yellow and pink were beginning to show as the willows and swamp maples prepared to send forth their foliage.

Up north, the natives would be wallowing in mud season. In Massachusetts, it mostly just looked dirty.

"The place was sealed off," Zerk was saying. "And, of course, I can't arrange to sell it until we clear probate. We'll have to look around, see what there is to dispose of. And you'll have to figure out what to do with it all."

"As the executor."

"Right. As the executor of the estate."

"No heirs, huh?"

"Both her parents are dead. No siblings. Her instructions were simply to donate everything to a charity. That means," he said, turning to me, "a charity of your choice."

"I want to do something special with her photographs," I said. "Perhaps arrange a showing, or try to get them printed in a book. They're damn good."

We pulled into the parking area adjacent to Heather's place. I hadn't been back since the night she died.

We walked up to the door. Zerk pulled a key from his pocket and stuck it into the lock.

I lifted the loose shingle beside the door, and Heather's spare key fell out. I picked it up and handed it to Zerk. "She was always forgetting her key," I told him. "This is how I got in that night."

He pushed open the door, then turned to face me. "Are you all right?"

I nodded. "Sure. Fine."

The place was as I remembered it. The forensics experts had presumably bustled around with their little plastic bags, dusting, vacuuming, and otherwise searching for clues. As far as I had heard, they had found nothing. And with the suicide of David Lee, they had abandoned their quest.

I wandered among the downstairs rooms. Somebody had had the foresight to clean out the refrigerator and throw out the potatoes that Heather had peeled and left in the sink. But the salad bowl was still sitting there, waiting for her to tear up the lettuce and slice the cucumbers and sweet onions.

I went into the living room and sat on the sofa. "She exercised to classical music," I said to Zerk, who was standing in the middle of the room with a notebook and pen in his hands. "The first time I came here, it was Wagner. She played it very loud. She looked terrific in a leotard."

Zerk sat down beside me. "This might not have been such a great idea, coming back here."

"No," I said. "It's all right. I wanted to. I've got to pick up those journals."

"Interesting stuff in that diary, huh?"

"Very interesting," I nodded. "If I can put the journals beside the diary, I think I might really have something."

"Wanna tell me what you're thinking?"

"Not yet."

"I've got to get a real estate appraiser out here, get a market value for the place," said Zerk. "What do you think about the furniture?"

"Sell it all. You don't think there will be great-aunts and third cousins coming out of the woodwork to pick over the stuff, do you?"

"As far as I know, you're it, big fella," said Zerk. "I've got to look around, make some notes." He got up and headed for the stairs. "You coming?"

"I really don't want to go up there."

He nodded. "Okay."

After Zerk disappeared up the stairs toward Heather's bedroom, I went over to her desk where, I knew, she had kept Stu's journals. She had once showed me the stack of neat notes she was making as she worked her way through them. She had copied out quotes—descriptions of the men Stu had met, little anecdotes about their backgrounds, street scenes, possible captions for the photos she intended to take—and had written reminders for herself in the margins. She'd liked to lay out the papers on the top of the desk, which was otherwise bare except for a lamp and a ceramic beer mug of pens and pencils. She'd kept the journals and her notes in a big manila envelope in the bottom left-hand drawer.

I pulled open the drawer. The envelope wasn't there. Nor was it in any of the other drawers in the desk. I went back into the kitchen. Once in a while, I knew, she would spread all the papers out on the kitchen table to work on while something was roasting in the oven. I went through all the cabinets and drawers. Then I went back into the living room and conducted an orderly search through all the bookshelves. I looked under the sofa. I prowled among the coats and boots and the stack of games on the shelf in the hall closet.

Then I went upstairs.

Zerk was sitting on Heather's bed, writing in his notebook. "You haven't seen a big manila envelope, have you?" I said.

"No. Haven't really been looking, of course."

"Well, help me look."

He nodded, and together we went through the upstairs. I took the bathroom and the spare bedroom. Zerk rummaged through her underwear and sweaters in the bureau and moved the stuff around in her closet.

Then we went back downstairs and did it all over again. Stu's journals, and Heather's notes, were not there.

"Maybe she hid them someplace," said Zerk. "Like she hid her spare key."

"She wasn't hiding the key. She was just keeping it there. There's a difference. She wasn't the sort of person who hid things." I shook my head. "I don't understand it. You're sure the police didn't take them?"

"The police took nothing," he said. "I'm sure of that. Look. Maybe she had some other place for them. An office, safe deposit box?"

"No. She had no reason to secure them. She was working on them. This is where she worked. The stuff should be right here, in the drawer."

Zerk peered at me. "You thinking what I'm thinking?"

I nodded. "They've been stolen. Yes."

"Well," he said, "that's a damn shame. That'll make it pretty tough to make sense out of that diary, huh?"

"As a matter of fact," I said slowly, "now that I think about it, it actually makes things clearer." I nodded. "Much clearer."

I got an answering machine at Gus Becker's number. An efficient female voice repeated the number I had dialed and instructed me to wait for the tone and then leave my own name and number and state my business, and Mr. Becker would get back to me as soon as he could.

"This is Brady Coyne, Gus," I said to the machine. "I've got something that I think will interest you." I said I'd be home for the rest of the evening and left my number. Then I sat back and lit a Winston.

Becker called back before I finished the cigarette. "Sorry about the machine," he said. "I've gotta do it that way, now."

"Heavy cloak and dagger stuff, huh?"

I heard him chuckle. "I know, I know. You're familiar with that ploy. I keep forgetting. So what's up?"

"I found Stu Carver's diary. You still interested?"

He hesitated. "Well, yeah, I guess I am. I had more or less abandoned that line, but, sure, I'd like to see it. Want me to come by and pick it up, or what?"

"Whatever you want," I said. "I could meet you someplace."

"Yeah, okay. That might be easier. Tonight?"

"Sure," I said. "Tonight's fine. You name it."

He paused for a moment. "Well, how about Choo Li's? That would be convenient for me. Know where Choo Li's is?"

"Afraid not."

"Beach Street. You can't miss it. Pretty good food. Never crowded. Drinks are generous. I'll treat you."

"That's in Chinatown, right?"

"Right. Can you find it?"

"Choo Li's on Beach Street. I'll find it."

"In an hour?"

I glanced at my watch. It was a little after eight. "Better; make it around ten-thirty. I've got a few things to do first."

"Ten-thirty, then. Hey, Brady?"

"Yes?"

"Have you had a chance to look over the diary?"

"Aw, shit, Gus. It's all scribbles. I'm not really interested, anyway. I'm just trying to help you out."

"Sure. Appreciate it. Probably means nothing anyway. Know something, though?"

"What's that?"

"I've been thinking about those murders. The girl, the old guy, and the Carver kid. Now, I'm not at all convinced that it has anything to do with the drug thing I'm working on. That's hard to fit together. But I'm not sure that I like Lee as the murderer, either. Some pieces just don't fit."

"I've been thinking the same thing," I said.

"We can talk about it."

"At Choo Li's. I'll be there."

18

Boston's Chinatown is contained within just a few city blocks, crammed into a corner between the Combat Zone and Atlantic Avenue. It's right next door to the Tufts Dental School, a short walk from the Sow's Ear, and a somewhat longer stroll from the St. Michael's mission.

A red and green neon sign in the window of Choo Li's advertised "Authentic Chinese and American Cuisine." The dining room was small, dimly lit, and almost deserted. Several Chinese waiters stood in a cluster, sharing a private joke that seemed, by the way they kept looking over at me, to be at my expense. They were all young, smooth-faced men, and all wore identical yellow silk shirts and tight black pants.

The one who silently steered me to a corner table and handed me my menu, I quickly learned, would not acknowledge that he understood English. I managed to convey to him how I wanted my Mai Tai built. I told him with gestures that I expected to be joined shortly by another person.

By the time Gus Becker arrived, I had lined up two empty Mai Tai glasses and was sipping from my third. He stood in the doorway for a moment, squinting. Then he saw me, grinned, and came over.

"Been waiting long?" he said, taking the chair across from me.

I gestured at the two empty glasses. "Few minutes. No problem."

"What're you drinking?"

"Mai Tais," I said. "Delicious. Love 'em. Want one?"

"You better take it easy on those things," he said. "They can sneak up on you."

"The hell, you're buying, right?"

He shrugged. "Sure. Have all you want."

The waiter came over to the table and lifted his eyebrows. Becker pointed at my glass. "One of those," he said loudly, as if he could overcome the language barrier by force. He glanced at me. "These boys don't speeka da English, you know?" To the waiter he said, "A Mai Tai, Sonny. And another one for my friend."

The waiter shrugged. Becker pointed at me, then at my glass. "More Mai Tai. Another drinkee." The waiter dipped his head and left.

Becker took a plastic-tipped cigar from his jacket pocket, removed the cellophane wrapper, and clenched it between his teeth, which gleamed from behind the curly bush of his molasses beard. "So," he said, holding a match to the cigar, "how've you been, my friend?" He lounged back in his chair and peered at me through a cloud of smoke.

"Getting by," I said. I drained my glass. "Managing, as they say."

"Sometimes getting by is doing pretty damn good."

The waiter came with the drinks. Becker said to me, "How about a Pu-Pu platter?"

I shrugged. "Sure. Whatever."

He looked at the waiter. "Pu-Pu platter." The waiter twitched his shoulders. "Jesus," said Becker. "How the

hell do you guys make a living? Look. Here.'' He pointed
at the menu. ''One of these, okay? Let's go. Chop chop.''

The waiter bowed, his eyes black pieces of stone, and
slid away.

Becker sipped his Mai Tai through a straw. ''So. You
got the diary.''

There was a little paper parasol sticking out of my Mai
Tai. I removed it and picked out a chunk of pineapple with
my fingers. ''I got the diary,'' I said, popping the fruit into
my mouth. ''The old man, Altoona, had it. He left it for
me at St. Michael's. You know, the mission where he
stayed. Very interesting, that diary.''

''I thought you said you couldn't read it.''

''Messy. Ol' Stu had messy penmanship.'' I took Stu's
diary out of my coat pocket and put it on the table. ''Certain words, though, they just jump out at you. Know what
I mean?''

''No. What do you mean?''

I gulped down half of my drink. ''Mmm. Good.'' I
wiped my mouth with the back of my hand. ''Stu was
interested in foreign policy. Haiti in particular.'' I took out
a Winston. I closed one eye in order to line up the flame
of my lighter with the tip of the cigarette. ''The diary's all
about Haiti,'' I said, smiling at Becker.

He picked up the diary and dropped it into his pocket
without looking at it. ''No kidding?'' he said. ''Haiti, huh?''

''No fucking kidding,'' I said. ''Remember that Cuban,
tried to shoot the State Department guy, there? Lampley?''

Becker nodded, frowning. ·

''Stu had a theory. A very interesting theory.''

Our Pu-Pu platter arrived. Ribs and sirloin tips. Deep-
fried shrimp and chicken. Egg rolls and chicken wings. All
arranged around a flaming can of Sterno. I took one of the
shrimps and popped it into my mouth. Becker was staring
at me. ''What was his theory?'' he said.

''Have one of these shrimps,'' I said. ''They're great.''
I took a swig from my glass. ''Stu says in this diary of his

that it was a setup. He says somebody put the Cuban kid, Felix Guerrero was his name, up to it. Recruited him off the streets. Gave him the gun, paid him to try to assassinate Lampley.''

''Sure,'' said Becker. ''He was a Cuban. They're behind the thing in Haiti anyway. It was the Cubans put him up to it. Everybody knows that.''

''Uh-uh,'' I said, shaking my head vigorously. ''See, that's exactly what it was supposed to look like. Supposed to look like the Cubans trying to kill the enemy American government man. That's how the papers interpreted it. That's what government press releases said. But Stu heard different. Stu heard it was an American who set it up. Somebody from the American government, but who was acting on his own, setting up the hit on the State Department guy.''

Becker was frowning. ''That makes no goddam sense,'' he said. ''Did he mention a name? Did he say who it was who supposedly set up this assassination?''

I wagged my finger at him. ''He didn't have to. Stu said this federal agent recruited the Cuban kid from a bunch of displaced Miami street kids. Ol' Stu got around, mixed with all the ethnics, got wind of this. He figured the idea was for the Cuban to snuff Lampley, then for the kid to get whacked, and there'd be this big shift in public opinion. Get support for goin' into Haiti with gunboats blazing. Far out, huh?''

''Far out,'' muttered Becker.

''So what I figure is this,'' I said. ''Knowing Stu, he was asking questions a mile a minute. He realized he had a great story here. Decided to keep his notes separate from the stuff he was doing on the street people. Kept a little diary just for the assassination story. I figure this American agent found out that Stu knew about it. So he arranged to meet him New Year's Eve. Probably promised him more information. Instead, he stuck an icepick into Stu's ear. But he also knew that Stu was keeping journals, so he had to track them down. Clean up his mess, see? Bad for him, if anybody got wind of what really happened. Bad for him, bad for the government. Terrible PR. Killed Stu. Killed poor ol' Altoona, too, just in case the old guy might've known something. Had to kill Heather, 'cause she had seen the journals. Then took the journals from her.''

"That's very imaginative," said Becker. "I think you've had too many Mai Tais, Brady."

I grinned. "I could use another."

Becker lifted his hand, and our waiter disengaged himself from the group across the room. Becker pointed at my glass. "Another Mai Tai, Sonny." Then he peered at me. "You got any proof of this?"

"Ah, Gus. Good ol' Gus. Always there when I need him. This federal agent Stu talks about. The street people, those Cubans, they called him Redbeard. Stu didn't know your name, Gus. But he figured out it was you, didn't he? Redbeard. That was you. You killed my girl, Gus. You killed Heather and you took the journals. She didn't know anything, and you had to kill her."

Becker sighed. "You're drunk."

"No, listen," I said. "You misunderstand me, Gus, ol' buddy. I know how it is. You gotta do what you gotta do."

He squinted at me. "What are you talking about?"

"Hey, shit. Raison d'état. National security. L'état, c'est moi. All that stuff. Better dead than red, huh? Can't have the damn commies sittin' there on our doorstep, now, can we? I mean, war is war. War is hell. There's always victims, you wanna have a war." I held up my hand. "Don't worry, Gus, old friend, old Redbeard. Ol' Brady can keep a secret. Just too damn bad you hadda kill my girl. Goddam shame.''

"Can you?" he said. "Can you keep a secret?"

I nodded eagerly. "Oh, sure." I held my forefinger to my lips. "Mum's the word."

"Good," he said, "because I want you to listen carefully." He leaned toward me. "The secret is this. You're dead wrong. That's the secret. I don't know what the fuck you're talking about. Okay? So why don't you just go home and sleep it off, huh? I mean, I understand how you feel about the girl. A tragedy. And the two guys, that's a shame, too. But these things happen, you have a whacked-out faggot like David Lee. I guess I can understand, you'd like to lay it on me, try to elevate the whole thing, make it less grubby. But, shit, things like this, they're usually grubby, and there's not a damn thing you can do about it. So why don't you just go home and forget it."

"I found out some things about you," I said. "You're quite a guy, Gus. Quite a guy. A goddam hero. A hero for our time. Green fucking Beret. Four years in Nam and Cambodia. You can kill people with a belt buckle or a boot lace or a goddam palm frond. POW, right? Escaped, too. Crawled forty miles through the jungle with a busted leg. Hero. Kind of a renegade, even by Special Forces standards. But a goddam hero. Then back in the good old U.S. of A., working in different jungles. Still a lone wolf. But a result getter. Busted up a big cocaine ring in Miami just last fall. Singlehandedly. Yep. Miami, where all the commie Cubans are. You probably talk pretty good Cuban Spanish. Still got that hair across your ass about the commies. What's it they say? A man can leave the Special Forces. But the Special Forces never leaves the man."

"Where'd you hear all this?"

"I got a buddy over at Justice, Boston office. All that stuff's on their computers, Gus. Part of the record. Nice record. You gotta be proud, record like that."

My Mai Tai arrived. Becker said to the waiter, "Give me the check, will you? Bet you understand that." The waiter nodded and dropped the check onto the table. Becker picked it up, glanced at it, extracted some bills from his wallet and laid them on the table. "Finish your drink," he said to me. "I'm going to get you home, let you sleep it off. You'll feel better in the morning."

"I feel fine," I said. I gulped down the drink. "I'm awful mad at you, though, Gus. I loved that girl."

He shook his head. "Come on, Brady. Let's go."

I put both hands onto the table and slowly pushed myself up. My chair toppled over backwards behind me.

Becker came around the table and grabbed my arm. "Come on. I'll help you."

He put his arm across my back and half carried me out. We stood in front of the restaurant breathing in the chilly March air. "I'm going to put you into a cab," said Becker. "Come on. This way."

We started up the street. "Where we goin'?" I said.

"Find a cab. Won't be any around here this time of night. We'll head over to Washington Street."

The lights were still on in the restaurants along Beach Street, but the narrow sidewalks were deserted, and there was no traffic moving in Chinatown.

"I gotta take a whizz," I announced.

"Good idea," said Becker.

"Very good idea."

There was an alley. I lurched toward it. "Gotta get outa sight," I said. "Don't want to get picked up. Indecent exposure, huh? Pissing in public."

Becker kept his arm on me as I moved into the shadows. There was a bare light bulb glowing over a doorway down the alley. It illuminated rows of plastic trash barrels and stacks of cardboard boxes, creating big distorted shadows on the blank, windowless brick walls.

I stood to face the wall, propping myself up against it with one hand while I fumbled at my zipper with the other. Becker stood behind me.

"Don't you have to go?" I said. "Those Mai Tais, they go right through you."

"You had more than I did," he said. He was standing close behind me, his voice a low whisper in my ear. "You had an awful lot of those Mai Tais, Brady. And you talked an awful lot. Said terrible things. You said things you really had no right saying. You hurt my feelings, Brady."

"Ah, we're friends, Gus. We can talk."

Suddenly his forearm levered against my throat and forced my chin up. His body was a heavy weight against my back. "Hey," I managed to gasp. "What the hell are you doing?"

"I told you," he said softly into my ear. "You talk too much."

I reached up with my right hand and grabbed his arm. Beneath his coat I could feel his forearm, as hard and unyielding as a hunk of oak. He increased the pressure on my throat. "Come on," I wheezed. "I can't breathe."

I was bracing myself against the wall with my left hand. The weight of his body was pushing against me. My knees were beginning to buckle from the bulk of him, and he was slowly forcing my chin up and back, constricting my windpipe.

I managed to shift my weight onto my left leg. Then I lifted my right foot and smashed backwards with my heel as hard as I could. I caught him on his instep, and he grunted in surprise and pain. And for an instant his grip on my throat loosened. I ducked my head and pivoted, swinging my left elbow backwards. I heard the whoosh of his breath as I connected with the pit of his stomach.

I turned quickly and went at him. I was bigger than Becker, and it raced through my mind that I could overpower him the way I once had been able to push opponents around when I played tight end, compensating for my lack of gracefulness with strength and bulk. I hit him with my shoulder and we went down together. I fell on top of him. I tried to get my forearm under his chin, but he managed to twist away from me. I clawed at his face. I wanted to get my fingers into his eyes or his nostrils and to rip and tear. I had no desire to fight fair. I knew Gus Becker was a killer. He wouldn't fight fair.

He tucked his chin into his chest. I couldn't get at the soft parts of his face. I smashed at his neck and throat with the side of my fist. All I hit was hard skull and shoulder.

Becker squirmed under me. He was quicker and leaner

and better conditioned, and I could feel my initial advantage slipping away. I tried to get my knee up into his groin, and as I did he thrust suddenly with his legs and rolled away from me.

I scrambled to my feet. My breath was coming hard and raspy. All those damn cigarettes.

Becker had managed to circle around beside me. I turned to face him. He was bent forward. I noted with some satisfaction that he was panting, too, and he was holding his side with his right hand.

In his left hand something glinted in the dim light.

I kicked at him and caught him high on his thigh, a harmless, amateur, glancing blow. He jumped back, crouched, both hands held low, a knife fighter's stance.

"Come on," I said. "Come on, Becker. Try somebody who isn't drunk or old or an innocent little girl. Come on, you fucking Green Beret."

He swayed back and forth, feinting, low and alert, like a cobra looking to strike. He was grinning, now, sure of himself. I backed up carefully until I felt the wall against my back. "Gonna be messy, boy," he whispered. "Coulda been neat and quick. Too bad."

He lunged at me. I turned my body and threw up my arm. I felt a sudden dart of pain near my elbow. I stumbled away from him, moving back deeper into the alley. Becker came at me, stalking me, his teeth glittering from inside his beard, his eyes narrowed. I held my wounded elbow. Warm blood soaked my coatsleeve and oozed between my fingers. The arm felt numb, and I had to cradle it with my other hand to keep it from dangling uselessly at my side.

"I thought you were drunk," he said, grinning, coming at me. "You can hold your Mai Tais, I'll give you that."

The pain in my elbow was moving up, searing into my armpit. Becker kept coming at me, an animal with the powerful whiff of his wounded quarry's blood flooding his nostrils.

"Why don't you give it up, Gus," I said, edging backwards. "It's all over."

"You said it yourself," he said, light and shifty, up on the balls of his feet. "Gotta clean up the mess."

He lunged at me again. I ducked away. Too late. I realized he had faked me, and I was off balance, stumbling backwards. He rammed me with his forearm, knocking me onto my back. Then he was on me, his knee in my stomach. "Let's make it quick and painless," he whispered.

I tried to twist away from him. He shoved the heel of his hand against the side of my face, smashing my head onto the rough pavement. I clawed at him with my one good hand. But I felt weak, and there was nothing to grab.

Then the alley was filled with a blinding light. This, I thought, is that great flash that you see inside your brain when an icepick slides in. Then it goes black and it's all over.

"Drop it, Becker!" came a loud voice.

I felt his weight shift on me, and I kicked hard and rolled quickly out from under him. I scrambled away from him on my one good hand and both knees and dragged myself into a sitting position against the wall. I looked toward the end of the alley. The light blinded me. I glanced at Gus Becker. He was crouched there on all fours staring into the spotlight, looking like a red-bearded raccoon that had been caught robbing a garbage pail.

Then the alley was full of people. Two uniformed policemen grabbed Becker by his arms and led him away. Becker did not fight it. Then Al Santis was kneeling beside me.

"You all right, there?"

"Shit," I said. "Had him right where I wanted him."

Santis grinned. "Sure didn't look that way."

"You guys cut it awful close," I said. "What were you trying to do?"

"Wanted to see how well you could handle yourself." I shook my head. "Not that well, to tell the truth. I expected you sooner, or I wouldn't have been so cocky." I held up my right elbow to look at it. The coatsleeve was wet and shiny with blood.

"Let's have a look at that," said Santis.

"It's okay," I said. "Help me up, will you?"

He put his arm around my back and helped me climb up onto my feet. "The transmission wasn't very good," he said. "We kept waiting to get something we could use."

I took the little transmitter out of my pocket and unhooked the wire that led to the tiny microphone pinned to the inside of my shirt. I handed it to Santis. "You mean, you guys weren't right there all the time?"

"Oh, we weren't far away. Picked up your voice just fine, most of the time. Couldn't hear what he was saying very well, though. Maybe the recorder got it all. What *did* he say?"

"Nothing," I said.

"Mm," he muttered. "Well, anyway, we've got an assault here, and a weapon." He showed me what looked like a miniature icepick, with a wooden handle and a thin steel shaft perhaps five inches long.

"That's not an icepick, is it?"

"Looks to me like a pickle spear," said Santis. "Seventy-nine cents at any five-and-ten. You use them to fish pickles out of a jar."

"Or to stick into people's brains."

"That, too." He held it up to the light. He was holding it gingerly with a handkerchief. "It's got your blood all over it. Maybe we can find traces of other blood on it, too."

We walked out of the alley. Becker had already been carted away. Two policemen stood beside a squad car, waiting for Santis and me. He said, "Hop in. We'll drop you off at the hospital, get that arm looked at."

I climbed into the back seat. Al Santis slid in beside me. "Now what do we do?" I said.

"Now we get that arm cleaned up. Then we go over to the station and talk about what happened."

"Nothing happened," I said. "I pretended I was drunk.

I told him what I believed he did. He didn't say anything. He admitted nothing. Then we went outside, and he tried to kill me."

"Well, we'll go over it, anyway."

The police car got onto Washington Street, heading toward Mass General. It traveled sedately. No sirens or flashing blue lights. It comforted me that no one seemed especially concerned about the wound on my arm. I put my head back against the seat and closed my eyes.

"How did you arrange that, so Becker would think you were loaded?" said Santis.

"I made a deal with the waiter. He brought me Mai Tais minus the booze. Just fruit juice. I can drink a lot of fruit juice without getting loaded. It does make me have to pee, though."

"Well, anyway," he chuckled, "you evidently made a pretty convincing drunk. Becker's no dummy."

"I've had lots of practice," I said. "The thing is, I never did get around to taking that leak. Can't we move it a little faster?"

Epilogue

Al Santis called me a week later. "How's the arm?" he said.

"I'll be pumping iron in no time," I said. The truth was, it hurt like hell. When I was younger, things seemed to heal faster. I had no desire to lift weights, anyway.

"Wanted to bring you up-to-date on the Becker case," said the detective. "Figured you were interested."

"I am."

"The DA has hated the case from the start. Screaming for evidence."

"Evidence? Jesus . . ."

"Listen," said Santis gloomily. "Becker's name is never even mentioned in the diary, okay? I mean, a few references to Redbeard just ain't the same as spelling it out. Carver didn't know Becker's name, that much is clear. The whole goddam thing is hearsay, anyway, and there's no convenient way to interrogate your friend there, who wrote it. In terms of evidence, it's just a story. Pure imagination, for all we know. What we could use is, we could really use a witness."

"I can certainly testify to an assault," I said.

"Big fuckin' deal."

"Yes. I get it. What about the weapon? The pickle spear?"

"Negative."

"And Becker won't talk?"

"He smiled a lot, and his lawyer had him out on bail lickety-split. The assault is all we could charge him with."

"He did it, you know," I said. "Heather. Stu. Altoona. He set up that assassination. Becker did it all."

I heard Santis sigh. "Maybe he did. Sure, he probably did. Whatever. It's all academic now, anyway."

"What do you mean?"

"He's gone."

"Gone?"

"Gone. Couple FBI guys were around yesterday. They had papers. Jurisdiction, know what I mean? It's now a federal case. Becker's in their custody. It's out of our hands."

"I don't understand. I know the law, and—"

"Me neither," Santis interrupted. "All I know is, the DA ain't fighting it. I personally think he's relieved. Not that much fun, putting a federal drug agent on trial. Especially with the kind of case we've got. Becker's gonzo."

"Politics," I muttered.

"Ah, we didn't have a case anyway. If you'd been able to get him to say something into the tape . . ."

"Christ! He came after me with that pickle spear."

"I know how you feel. I'm sorry."

"So now what do we do?"

"Do? We do nothing. We go back to work, that's what we do."

"Not me," I said.

* * *

"That is one hell of a story," said Mickey Gillis, her monkey face breaking into a toothy grin. She snapped off the tape recorder that sat on the sofa between us. "Carver had himself a Pulitzer there. Another fuckin' Watergate. And talk about plugging up the leaks. Three murders. Wow!"

"Nearly four," I said.

"Yep. You would have made four," she said. "That would have made the story even better."

She lit another little cigarillo, her fourth during the nearly two hours we had sat in my office while I told her the story. "Go over that part that your pal McDevitt told you again, will ya?"

"I told you," I said. "You can't mention Charlie Mc-Devitt in this."

She waved her cigarillo impatiently at me. "Yeah, yeah."

"About Becker's stay in the prison camp, you mean?"

"That's it. That's what explains it all."

I shrugged. "It's not that clear exactly what happened. The VC had him for about nine months. He went in a clean-cut American boy and came out a bitter, twisted fanatic. A very heroic escape. He had to crawl through about forty miles of jungle with a broken leg."

"It was broken because some communist interrogator had kept hitting it with a sledgehammer," said Mickey, her eyes glittering.

"Yes, evidently. He had dozens of cigarette burns on his face. That's why he grew a beard. To hide his scars."

She nodded. "He kept most of his scars pretty well hidden. But they ran deep into his soul."

"He hated the hell out of anything called communist, that's for sure," I said. "He was waging his own private war. Chasing down drug dealers wasn't direct enough for him. But it gave him the access and the freedom. This thing with Lampley was obviously completely wacko. But he damn near carried it off. If it hadn't been for Stu Carver . . ."

Mickey touched my arm. "And you, Brady Coyne. Don't forget yourself." She held her glass to me. "More, huh?"

I went over to the cabinet and sloshed some Scotch into her glass. "Can you write this story?" I said, handing her drink to her.

"Damn straight I can write it. This is a career story, Brady, old pal. Methinks I'll do a three-parter. Part one, the assassination story. Once upon a time there was this drug agent they called Redbeard, a Rambo type, who thought he could make foreign policy by staging an assassination, then making sure the assassin himself got it so he couldn't talk. Part two, the murders. Three interesting victims, any one of whom might have been able to blow Redbeard's scheme right out of the water. And part three, the official coverup, in which the Feds come along like the Apaches to whisk the drug agent away from the intrepid local police before they can properly apply the full and just measure of the law. This'll get national attention. No question about it. I'll probably have to run down a few details. But it's got it all. This is a biggie. I love it."

I sat down beside her. She put her hand on the inside of my thigh and leaned her face close to mine. Her breath smelled masculine, a mixture of tobacco and whiskey. Her hard little breast pressed against the side of my arm. "Whaddya say?" she said in a raspy whisper. "For old times' sake, huh? This sofa pull out, or what?"

"No, Mickey," I said. "Sorry to say, it doesn't pull out."

"Your loss," she said with a shrug.

I checked the paper every day for two weeks. Then I called Mickey.

"When are they going to print the story?" I asked.

"They aren't."

"What do you mean?"

"They killed it."

"Who? Who killed it?"

"How the fuck do I know? They. You know. Them. It's dead."

"So what are you going to do?"

"Me? I'm gonna write other stories. That's what I do. I write stories."

"That's it?"

"Unless you got a better idea."

"No," I said. "I don't have a better idea."

Ben Woodhouse called me on April Fool's Day. "Brady," he said, "I think it's time you quit sulking."

"I'm not sulking, Ben. I don't sulk."

"Then it's time you came back to work for me."

"You misunderstand. I don't work for anybody. I am nobody's employee. I have clients. You used to be one of them."

He chuckled. "Well, then, we have a misunderstanding, that's all. We can work it out. I need you. You're the best."

Ben Woodhouse used to be the consummate politician. His tools had not rusted noticeably in the years since his retirement from the arena. He was deft with flattery, deadly at negotiation.

"You're not my client anymore," I told him. "I haven't changed my mind."

"Dammit, Coyne. I'm warning you—"

"Don't try to threaten me, Ben. That won't work, either."

"You'll regret this."

"I seriously doubt it. Give my regards to Meriam."

I hung up before he had a chance to.

A few days later I strolled through the early spring sunshine to the St. Michael's mission. Father Joe Barrone accepted the check I handed him with a nod and a smile.

"This is most generous, Mr. Coyne. I assure you, it will be put to good use."

Heather Kriegel, I thought, would have been pleased with the way I had chosen to execute her estate.

Charlie McDevitt was swinging his driver back and forth while we waited for the twosome in front of us to hit their second shots. The fairway was beginning to green up. Springtime had begun its annual healing of the scrapes and abrasions that winter had inflicted on the earth. The April air smelled warm and sweet. It was good to be outdoors.

"You hear the one about the lawyer who died and went to see St. Peter at the pearly gates?" he asked.

"You told me that one," I said.

"Too bad," he said, swiping the blossom neatly off a dandelion with his driver. "Good story. You think I can hit now?"

"You could have hit a long time ago," I said. "You'll probably swing and miss anyway."

"Probably will, this being the first hole of the season and all." Charlie took another practice swing with his driver and peered down the fairway at the two golfers who were disappearing over the rise.

Charlie teed up his ball, then stepped back. "I think I'll wait another minute. If I catch it just right I could hit those guys."

"Not likely," I said.

He propped himself up on his driver. "Remember your friend there, Gus Becker?"

"He wasn't my friend."

"I know. Anyway, something came over the wire yesterday. He'd been assigned to a tough case in Lima, Peru. Maybe you heard."

"I've heard nothing about him since the FBI took him away from the Boston police," I said.

"Well, they sent him to Lima. Yesterday on the wire it

said that he was found in the trunk of his Buick. Big bullet hole in his forehead."

"So there's some justice after all," I said. "Those South American cocaine dealers play rough, huh?"

"That's what we're expected to believe," said Charlie.

"And what the hell's that supposed to mean?"

Charlie shrugged elaborately. "Like you said, justice gets done, one way or the other."

"I don't get you."

Charlie peered of down the fairway. "If anyone was to calibrate that hole in Becker's forehead, I suspect it would measure just about standard United States government is- sue point-forty-five." He turned to lift his eyebrows at me.

I shook my head. "American justice. I'll be damned."

"I'm gonna hit now. Think it's okay?"

"Keep your damn head down."

He stepped up and hit it well. Then it was my turn. I was eager to get the new season under way.

ABOUT THE AUTHOR

William G. Tapply has lived in New England all his life.
He has taught history in both private and public schools
and has written for *Field & Stream* and *Sports Illustrated*.
He lives in Concord, Massachusetts, with his wife, Cyn-
thia, and their three children, Michael, Melissa, and Sarah.
He is the author of DEATH AT CHARITY'S POINT,
DUTCH BLUE ERROR, and FOLLOW THE SHARKS,
previously published by Ballantine.

RICH
with Mystery...
William G. Tapply

Brady Coyne, a Boston attorney, makes his living doing trusts and estates for the Boston elite — but at the request of his wealthy clients he finds himself in one murder investigation after another.